THE DARK OF KNIGHT

Gentlemen of Knights
Book Four

Elizabeth Johns

DRAGONBLADE PUBLISHING, INC.

Dragonblade Publishing, Inc. is an imprint of Kathryn Le Veque Novels, Inc.

P.O. Box 7968

La Verne CA 91750

ceo@dragonbladepublishing.com

Produced in the United States of America

First Edition December 2020

Print Edition

ARE YOU SIGNED UP FOR DRAGONBLADE'S BLOG?

You'll get the latest news and information on exclusive giveaways, exclusive excerpts, coming releases, sales, free books, cover reveals and more.

Check out our complete list of authors, too!

No spam, no junk. That's a promise!

Sign Up Here

www.dragonbladepublishing.com

Dearest Reader;

Thank you for your support of a small press. At Dragonblade Publishing, we strive to bring you the highest quality Historical Romance from the some of the best authors in the business. Without your support, there is no 'us', so we sincerely hope you adore these stories and find some new favorite authors along the way.

Happy Reading!

CEO, Dragonblade Publishing

Additional Dragonblade books by Author Elizabeth Johns

Gentlemen of Knights Series
Duke of Knight (Book 1)
Black Knight (Book 2)
Knight and Day (Book 3)
The Dark of Knight (Book 4)

CHAPTER ONE

THE SKY WAS clear and black save for the stars and moon. The breeze was warm, with the scent of citrus and night jasmine in the air—a perfect night for scaling walls and housebreaking. If only he knew what he was looking for. Felix knew nefarious deeds happened by the light of day, but why take the extra chance of being seen? He was a guest at the ball happening now, in this very house, which was full of dignitaries and the military elite, but he had slipped out via the rear courtyard to scale the wall and look for some sign of treason. Then he would rejoin the party with no one the wiser... if all went as it should.

He looked up at the wall – these Spanish villas had lovely iron railings around the walls, which made it easier to climb. Any reduced risk of breaking his neck was always appreciated. He looked around discreetly, using the pale moonlight to seek any watchful eyes. Seeing none, he began to climb to the third window from the left on the next story above. Those were the directions he had been given when he had received his orders to investigate the owner of the villa. He found himself on a balcony of sorts, the doors open and sheer curtains blowing outwards as if in welcome.

Nice of them to be so obliging, he thought to himself. It hardly made this a challenge. He stood for a moment in the shadows outside the doors, catching his breath. Even something so simple could give an intruder away. The scent of roses wafted to his nose. Had he come to the wrong room? No, he was certain he had counted properly. Being a spy tended to make a person careful about details. Was there someone else in the room with similar ambitions?

Felix leaned forward to listen, but there was nothing beyond the distant hum of the music in the ballroom. Slowly, he pulled back the sheer curtain and crept in behind it, pausing a few moments for his eyes to adjust. This was a study of some sort, a sofa and fireplace set to one side while a wall of books and a desk occupied the other. It was a masculine room, with the underlying odors of tobacco and leather. The rose perfume was distinctly out of place. There were papers on the desk which had been strewn about. Had he interrupted someone on the same task?

He looked around very carefully. Besides the scent, it appeared he was alone—no heavy breathing, no minuscule movements by which the amateur would betray themselves. Felix slid a knife from his inside pocket and decided to reassure himself anyway. He crept around the room, deftly and silently checking every spot where he himself would hide. Finding nothing, the only other place someone could be was beneath the desk. It would not be impossible for a person to escape the other side of the desk, but Felix must have a look at those papers. Who had he interrupted? There was no one else assigned to this task, after all, and he did not think any French would be about. But he could be wrong.

He went over to the desk, paying mind to the fact that someone might be hiding beneath it, and began to ruffle through the papers on the top. Holding the documents up to the thin ray of moonlight, he could see familiar script—troop movements, cargo shipments, dates, names... all of this information should be closely guarded. Either Felix had caught someone in the act of stealing these reports, or they had been deliberately placed here. Folding them carefully, he placed them in an inside pocket of his jacket and made to leave, ever conscientious of timeliness and being missed from the ball downstairs.

Unable to help himself, he gave one shove with his boot beneath the desk and heard a tiny grunt.

He should always trust his instincts... yet who could it be? Another spy? Or someone waiting for a clandestine engagement?

He risked being seen as much as they, and he hesitated to reveal himself. However, if there was a traitor in the midst, it would be best to know.

"Do you intend to reveal yourself, or do you intend to make this difficult?" he asked in a low, disguised growl.

A negative noise came from beneath the desk. It was either a young boy or a woman. Felix hesitated. No spy worth their salt would wear perfume. He had the papers he needed. Should he risk his own exposure?

He knelt down, but in the dark could not see the face of the figure huddled beneath the furniture.

"Why are you in here? Are you in trouble?"

"Why I am in here is my own concern, and I am perfectly well, thank you," a female said in a well-bred Spanish accent.

Felix relaxed. She was doubtless an unlikely traitor. "I will leave you to your assignation, then, ma'am. I am sure neither one of us wishes to be revealed."

"I should ask why you are here," she said, seemingly as an after-thought.

"As you say, it is none of your concern."

Felix should have already been done and gone, but there was something drawing him to this person. Dallying was the ruin of any good spy.

"Adios," he said, standing up and leaving via the balcony as he had come. He hesitated to return to the ballroom immediately, wondering if his mystery lady would also escape that way, but he had already been gone too long. He straightened his coat and slipped back in through the terrace doors towards the wall. Taking a drink from the tray as one of the footmen passed, he then joined Captain Everleigh and some other British soldiers. One would not guess, by looking at the glamorous picture before them, that they were in the midst of conflict. It was one of the great ironies of war. He repressed a sigh, disliking the idea of dining and dancing while common soldiers barely had enough food to eat and slept out of doors in the harshest conditions.

Felix gave Everleigh a quick signal to indicate he had found something. All attention, it seemed, was drawn to the other side of the room.

"The Lady Catalina has just arrived," Everleigh said by way of explanation.

"Therefore I was not missed," Felix replied dryly.

"Not by any of the men," Everleigh agreed, as they both watched the horde of men surround the beauty.

She was the daughter of General Mendoza, one of the most powerful men in the Spanish army. Many said she was his greatest weapon. Men would kill for just a dance with her. Felix had never thought any woman worth violence, and had often said so. The world was full of beautiful women; in fact, this ballroom alone held several. It was more than the physical attributes of a woman that attracted him. Irrespective of his own thoughts on the matter, the sea of uniforms parted like the Red Sea for her to enter, as though she were the great man himself.

Felix looked to see what all the fuss was about. It took him a moment to find her. Once he had, he took full advantage of being able to examine freely from afar. A beauty to be sure, he mused, but there was definitely something more, something unique about her. She was petite, yet perfectly proportioned, with ebony hair and skin as fair as snow. There was a radiance about her that made her shine and everyone around her seem dull. She would be very, very dangerous. He watched as she smiled and charmed her way through the crowd of gentleman surrounding her.

Felix hardened himself against her. Women were an unnecessary distraction in this business and had led many a better man than he to his death.

❯❯❯❯❮❮❮❮

HOW HAD SHE been so careless? She had almost been caught! Strictly speaking, she *had* been caught, but for reasons she could not fathom, the man had chosen not to reveal her presence or seek her identity. As soon as he left through the window, she scrambled out from under the desk and ran down to the ballroom. It was imperative that she be there before him—whoever he was. She stopped before the glass in the hall to shake out her dress and make certain everything was in its proper place. Her heartrate and ragged breaths, she reflected, might never return to normal after that scare.

Outwardly, she seemed the picture of maidenly innocence; she had chosen a light silver gown with no frills, only a delicate overdress of fine lace. Even in the candlelight her black hair shone in stark contrast to her porcelain skin. She looked everything that was proper. She tucked one loose curl behind her ear and paused to still her breathing and put on her best society mask. If anyone knew what she was really like, they would laugh themselves silly. This character she assumed was not the real Catalina Mendoza y Elizondo. If only they knew she preferred to be at home, alone with her dog and horse, not following the drum or playing the society lady. She wanted nothing to do with any of these men who made themselves foolish over her.

Her father was waiting for her when she came down the stairs. "What took you so long?" he asked her.

"Complications," she answered blithely.

"You look perfect now. Let us go, we are later than usual." They always arrived late to make a grand entrance. That was quite acceptable to Catalina. The less time she had to spend pretending to enjoy the attentions of men, the better.

They entered the ballroom and were announced. Immediately, she was surrounded by gentlemen and officers and her father drifted away, a look of satisfaction on his face.

Instantly, Catalina knew *he* was in the ballroom. She could feel his eyes upon her while she greeted her court of usual gentleman, Father's Lieutenant Dion amongst them. She was uncertain whether that was a direct order from her father or entirely his own idea. Lord Rollings, Major Silva and Captain Molina had all asked for dances. She did not think she knew this gentleman spy. Her senses would have told her. Perhaps she might recognize his scent, though it had been faint: bergamot and tobacco, she rather thought.

She smiled and took Lord Rollings' arm as he led her out to the dance floor. With every step, she could feel his gaze upon her. Did he know who she was? That was doubtful, but did he feel the strong attraction she did? It was going to drive her out of her senses. Besides, if they were looking for the same thing, would they be doing each other harm or a disservice?

"You grow more beautiful each time I see you, Señorita," Lord Rollings said.

Catalina forced herself to look up and smile. He was an important minister of some sort, and Father would want him to be kept happy.

"You flatter me, my lord. There are any number of ladies more beautiful in this very room."

"Not to my eyes." He looked at her meaningfully. Oh dear, she must change the subject quickly.

"How long do you think we will be in Salamanca?"

"It all depends on the French. Wellington is rarely the aggressor unless necessary," he answered, in a tone indicating he was placating her.

"I quite like being near to my home, though I do not wish there to be any battles here."

"I cannot agree with your father's decision to have you so close to the fighting, but I benefit from that, of course." He gave her another meaningful look, heaven help her.

Catalina kept the smile on her face but did not encourage him any further. Her gaze wandered around the perimeter of the room for any new faces. She saw only one or two people she did not know and one of those was standing near Major Silva. Perhaps she could gain an introduction. As the music drew to a close, she decided she must meet the new guests. She could feel it in her bones that she would recognize the man.

"Major Silva is my next partner. Would you please escort me to him?"

"I suppose I cannot keep you to myself the entire evening." A jealous man would drive Catalina to distraction. Lord Rollings might be handsome and well connected, but he would smother her independence.

She rapped his arm with her fan. "Of course not, my lord," she said playfully.

Major Silva was standing amongst a group of British soldiers. Catalina proceeded towards those she knew. Captain Everleigh and Captain Owens she had met many times, but between them was a tall, broad shouldered yet lean man with dark, brooding eyes. He was watching her as a predator watched his prey, not with any sense of adoration as did all the other men. Instantly, she was intrigued.

"Who is this new gentleman come among us?" she asked flippantly. "I do not believe we have met."

Major Silva and Lord Rollings exchanged looks of annoyance.

"Devil take it, Knight, did you have to be sent here? None of the ladies will pay us any mind now," Rollings drawled.

"You may have them all, I assure you," he drawled in a deep, bored voice.

Catalina searched her mind for the name "Knight", but could think of no one to whom she might attribute it. If he was a soldier, where had he been? His face was not one she would forget. Despite herself, she felt an attraction. Could this be the man?

"Lady Catalina Mendoza, this is Major Lord Felix Knight." Captain Everleigh made the introductions.

She held out her hand. She needed him to touch her to know. Instead, he bowed over her hand and kissed the air above it.

The other men exchanged sly glances. They had noticed the slight, evidently. It almost confirmed her suspicions. He wanted to play games? So be it.

The orchestra signalled that it was ready to begin the next song, and many of the officers excused themselves to find their partners for the next dance.

Another Portuguese officer came over to speak with Major Silva, leaving her standing near Major Knight. She tried not to let her annoyance show. Surely she was not so shallow as to be angered by his failure to pay homage? That would require further consideration later. In this moment, she needed to find out more about him.

Major Silva looked up. "Unfortunately, Señorita, I must go and speak with my commander. Knight, would you be a good fellow and dance my dance with the lady?" He looked back to Catalina. "I will make this up to you later." He took her hand, and kissing the air above it, walked away without waiting to hear Knight's answer.

She looked up into the Major's dark eyes and could read nothing. "You need not feel obliged to dance with me, sir."

"I never feel obliged to do anything," he said, in a deep voice that assured her he meant it. She also sensed that he was reluctant to dance with her.

"Perhaps you would escort me back to my father, if you do not wish to dance," she said, more curtly than she wished.

"I did not say I did not wish to dance." He was now toying with her, to judge by the look of amusement in his eyes.

"Then what do you wish for, sir?" What a ridiculous question. Her wits had deserted her around this man.

"Many, many things. But for now, we should dance." He held out his arm and the moment she placed her hand on it she knew. A deep breath to smell his unique aroma was not necessary, for there could be no doubt it was he.

He took her hand in his and placed the other on her waist. Her body trembled at the touch. She scarcely knew if her feet would be capable of moving.

Fortunately, he took the choice out of her hands and swept her into the waltz. It was a new dance that Wellington and his officers seemed to favor. It was a beautiful movement, as two bodies moved in perfect harmony, but never before had it affected her senses as it did now. She tried to stop thinking and just flow with this enigma of a man, for he did not seem inclined to speak. That was acceptable to her, for she did not think she was wise when in his company. How could she let him know they were on the same side and should work together? He would not know she had been the one in the room with him. How could he?

The waltz drew to a close and no more words had been spoken, even though their bodies had communicated with a language all their own.

Instead of leading her to her father or next partner, he led her towards the terrace doors. Suddenly, she feared him. Not for threat of assignation; no, he did not harbor an interest in her for something so simple. She thought about resisting, but knew it would be futile and only make a scene. She let him lead her and waited. Once they had passed beyond the light of the ballroom, he pressed her up against the wall and inhaled deeply.

"Roses."

She should be afraid, but she was not. Boldly, she tilted her head to look up at him.

"Would you care to tell me what devil's game you are playing, Señorita?"

CHAPTER TWO

FELIX WAS ANGRY. He knew, from the moment Lady Catalina stood before him, that she was the woman from the study, and she was toying with him. She sought an introduction and it would not surprise him if she had arranged to dance with him. But why? He waited for her answer.

"I do not know what you mean, sir. I play no games."

"No? I could have killed you."

"Why didn't you?" She looked boldly up into his face and his body reacted despite his decision to remain unmoved. Small she might be, but she was fierce.

"I do not normally strike unless threatened."

She held up her hands in a defenseless gesture. "I am no threat."

"I would like to know exactly what you are. Why were you in the study?"

"Why were you?"

"And you claim that you don't play games. If you are trying to be a spy, I will speak to your superiors because you will be killed. This is no place for amateurs."

"I admit I made a mistake. I have never been caught before. What gave me away?"

"The truth?"

"Of course." She almost spat the words.

"Roses. I could smell your perfume. It was most out of place in a man's domain."

"Humph!" she muttered under her breath.

Felix still had his arms against the wall on either side of her, and found himself reluctant to move.

"It seems we have come to an impasse, sir," she said at last. "And I am certain people will have noticed my absence by now."

He pushed back from the wall and held out his hand for her to pass. "Cease your attempts at spying, Señorita," he could not resist saying as she passed.

"I am sorry to disappoint you, sir," she said sweetly. "You should work with me instead of against me." She walked away but then said over her shoulder, "Until we meet again." Turning fully, she proffered an irreverent curtsy.

Felix remained where he was and watched her retreat, cursing himself. What was he to do with her? Who authorized such an atrocity?

He shook his head and went back inside to speak to his fellow officers. Captain Owens was laughing with two Portuguese officers they all knew from Badajoz.

"Someone looks as though his rations have been stolen," Owens said, looking much amused.

Felix sent him his most fierce glare, which only made Owens laugh more. He himself would do the same were their positions reversed, but it did not make him feel any better about the situation. Lady Catalina was a nuisance and he did not know what to do about her. He suspected no one ever told the little beauty "no" and now she wanted to play at being a spy.

Felix watched as Major Silva bullied some lieutenant into giving up his dance with the lady. He shook his head.

"Was England's Romeo rejected by Spain's fair Juliet?"

Felix snorted with disgust. "You would not believe it if I told you."

"I sense a delectable story," Owens responded. "Let us go and find Everleigh. We have paid our dues for the night."

They excused themselves from the Portuguese officers and found Everleigh in the card room. They waited patiently for him to rout his opponent and then they took their leave.

They elected to walk back to Headquarters in the warm spring evening. The city still had a fair amount of life at this late hour, as music and laughter was heard from open windows throughout the streets. The moon had shifted past the midnight hour on its way towards another day.

Owens whistled a merry tune, and to any passersby, they looked like carefree British soldiers on their way home from a night of revelry. They could not be more wrong. They were three of the most dangerous spies Wellington had up his sleeve in defense of the allied army.

"I cannot wait to see what you found," Everleigh said once they were too far away from the villa's gates to be overheard. The common man in the streets would not understand English at the low cadence he spoke.

Felix let out a heavy sigh. "My most interesting find is not what you would suspect."

Both Owens and Everleigh looked at him with a mixture of suspense and curiosity.

"Why do I already know I am not going to like what I hear?" Everleigh asked.

"And I am exceedingly curious about what happened with Lady Catalina on the terrace," Owens mused.

"I need a drink," Felix replied, as though he were dealing with an exasperating sibling. Everleigh and Owens were like brothers to him. He dearly loved his family, but he had been glad to escape the suffocating domesticity. At least his sister, Eugenia, had been unapologetically feral during his most recent visit.

They climbed up the steps to their billet, a pleasant house off the High Street in the center of town. They shared it with their immediate superior, Colonel Hill, cousin to the famous General Sir Rowland of the same surname. Hill was waiting for them in the study, a healthy glass of brandy in his hand. He waved them towards the leather chairs surrounding him around a small reading table in the center.

They removed their hats and dress swords, placing them on a side-table near the door. Owens went to the cupboard and poured three glasses of brandy while Felix went to one of the chairs and sat down, stretching out his legs and throwing his head back. He hoped he appeared relaxed, but in actual fact he was anything but. He was strung as tight as a fresh bow and his blood was simmering just beneath the surface, rather like a volcano ready to erupt.

Colonel Hill waited for them all to be seated. He was a plump man with a deceptively kind face and long, thick whiskers, which he was stroking. "What is there to report?"

Owens shook his head. "Nothing from me. I simply had a charming night, dancing with wallflowers and generals' wives while Knight had all the fun."

"I cannot wait. Everleigh, anything?"

"Nothing definite, but my instincts tell me to be suspicious of Lieutenant Dion, Mendoza's aide."

"The one you were sharping at the table?" Owens asked casually.

Everleigh smiled. "The very one."

"I need more to go on than your instinct. What made you suspicious?" Colonel Hill asked.

"The questions he asked—he delivered them a fraction too eagerly. as though he wanted the information first." Everleigh shrugged. "He could just be a toady, trying to win his superior's favor."

"He would not be the first." Colonel Hill snorted and took a long drink before turning his knowing gaze on Felix.

Having regained a measure of calm over his broiling thoughts,

Felix had begun to unbutton his jacket in order to retrieve the documents he had taken from the study.

He unfolded them and placed them on the table in front of him. "These were left out in the open, on the desk in the study."

The colonel thumbed through them with a frown on his face.

"If you look closely, the information is incorrect. It is a fair imitation, with just enough accuracy to be believable," Felix said.

"I see that," Hill agreed. "A deliberate decoy, then. But why? It was not authorized."

"Someone clearly suspected an intruder tonight, but who? And why was I not apprised of this?" He could have walked into a trap if he had been dealing with a professional.

The colonel stood up and began to pace around the room. He did that when he was thinking. Meanwhile, Felix knew he needed to tell him about the other intruder in the room, but he was not certain if he wished to divulge her name yet.

"There is one more thing, sir."

Hill looked up at him, waiting for him to continue.

"I was not the first person in the room."

"I suppose there is a good reason why you did not tell me this at once?" Hill asked in a stern voice.

Felix gave a casual shrug. "I suspect the other person was the one to find the documents. I do not think they were left out on the desk."

Hill waved his hand impatiently.

"The intruder was hiding under the desk, and I am not certain I would have discovered them, except…"

"Except what, Knight?"

"Except I could smell perfume. I suspect the intruder was female."

Hill narrowed his gaze and took another long drink. "Many a nation has been brought down by a wily female."

"But whom?" Everleigh asked keenly. "The villa was guarded more closely than Napoleon's boudoir."

"That is what I wish to know," Felix said candidly. "We had no one else authorized to be in that study."

"A free agent?" Owens suggested.

"If so, nothing good will come of it," Hill remarked. "It means there is distrust amongst the allies. Knight, I want you to discover who this person is—male or female. It had to have been a guest at the ball. I will have the guest list sent over in the morning. Woo every single lady if you must until you discover who it is." He drained his glass and set it down on the table with a heavy thud. "I am for bed."

They watched Hill leave and shut the door behind him.

They drank in silence for a few moments. This was an unforeseen complication that none of them had anticipated.

"Why did you not tell him?" Everleigh asked, once just the three of them remained.

Felix thought carefully before answering. "I want to see what she is about."

"And your time on the terrace with her revealed nothing? You must be losing your touch."

Felix stood and placed his finished drink next to Hill's. "Perhaps I am, but delivering her up would reveal nothing. I must uncover what she is about."

Everleigh shook his head and set his own glass down. "I do not predict a good ending to this."

Owens also rose, his glass joining the others on the table. "Nor I, but it will be a jolly good show."

CATALINA COULD NOT remember being so angry. As if she had not been humiliated enough, the arrogant Major had been there to rub her face in her shame. To make matters worse, he did not think her a worthy adversary! She would prove it to him if it was the last thing she did!

She had been spying for a couple of years, now. It began when Lieutenant Dion had discovered her influence over men. They tended to lose their heads when in her company and spill secrets. "No one would ever suspect her," he had said. Her father had reluctantly agreed.

What she could not understand was why the Englishman was so angry. Were they not on the same side? Although his meddling could cost Spain a great deal. He should not have been in that study tonight. Who had sent him?

She had done the difficult task and he had had the gall to insult her and take her work! Thankfully, he had not arrived in time to do more than find her hiding. It proved nothing. She changed out of her ballgown into her nightclothes and waited for her father. He would not be pleased by the interference of the Englishman.

It felt like an eternity that she waited, even though in all likelihood it was no more than twenty minutes. He knocked on the door twice as he always did.

"Come in, Papa."

Thankfully, he was alone. He looked very tired. She hoped this war would be over soon and they could move back to Villa Blanca.

He sat in the chair near her window and smoothed his fingers down both sides of his graying mustache.

"Tell me," he commanded.

"I was interrupted. Someone else was searching the room."

"Did he see you?"

She shook her head furiously. "No, but he knows who I am."

He narrowed his gaze. "And who is he?"

"An Englishman. A Major Knight."

"I have heard of him. He is close to Wellington—one of his favored aides."

"Why have I not seen him before?" she asked, trying not to be irritated that her father had not warned her.

"He was being held in a prison camp. I was unaware he had been released. Did he take the papers?"

"Every last one. He seemed very suspicious."

Her father grew very quiet when he was angry. He was now very, very quiet. Catalina knew this meant that there was a traitor amongst his people. He had laid a trap, and now the English would know about it.

"You must retrieve the papers."

"How am I to do that? Do you propose I break into the British Headquarters?"

"If you must. But I saw you dance with him. Use your influence on him."

"I am certain it is already too late. I could not get close enough when dancing or even on the terrace. He knew it was I in the study, so was very cautious."

"Then take Dion to help you break in tonight. If they do not have the documents, they have no proof. Perhaps they will not have read them yet."

She could feel herself scowl. "I will be better alone."

"You may not travel the streets of the city by yourself. You may do the rest alone, but he will accompany you there. Do you even know where it is?"

She waved her hand dismissively. "It will be easy enough to discover."

Her father stood. "Report to me when you return."

He kissed her on the cheek and left, no doubt to seek his bed. She stared at the ceiling for a moment, her feet exhausted and her eyes heavy with the desire for sleep. Now she must go and retrieve the papers from that *cerdo*.

Shaking her head, she muttered to herself the entire time she was making ready. She pulled on dark-coloured breeches and shirt, along with some well-worn boots that were useful when climbing. She wound a scarf around her neck—with which to hide her white face when needed—then hurried down the stairs, considerably irritated.

As if she had not suffered enough indignity, now he insisted Dion accompany her! She had asked for this, and relished the independence, but there were limits to what she could endure.

Dion was waiting at the bottom of the stairs and she barely acknowledged him as she whisked past to the study. She took her father's gun from the desk, and having checked it, hid three knives about her person. One she slid inside her boots, one in a sheath at her waist, and one inside the jacket pocket. Next came a rope that she wound around her body and clipped to her belt. One never knew what tools would be useful when breaking and entering.

They rode silently into the city. A couple of streets away from the British officers' lodging-house, she directed Dion to hold the horses and wait. The less he had to do with this operation, the better. She did not know why she resented the man so much, but he seemed to have a layer of oil surrounding him that made her skin crawl. She trusted him not at all.

"You will whistle if you have need of me?" he asked, which she appreciated more than she cared to admit. She pulled out the tin whistle which hung from a cord around her neck and showed it to him.

"I will walk the horses if they grow restless, but I will not be far."

Catalina gave a nod and then crept away into the darkness, slinking along beside the buildings, behind trees and bushes when able. When she reached her objective, she stood across the street and surveyed the unobtrusive house. It was housing several British officers. She knew these houses well. All the dwellings in this part of the city were of similar build. Constructed of golden stone with a tile roof, this one also had a green door. The kitchens would be in the basement and the reception rooms would be on the first floor, with the bedrooms and servant rooms located on the floors above. There were no lights shining from any of the windows, and many were open on this warm night to allow in a breeze.

She smiled wickedly. This was too easy. She crept across the street and hid beneath an almond tree in front of the house while plotting her next move. The open window on the floor above would be a drawing room or dining room, in all likelihood. It would have been helpful had Dion been there to give her assistance, but she would not be deterred. She was light enough that the railings on the windowsill would hold her. A row of rosebushes were arranged in a line beneath the windows in front of the house, daring her to fall into them.

Roses, he had said. She took a knife and cut one off before tucking it behind her ear in defiance.

A rush of excitement came over her as she began her climb upward. She jumped and her hands took hold of a railing while her body dangled beneath. Her fingers immediately burned beneath the weight. There was no good place for her feet. Using only her arms' strength, she pulled her body up until one knee could balance precariously on the sill, for she needed her other arm to open the sash.

The wood had warped and was difficult to slide; she struggled to create a gap wide enough to slip through. With the force needed to push the window open, she slipped and her body tumbled forward into the room. She caught herself before she made a loud thud.

She rested where she lay on the floor for a moment, catching her breath and letting her eyes adjust. That had not been completely smooth, but it appeared she was still undetected. The smell of spirits, tobacco and maleness lingered in the air. She was in a man's domain. They had not been gone long, she thought, but it did not deter her. She crawled along the floor toward some leather chairs set around a table, and she could picture Major Knight and the others discussing what had happened. Had he given her away?

She scanned the room for where they might have hidden his booty from the night, and wondered if he would be so foolish as to leave it on the same floor with the windows open. She crawled forward to the table and felt paper beneath her hands. She stopped and came up to her knees. Four glasses sat on top of the documents in a perfect square. She frowned with disappointment. Was it to be so easy, then? Had they realized they were false?

She moved the glasses gingerly and rolled up the papers, then rearranged the glasses as they were before. As she was about to leave, a moment of devilment came over her and she laid the rose between the glasses. He would know it was her, she thought with satisfaction.

"Enough of such foolery," she told herself shortly. Tucking the papers securely into her coat, she climbed out of the window, not troubling to close the sash again.

She pushed away from the wall to avoid the roses, and released her hold. Her ankles smarted from the drop when she met the stone. Glancing up from her crouched position, she allowed herself to imagine Major Knight seeing her for a brief moment before she ran away. She smiled up at the window for good measure—just in case—before dashing away to find Dion.

The lieutenant grunted with satisfaction when he saw her and cupped his hands to aid her to mount before they rode off into the night.

CHAPTER THREE

FELIX WAS AWAKENED the next morning by an angry colonel, who was leaning over his bed holding a rose under his nose.

"What is the meaning of this?"

There was not a soldier alive who could not wake up in an instant, but Felix still had to blink a few times. He had no idea what Colonel Hill was asking him.

"I beg your pardon, sir, I do not know what you mean."

"The papers are gone and a rose was left behind."

"A rose?" Suddenly, Felix knew exactly what had happened. He cursed himself roundly. "I believe I was taught a lesson, sir."

Hill dropped the rose on his chest. "Be downstairs in five minutes to explain." He turned and stamped from the room, slamming the door behind him.

Felix threw his head back on the pillow. She had made a point, he supposed, but what else was she about?

He dressed hastily and went downstairs to report to his superior.

Hill did not look up from his desk. "Explain."

"The person in the room last night smelled of roses. I believe I know who the lady is—and that she was trying to prove a point by retrieving the documents."

"And leaving the rose?" Hill looked at Felix over his glasses, unamused. "Is this some sort of game, Knight? It had better not be a lover's spat."

"Not at all, sir. I will go and have a word with her this morning."

"You do just that, and have a good explanation when you return. I will expect names, which you so pointedly avoided giving me last night."

"I did not want to besmirch a lady's name without verification, sir, but I am quite certain it was Lady Catalina Mendoza." There was no sense in prevaricating any longer.

Hill sat back and pulled off his glasses, biting the end of an earpiece while he looked deep in thought.

"Do you know aught of her history in espionage?" Felix dared to ask.

"No, her name was unknown to me, but things begin to make sense," Hill replied slowly. Felix waited. "We have suspected for some time that someone was leaking information, and we deliberately planted false information to narrow down the source." He hesitated. "We believe the leak comes from the Spanish contingent, more specifically Mendoza."

Felix frowned. Hill waved him to a chair. Taking a plain armchair with a faded gold fabric seat not unlike a camp chair, he perched on the edge, leaning towards his commander.

"If Mendoza was aware of this leak—presuming he was not involved—he could have planted these papers in order to catch the traitor himself."

"It would explain why he wanted the papers back, certainly," Felix agreed. He tried to picture the petite beauty scaling the walls and stealing into their house during the night. He smiled despite himself. "Should I confront her?"

"We must to do something," Hill remarked. "To leave as good as a signature behind..." He shook his head. "I should have your neck if you did such a thing."

"Except she knew that I knew. I accused her of being an amateur and she was making a point."

Hill raised his brows much like Felix's brother, the duke, would in a silent reprimand. He put the tips of his fingers together in a steeple shape and placed his forehead on them.

"Go and speak with her and tell her we know what is afoot."

"Call her bluff, you mean?"

"If it is one," he agreed. "It certainly points to Mendoza's personal innocence. Tell her we will help find their traitor. We have new intelligence from Hookey this morning, just come in on a dispatch. The Spanish contingent will be the last to receive the order and you will be the one to give it to Mendoza directly. Wellington is ready to move in for the kill and nothing had better leak."

"Yes, sir," Felix answered. "Do you have any suggestions on how I might be received by Lady Catalina without a chaperone?"

Hill smirked at him. "I have no doubt, with your reputation, you can determine how to woo the lady. Your particular talents will be greatly appreciated by your country."

Felix snorted.

"Dismissed," Hill said and returned his attention to the papers on his desk. Felix had risen and walked towards the door when Hill's words stopped him. "Oh, and Knight, you might want to re-button your jacket before you go a-courting."

Many unkind retorts came to Felix's tongue, but he simply saluted, as a good subordinate officer did, regardless of what idiocies came from his superior's mouth.

He climbed the stairs and corrected his toilette before calling for his horse and riding off to Mendoza's lodgings across from the Parque de los Jesuitas. It was not far enough away for Felix to blow off his anger, and he still had not decided what to say to Lady Catalina when he reached up to knock on the door. It was answered by Lieutenant Dion instead of a servant. Everleigh's suspicions of the man sprang to mind.

"Major Knight to see the Lady Catalina," Felix said.

The Lieutenant scowled but opened the door. "Join the throng." He held out his hand to indicate the way to the drawing room.

It was barely a civilized time of the morning, and yet the drawing room was full of suitors? Felix wished he could leave her to them, but this must be dealt with. He stood at the doorway, not bothering to hide his displeasure. Turning at his arrival, several of the young men looked afraid of him. Good. Perhaps they thought he was vying for the lady's hand, but nothing could be further from the truth. However, it was a useful tactic to employ at this point.

Lady Catalina looked up and inclined her head to him, a smug smile of satisfaction on her face.

"Major Knight," she said with false sweetness.

He stepped forward, this time taking her hand and boldly kissing it. "I have come, as you see, to fulfil my obligations. We are engaged for a walk in the park." He then pulled her to her feet, holding her firmly by the arm. He would not give her a chance to refuse.

"Indeed? It must have slipped my mind."

Several of the young fops groaned their displeasure.

"Forgive me, gentlemen. I cannot cry off an engagement. I will see you all later."

She stepped over some of the men who were attempting to scramble to their feet and Felix led her out of the front door. Dion began to hasten after them, which brought a surprising look of annoyance to Lady Catalina's face. That was an interesting revelation. However, having the lieutenant trail behind—much though it might amuse—did not suit his purposes.

"We will go no further than the park. You may watch from the window if you choose," Felix ordered.

Dion looked displeased, but clearly dared not argue with a superior officer, even if he was English.

Felix continued to hold firmly on to Lady Catalina's arm until they crossed the street into the park. Once there, he loosened his grip.

"Thank you," she said, with genuine relief.

He looked sideways at her. "I did not expect those to be the first words from your lips."

"You think I enjoy having ridiculous young men spouting sonnets to me and languishing at my feet? It is my father's wealth they seek, not my heart. I do my duty and nothing more. And then that imbecile insists on following me like a duenna." She growled in the back of her throat, making him smile despite his annoyance. Whatever else she was, she was not just in the common way. "Why are you here? I doubt it was for my rescue."

"Need you ask?" He shook his head in disbelief.

"Oh, you found my gift."

"My superior found your gift," Felix corrected.

"Did you get into trouble?" she asked, sounding very pleased with herself.

"Not at all. Many things became clear to us with your gift, as you call it."

She tilted her face up to him. "Please enlighten me."

They walked towards a bench, ironically set amongst a garden of roses. He directed her to be seated and joined her, after looking around to make certain they could not be overheard.

"I believe you planted those papers there deliberately in order to trap someone."

"Very clever," she remarked, as though she thought he were anything but.

"We have been aware for some time that there is a leak from within your father's camp."

She stared straight ahead, but he could sense her anger in the way she fidgeted with her gloves.

"Why are you telling me this?"

"Because we are on the same side. I want to help you."

"How do you know? Such a traitor could easily be me. You caught me yourself."

"I suppose that is a risk I—we—are willing to take."

"And how do you propose to help?"

"We work together. The orders go directly from you to your father. No middleman."

"And if my father disagrees? He is rather attached to his lieutenant."

"Your father is not in a position to disagree," Felix answered firmly. "Just as I am not able to object to working directly with you."

She turned, then, and openly glared at him. "Because you think a female incapable?"

"You would not ask that if you met my sister," he drawled. "No, it is because you made a deadly mistake last night, then proceeded to leave a signature, simply to prove a point."

"Did it work?"

He sighed heavily as his answer.

"How do you propose we work together?" she asked, continuing to be coy.

"Unfortunately, there is only one way. I must pretend to court you."

⟫⟫⟫✠⟪⟪⟪

"YOU MAKE IT sound as though you have been asked to drink poison," she snapped.

"That might be less painful," he retorted unkindly.

"All this because you smelled my perfume? Other ladies wear the same fragrance, you know." She stood up abruptly. "I do not agree with this dictum. You merely wish to play nursemaid to me and I will not have it."

He had risen, as a gentleman did, and was now looking down at her. "I wish nothing of the sort. This was not my idea."

"I will speak to my father."

"Alone," he ordered.

"Alone," she conceded. "Dion is not my favorite, either."

"That is one thing we can agree on. What do you know of him?"

"Very little. My father trusts him with everything. He is also from the north. He has been with us for two years now."

"Might I suggest you make it your duty to discover more about him? If he is from the north, he could have ties to France."

Part of her would love nothing more than to be rid of Dion, but it would humiliate her father.

He read her mind. "This will not reflect poorly on your father. He would not be the first man to trust the wrong person. But do consider: Dion is a name found in both Spain and France. This close to the border, loyalties could be divided."

Catalina knew it was possible. When she had been a child, France had not been the enemy. They had visited there several times. The Basque country was a mixture, even now.

"I do not like Dion, but I do not believe he is a traitor."

"I will be pleased if he is not. However, you must be very careful. He is often your chaperone, is he not?"

"*Escort*, on occasion. An elderly aunt lives with us at Villa Blanca, but she cannot follow the drum. And my maid…" She shook her head. "She is useless." *Except for her talent with hair and clothing*, she amended to herself.

"Does Dion help you in your spying activities?"

"Help is a very strong word. He accompanied me to your head-quarters last night and waited outside for me while I took the papers."

"I see." He took her arm and began walking her around the park towards the fountain. "Are you certain you can persuade your father?"

"He will not be pleased," she conceded.

"I suspected as much. May I suggest a diversion for the lieutenant?"

Despite herself, Catalina was pleased. "And how do we do this?"

He pulled out a sealed note and held it out to her. "I have an official letter here for you to hand to Dion. It tells partial truths of our plans to attack. It is our hope it will send the French running into the Pyrenees, towards France."

"And by telling him this, he delivers the information and is also out of the way?"

"Precisely."

"When am I likely to see you again? I can hardly send over love notes to you at headquarters."

"I will find a way to send word to you. Wellington arrives soon and he will want entertainment." He turned and led her back to the house, where he bowed over her hand at the front door. He did not escort her back inside. She watched him walk away in the direction of the stables before she turned to enter the house.

Dion was waiting just inside the door, like a dog for its master. *If only he had a tail to wag,* she thought, in some amusement.

"You were gone a long time."

If looks could give set-downs, then Dion should be six feet under, she mused. Alas, they were lost on him. She glanced at the clock on the wall. Its pendulum was swinging comfortably, marking the passage of time with no sense of human conflict.

"I have not been absent above half an hour," she responded shortly. She did not doubt he had watched every solitary minute. It would not surprise her if he had had a sailor's spy glass trained upon them the whole while.

"What did he want?" he asked, not bothering to hide his curiosity.

She waved her hand flippantly. "To court me, of course."

He watched her suspiciously. "He does not behave like your usual suitors."

"Major Knight is not the usual stamp of gentlemen." She tried to look dreamy. It was not a practiced look, nor yet an emotion with which she was familiar.

"I cannot like you associating with him," Dion said, still scowling.

"You presume too much. It is not your place to comment upon what I choose to do," she snapped. "Where is my father?"

"In his study, *your ladyship*."

Ignoring this insolence, she turned to walk away. However, Dion's footsteps echoed behind hers. That would never do. She spun around and glared at him. "I do not need a shadow!"

"My work is in there."

"Very well." She stalked down the hall and opened the study door. Seated at his desk, her father looked up. "Father, I need to speak with you. Alone." She emphasized the last word and only just kept herself from fixing Dion with a malevolent stare.

"Anything you can say to me you can say in front of Dion."

Dion smirked triumphantly back at her in the manner of a naughty child.

"Papa," Catalina pleaded in a voice that was sure to get his attention. He looked up. She tried to look embarrassed. "This is private." Let them use their imaginations.

"Why did you not say so?" He stood up. "Come with me for a walk. I have been sitting too long."

Catalina did not demean herself by gloating. She could tell Dion was eager to get his hands on the note from Major Knight, but she needed to tell Papa everything first.

Catalina did not speak until they reached the park. "I took a walk here with Major Knight not twenty minutes ago."

"I see," her father said quietly. "So, this is not about something a mother would discuss with you?"

"No, Papa. He asked me to go directly to you."

Her father remained quiet.

"They know information has been leaking from the Spanish camp and they have narrowed it down to those under your authority."

"They believe me innocent after finding you with the documents?" He turned and looked at her with disbelief.

"He said the documents were what proved our innocence." She shook her head, baffled as well.

"I find it interesting that the Englishman came straight to you."

"They know you trust Dion implicitly," she said carefully.

"They suspect him?" Her father did not trouble to keep the anger from his voice.

"They have to, can you not see that? If not him, they will instead suspect us."

They walked in silence until they reached the rose garden. Catalina smiled, then remembered what she was about and pulled the letter from her pocket where she hoped Dion could not see. There was little doubt he was watching every move they made.

"I have not read this yet, for I wanted you to see it first. It involves how they want to proceed."

Her father discreetly took the note and walked on again, to a bench farther along where he would be out of sight of the house to read its contents. It seemed he knew his lieutenant's habits quite well.

Catalina sat and waited while her father read the note.

"He is being given the rope with which to hang himself." Returning, he sat down beside her with a little groan.

Catalina placed her arm on his. "Perhaps. Yet this way he will still have an opportunity to prove his innocence. It is better to know, Papa. If he is the traitor, we must know. He has duped all of us."

He looked away. She knew he was upset. This was very personal for her father. "I had hoped to discover the betrayer myself and avoid the shame to our name, our country."

She had known he would feel this way. "Every country has traitors. Thankfully it has been discovered before anything truly bad has happened."

"I do not think we can know what the true damage is. And if the villain is not Dion, what then?"

"We will know soon enough. Major Knight is going to pretend to court me and deliver information directly to me that way." She tried not to sound churlish as she explained the plan to him.

Her father noticed the timbre in her voice and looked at her in a knowing fashion anyway.

"Be careful, *mi querida*. He is not one with whom you can play your games."

Catalina needed no warning that Major Knight was dangerous. Every instinct had told her that from the first moment she had been near him.

"We should return. I have no doubts Dion is champing at the bit to know what we have been discussing."

Catalina snorted rudely as she rose from the bench. "I have never been a friend of his, but I do not wish him to be a traitor."

Her father stood and took her arm to escort her back to the house. "There was a time when I hoped he might be a candidate for your hand, but it quickly became apparent you would not suit."

Catalina bit back a retort.

Her father sighed. She was well aware he carried the weight of the country on his shoulders. "He will soon be gone. I will send him away on this commission to Burgos. He will either prove his allegiance or commit treason."

Catalina reached up and kissed her father on the cheek. "He has never deserved your patronage, Papa."

"No, he has not. And he certainly does not deserve you, guilty or no."

CHAPTER FOUR

WELLINGTON HAD ARRIVED by the time Felix returned to Headquarters. He was anxious to push the French into the mountains, and wanted to move forward immediately. An invitation was sent for Mendoza and his daughter to join them for dinner, along with a couple of staff officers. Felix dressed with care, then went downstairs to brief the general on the plan he had made with Colonel Hill.

"Knight," Wellington greeted him as he entered the room. It was a drawing room that had been transformed into what they referred to as the war room. Tables had been lined up for meetings and work, large enough to accommodate maps and plan although at the moment they bore reports. Several maps covered the walls. The walls were plaster and the floors were of old Spanish hickory. A soft breeze wafted through the open windows, and Everleigh, Owens and Hill sat in worn leather chairs, while the commander surveyed some reports.

"Hill told me of his plan to send a lieutenant of Mendoza's to Burgos. I do not think I wish to let him out of our sight. It will set up his suspicions," Wellington said thoughtfully.

"Pray it is not already too late," Hill replied. "Knight delivered a letter to Mendoza this afternoon."

"Then let us hope he has not put anything into motion yet, or Knight will find himself chasing the lieutenant."

"Mendoza and his daughter will be here for dinner. We can ask him presently."

"Ah, yes, the lovely Catalina," Wellington remarked with an appreciative smile.

"Were you aware, sir, that she spies for him?" Felix asked.

"No, but I am not at all surprised. I have little doubt she could squeeze secrets out of a rock." He furrowed his brow.

"Knight discovered her when he went to examine documents at the villa. I have directed him to pretend to court her."

"As good a plan as any," Wellington agreed. He chuckled. "If anyone can be convincing, it is Knight."

"Please do not tell me I must take her to Burgos. Bear-leading is not my forte."

"For Lady Catalina, I could be persuaded," Owens teased in his flippant manner.

Wellington ignored that remark. "Tomorrow we press north. I have an excellent notion of how to surprise Jourdan and Joseph by surrounding them on four sides. I will tell Mendoza tonight I have already put the plan in motion."

"With respect, sir," Hill interposed, "is it wise to alert the Spanish? Might it not be better to wait until the last minute? Will such notice not give the surprise away to the frogs? 'Twas why we thought to send the lieutenant away."

"Enemies are better kept close," Wellington said to no one in particular, "but I take your point." He shook his head. "That puts all of your eggs in the lieutenant basket and the snitch could be any number of people."

"So, I am to court the lady and keep a close eye on the lieutenant?" Felix asked.

"Yes, and we will wait until the last moment to apprise Mendoza of our intentions, when it will be too late to alert the French." Wellington walked over to a map on the wall. "This is where I intend to push them, and we will surround them here, here, here and here." He stabbed the paper with his finger at four points surrounding the French encampment. "Of course, they do not always cooperate, and we will adjust as necessary. Owens and Everleigh, you will ride on towards Burgos, where Joseph is, no doubt, comfortable on his sofa with bonbons, admiring the Spanish jewels."

"The usual, sir?" Everleigh asked. "Asking discreet questions, pretending to look for billeting?"

"Aye, that should be enough. If that does not set them on the road back to France, I do not know what will. Knight, you will do similar with the Spanish contingent. I will think on it and let you know how I wish to proceed. We will travel with them."

A carriage pulled up in front of the house, and Wellington looked out of the window. "It looks as though our guests are arriving." He took some papers from the table, rolled them up and tucked them into his coat.

Felix could hear Catalina and General Mendoza being shown into a smaller parlor across the hall. They had all risen and straightened their dress uniform jackets in order to greet the visitors. One of their batmen had already begun serving wine; they performed a dual function since it was impossible to travel with a full complement of servants. Lieutenant Colonel Roberts and Lord Rollings also joined them.

Lady Catalina looked as perfect as the flamenco dolls Spanish shops displayed in their windows. Tonight she wore a lace mantilla over her dark locks, and a bright red and white flowing gown trimmed in the same lace. Felix would prefer to see her dressed in a simple gown, with her hair about her shoulders. He knew she would be even more beautiful thus.

As they greeted each other, Major Silva and Captain Molina were announced. They were the trusted officers from the Portuguese contingent.

Having old acquaintance, Wellington kissed Lady Catalina's hand. He was a great flirt and always enjoyed a beautiful face. However, Felix knew that he was looking at her in a new light and assessing her through the compliments he made. Wellington was very keen. He turned once more to speak with Mendoza and then led him off to one side, so Felix was able to claim Lady Catalina's attention while Everleigh and Owens distracted the Portuguese officers. They had worked together for long enough that it was a seamless operation.

"Good evening," he said, looking her in the eye as he kissed the air above her hand. She watched with some amusement.

"We play the game already?" she asked. Her violet eyes twinkled.

"But of course. We will make such an excellent show of courting that even our friends will question if it is genuine."

"In that case..." She batted her eyes at him, causing him to laugh. "It is good to know I have not lost my abilities. It is also good to know you can laugh."

"I am a man of many talents. I am certain you will soon discover that fact for yourself."

She raised her eyebrows and tilted her head *just so*, as Eugenia would phrase it. Lady Catalina was very good at playing this game of flirtation. Even Felix was not completely convinced it was just a game, but he would not let himself be drawn in to then make a fool of himself—at least inwardly. He was certain Lady Catalina, when she decided to marry, would catch a very big fish.

"Plans have changed since we spoke earlier. Has your father sent Dion away yet?" He leaned very close and almost whispered in her ear, as though he was saying something for her ears only. He was, but not what most people would suspect if they were watching them.

She smiled and flashed her eyes at him. "Papa has not said a word to him yet. He wanted to think it over and speak about it with Wellington, when he heard the commander was arrived."

"Excellent," Felix said and took his eyes off the lady to survey the room. "If looks could kill, Molina and Rollings would have flayed me alive. Were they serious suitors before?"

She waved her hand dismissively. "They will do you no harm."

"I do not wish to be called out, nevertheless."

"No promises have been made, Major."

"Good. I would hate to have to admit to them that this is a farce. Although, they who know me well, will not be fooled if I become sunshine and roses with you."

"It happens to the best of us sooner or later," she warned.

"I expect, my lady, that we can, and shall, remain professional." He felt the need to say that to himself and to her.

"Do not make it sound so charming," she retorted.

"Tell me about the lieutenant," Felix said. "What is he like in a casual setting?"

She narrowed her eyes to think. "My feminine instincts do not care for him. He toad-eats my father. I would not have thought him to have the shrewdness to be a traitor."

"Often, men like him are the puppets and there is someone else pulling the strings."

⤷⤓

THE NEXT DAY they packed up and began the trek north. With any luck, Catalina reflected, King Joseph would flee back to France, and the army with him. On some days she enjoyed following the drum but on other days, like today, she longed to be back at Villa Blanca. Sometimes spying was exciting, though she had never done anything horribly dangerous. Mostly, however, her task was to ferret secrets from people who thought a young female too silly to guard their tongues in her company.

So far, she did not know what to make of Major Lord Felix Knight. It was somewhat ironic that he be the one to pretend to court her when it was the last thing he had on his mind, she was certain. He was roguishly handsome and she had noticed how other ladies looked at him. He was not fond of the attention; nor was she, for that matter. In this, she could relate to him. However, Catalina still wanted to claw the eyes out of every female that fawned and flirted over him for purely empathetic reasons, of course.

"That will do, Maria," she said to her maid, who had finished putting up her hair to go under her hat. She intended to ride as much as possible today, for she always felt ill inside a carriage on the winding mountain roads.

After breaking her fast on some rolls and coffee, Catalina stood patiently while Maria pinned her hat atop her head. It was a blue riding habit with gold braided trimming in the style of the Spanish uniform. She thought it was rather clever, since she traveled with the army.

Outside, their luggage wagon and carriage were already piled high with trunks and supplies, and her grey Andalusian mare, Luna, was saddled and waiting for her, as were her father and Lieutenant Dion.

"Good morning, *mi querida*," her father said.

"Good morning, Papa, Dion." She reached up on tiptoe and kissed her father's cheek as she pulled on one riding glove. "How far do we travel today?"

"I could not say. We travel with Wellington and his staff."

Her eyes widened in surprise.

"Does this not please you? I thought you would want to be near your latest flirt."

"Papa, please." She swatted him with her remaining glove and felt her cheeks heat a little. "It matters not to me. I can keep up with any Englishman."

Her father laughed. "Of course you can, *querida*."

She pulled on her other glove and accepted her father's lift into the saddle. She settled her skirts around her while she tried to settle her insides. What was the matter with her?

They set off to ride the few streets to where Wellington was already waiting on Copenhagen with Major Knight and Colonel Hill.

Wellington tipped his tricorn hat to them and they fell into the line, two by two, Wellington beside Hill, Dion next to her papa, and Major Knight next to her.

"You look… patriotic this morning," he said, looking at her, clearly very amused.

She lifted her chin into the air and glared at him as their horses tried to greet each other.

"Is this how the English say good morning?" she asked tartly.

"I beg your pardon. You look ravishing. Is that better?" He did not look the slightest bit repentant.

She twisted her lips. "No, I think I prefer your honesty, even if it is brutal."

"Now, that is something my sister frequently accuses me of."

"Oh, I am to be treated like a sister. That is most reassuring," she said dryly, although it piqued her pride to know he thought of her as a little girl.

They negotiated traffic through the city, and once they were free of the narrow streets, she watched him in the saddle with approval and some envy. She would dearly love to ride astride for these long journeys, but Papa would not hear of her looking anything but the most proper lady. It was no small matter of pride for him to think he had raised her properly after her mother's death.

"Why the long face?" Major Knight asked. She had not known he was watching her as well.

"I was thinking of my mother," she admitted as they cantered through the countryside, a wide, pleasant valley dotted with trees and farms leading them north-east away from the cathedral city of Salamanca. The road was wide, smooth and well suited to travel by carriage, and they made good progress. Lines of cork oaks provided shade from the scorching sun, and there were far-reaching views to be enjoyed across rich pasture and fields of corn toward the distant mountains in the west.

"What was she like, your mother?" he asked, probably only to make conversation to help the miles pass more quickly.

Catalina laughed. "She was beautiful and spirited and witty. I miss her every day."

"My parents died when I was but three. I wish I had more memories of them."

Catalina nodded. "I was twelve, a very hard time for a girl to lose her mother. I was not a girl, but not yet a woman."

"I imagine that would be difficult. I remember my sister Eugenia trying to navigate those waters with four overbearing brothers to guide her. My eldest brother lost his own youth and became a parent to us all."

"You are lucky to have siblings. I think I would have managed better with a brother or sister. It was often lonely."

"I am one of five," Major Knight offered. "I am very blessed…" His voice trailed off as though he was lost in memories.

"Why do I sense hesitation?"

"I have recently come from England. I spent a couple of months with them." He shook his head. "I love them dearly, but I am not like them."

She nodded in comprehension. "Being a soldier is a very different life. I do not envy you when it ends and you must return to what people consider normal. They have no idea what you experience."

Their eyes met in understanding, but he looked away. Catalina wondered what this man had suffered. Papa *had* said that, until recently, Major Knight had been imprisoned.

"I am pleased we are going north," she said, changing the subject. "If I am lucky, we will go near my home."

"And where is that?" Major Knight asked.

"The Basque country. It sits in the valley below the Pyrenees. It is the most beautiful place on earth. Vineyards cover the hills, and on a clear day you can see the sea." She smiled. "I am biased, but perhaps you may see for yourself."

"I would like that. The rolling landscape reminds me of England," Felix remarked, with a bit of longing in his voice.

She smiled at him, and sensed that he had decided to treat her like his little sister. Perhaps it was safer, but she did not wish to be thought of in that way. She wanted to be taken seriously.

That night the company bivouacked in a wood and she was able to show the major that a night under canvas held no fears for her, although if truth be known, she was glad of a respite from the saddle. They set off again at first light and marched on all morning, the terrain gradually ascending as they crossed the central basin of the Peninsula.

They stopped for a few minutes, alongside the River Douro, to water the horses and have a light meal in the shade. A large group of soldiers encircled them as they ate. Catalina had known there were people in front of and behind them, protecting the commander's entourage, but she had not seen them until now.

The day was growing hot, with the sun high in the sky and no clouds. It was preferable to being sodden to the bone and bogged down with muddy roads, but it would not be a comfortable afternoon. However, she would not complain. No, nothing caused fellow soldiers to lose their respect more than complaining. She may not set her face against the enemy directly on the battlefield, but she considered herself a soldier, nevertheless.

"You are deep in thought, Señorita," Major Knight said from beside her. She had thought he had fallen asleep, since he was resting his eyes.

"I confess I was thinking about the bright sunny day ahead."

"You mean the sun-scorching, dry and dusty ride ahead?"

She laughed. "Yes, but I would never put it so inelegantly."

"No, you are quite the hardened soldier, used to the elements."

Catalina was certain he was making fun of her, but she chose to accept it as a compliment. Her eyes strayed over to the trees. Many of the men had retired some distance for privacy, but she noticed Dion and Lieutenant Colonel Roberts deep in conversation.

"Do you see what I see?" she asked Major Knight, who, she discovered, was watching keenly despite having a lazy look beneath his eyes.

"Señorita, I have done nothing but watch these past twenty minutes."

"Is there anything to worry about?"

"Have you noticed them speaking before?" he asked, as though interrogating her.

Her first impulse was to retort rudely, but she paused and considered. They were to be professional, she recalled.

"Now I come to think on it, I have seen them speaking once or twice, but it was always in a social situation."

"You mean, as one of your court," he said knowingly.

She nodded reluctantly. It sounded so shameful when he pointed it out.

"There's no need to pout, Señorita." He came to his feet in a swift motion like a lithe feline, and held his hand out to her.

She accepted his hand, wishing she could wear trousers and have the ability to move freely as the men did. His touch caused her to feel things, and she resented it. If he could remain ambivalent to her touch, then so would she.

Reluctantly, she prepared to mount again. Even though she was used to hours on horseback, it was still a strain on her body. The foot soldiers had to walk hours every day, often without proper boots, or rations to give them energy. Whenever she thought of whining, thinking of them made her grateful.

"Again the long face, Señorita?" Major Knight remarked, standing before her. "Are you so reluctant to ride again? I am certain room can be made for you in one of the carriages."

She shook her head. "It is not that at all."

He tilted his head and seemed to see straight through her. Instead of thrusting her up into the saddle in the conventional manner, he surprised her by putting his hands on her waist as she lifted one foot for his assistance. He lifted her up and they were nearly level, he was so much taller than she. Their eyes met and then he turned away. So much about this man disturbed her, but she could not become distracted. They had a traitor to catch.

CHAPTER FIVE

A FTER OVER FORTY miles of travel, Felix estimated, they crossed the River Douro via a ford below at the town of Toro. The enemy had destroyed the bridge and the river here ran deep and swift. A little downstream was a place fordable by cavalry, although the horses were forced by the strong current to swim diagonally and gain the opposite bank some yards below the entry point. Felix was exceedingly thankful to have himself on one side of Catalina and a burly sergeant on the other. Toro itself stood high on a cliff above the river, but the country before them was level and verdant with fine champagne vineyards. After a long march, it was in this pleasant country that Wellington decided to stop for the night, at the village of Miranda de Duoro.

Everyone began to set up camp as if by memory. After a long, hard day in the saddle, the main thing on everyone's mind was food and sleep. The men led the horses to the water's edge to drink, and many of the soldiers took the opportunity to wash themselves, Felix included. Never before had he given much thought to a lady following the drum, except that there had always been camp followers. Some of the officers brought their wives, but most ladies stayed in nearby cities in lodgings or hostelries.

As the men were leaving, Felix saw Lady Catalina and three other women heading down to the river. Most of the men watched the ladies walk past, some subtly and some not, doubtless wishing they could be like David and wash Bathsheba at her bath. He shook his head. Even he was not immune, but he would not be taken in by this temptress. Losing one's head over a woman was dangerous at any time, but often deadly at war. It was surely some kind of punishment for past sins that he had been placed in her company for this assignment.

He did not linger at the water and watch the ladies bathe, but he stayed nearby to watch out for other soldiers who might not have his sense of decency and strength of will. Even though a blanket was held up to shield them, it would not be difficult for those determined to watch.

When the ladies had completed their ablutions, they climbed up the hill and he began to escort them back. Lady Catalina cast him an amused glance as though she believed he had been loitering.

"I will not be accused of sins I did not commit," he said, guessing at her thoughts.

"You would be the first man to show such restraint."

"Are baths a frequent source of amusement, then?"

She gave a Gallic shrug. "There is little I can do to prevent it other than remain dirty, which I refuse to do. I do not put on a show, as you assume."

"I beg your pardon. I should not tease you so."

Several tents had been erected and two dozen fires were roaring by the time they had climbed back up to the camp.

They parted company and he did not see her again until it was time to eat. Surprisingly, she was standing at the table with some of the cooks, helping serve bowls of stew, dough boys and mugs of ale. She was garbed in a plain, dark cotton dress with an apron covering it, her hair twisted into a simple plait. She had never looked more beautiful to him.

Once everyone had been served, Lady Catalina approached the

campfire where he was sitting with a few of the other officers. They began to stand, but she waved them back down and sat next to him to eat her own meal.

There was something enchanting about being outdoors with a fire, far away from the city. The smell of burning wood and the crackle of the flames, with the river roaring in the background, was seductive to a soldier, and for this one night, it was easy to forget what their true purpose was. There was no artifice in any of them at this moment.

Some of the men left for their beds and one or two others left to seek card games or alternative entertainment. It was companionable sitting next to the lady, and he felt more disarmed by her in this setting than he did in any ballroom.

He glanced sideways at her as she sat next to him in a relaxed pose, the orange flames casting an angelic glow on her face. For a moment, he allowed himself to think of a settled life such as his brothers had chosen. He did not know if he could do it. Certainly, a few weeks of it sounded heavenly, but he knew he could not sustain the docile life of a gentleman farmer, or similar, for long.

"You did well today, Señorita," he said quietly, trying to interrupt his disturbing thoughts.

"You doubted I could keep pace?"

"Not at all. I knew you could keep pace—my sister could outride most men. It is the steady resolve with which you accomplished it that impressed me."

"This has been my life for eight years, now." She took a stick that had been placed by the fire for kindling and begin to play with it by twirling its tip in the flames.

"Do you ever wish to settle and lead a calm, quiet life?"

"I am not certain what such a life would be like, in all honesty, but I do wish for peace."

He gave a nod of agreement. "I would not like it if the fighting were this near to my home. Pray this war resolves soon. If Wellington's plan works, it will be so."

"What of your dreams? Do you wish for this calm, docile life that you speak of?" she asked.

A short laugh escaped his lips. "I do not think I am capable of such a thing. All three of my brothers have married this past year. At least, I assume the third brother will have married by now. It was quite a shock to go home and witness the change in them."

"What will you do when the war ends?"

"I imagine I will work in the diplomatic service. My brother has been pressing me to do so for some time."

A piece of log broke in half, sending sparks flying into the air. They watched the shower of light descend. Lady Catalina shivered, running her hands up and down her arms. As he watched, she covered a yawn and then laughed.

"I think it is time for me to retire."

He leapt to his feet and helped her to rise. "Which tent is yours?"

"This way," she said, and led him to the edge of the camp, greeting others as they passed. Felix kissed her hand as he bade her goodnight, for the benefit of those nearby, then waited while she went inside.

Instead of walking back through the camp, he went to the perimeter to think and scout a little. The day with Lady Catalina had been pleasant. She had not chattered incessantly or demanded special treatment. He had expected a spoiled shrew. Perhaps this would not be as tedious as he had imagined. She was definitely headstrong and opinionated, and he only hoped, if there was danger, that she would be able to yield and trust him. His eyes and feet were on alert in the darkness, scanning for anything out of the ordinary. There were soldiers sent to guard the perimeter, of course, but this turn about the encampment was a habit, something he always did before he could retire.

He passed a rowdy group who had very likely exceeded their rations of drink for the night. So far, they were jovial as they told stories and played a dice game.

Further on, there was a line of soldiers bivouacked into a natural crevice, covered by rough blankets and with their packs beneath their heads.

At the next corner, a quiet, contemplative-looking group sat drinking around the fire. He raised his hand to them as he passed by.

When he drew near to his own tent, next to the commander's, he could hear the familiar voice speaking with Colonel Hill and Lieutenant Colonel Roberts. Normally, he would have been in such a meeting, but he had been tasked with escorting Lady Catalina.

As he moved forward to the command tent, he heard a sound of movement and saw a slight shift of light within the shadows.

He froze as if turned to ice and narrowed his gaze upon the movement, reaching for the dagger in his coat at the same time. Where were the guards?

It was very dark at the side of the tent, the only light being the flicker of the dying campfires. Slowly, Felix began to move forward like a lion stalking its prey, years of practice serving him well. He could sense the moment whoever it was realized they were about to be caught. He leapt the last few feet and tackled the figure, throwing his arms around their chest and holding their upper arms immobile.

With a groan from the other, the pair hit the ground as the person fought back, flailing their lower arms in an attempt to injure Felix. He wrapped his legs around the intruder's, and they rolled a few times, the flash of a blade in the other man's hand causing Felix to tense.

The man was big and fit and in all probability, another soldier, used to fighting for his life. Felix held a dagger in his hand, but did not want to use it. At such close quarters it would be too easy to kill, and he wanted him alive.

People came from the tent when they heard the commotion and his captive tried desperately to escape. Writhing and butting with his head, for all the world like an enraged ram, he tried to throw Felix away from him.

"Enough!" Felix shouted, noticing Wellington and Hill standing before the command tent, guns cocked and pointed at them both. It was too risky for either to shoot and Felix knew he was on his own until he could subdue the man. Eventually, the man would tire. Felix could wait a little while, though his muscles burned with exertion. The intruder tried to roll away from the light. In that moment, he was able to free his hand enough to plunge a dagger into Felix's thigh, causing him to grit his teeth in pain. That was the final straw. Felix took his own chance and let go of the man's arm long enough to thrust the pommel of his dagger into his assailant's temple. Immediately, the man slumped in his arms.

"What the devil happened, Knight?" Wellington asked when he and Hill came over to survey the disorder.

Felix removed his neckcloth and wrapped it around his bleeding thigh while Hill rolled the unconscious attacker over.

"I caught him listening outside your tent."

"Dion. As you suspected," Wellington remarked. "If only this would put an end to it. It is my belief, however, we have but caught the bait."

⫸⫷

"I WANT THIS kept quiet," she heard a voice say. Catalina immediately became alert, though she did not move in her bed.

"What do you intend to do with him?" her papa's voice asked.

"Wring every ounce of information out of him first. I want to know who is giving him orders."

Something must have happened with Dion, she thought furiously, her eyes tightly closed while she pretended to sleep. General Wellington was speaking to her father in their tent, so it must be serious.

"I would like you to speak with him first, when he regains consciousness. My immediate concern is Knight. We have no surgeon with us at present and I need to ascertain how deep his wound is."

"Catalina can sew. You should take her."

"I hate to wake a sleeping beauty, but he might very well need her."

"I will wake her and we will both meet you at your tent. I must consider what to say to Dion so I do not kill him myself."

"They become like sons to us, and the betrayal is deeper because it harms not just ourselves but our countries," Wellington said sympathetically.

Her father murmured something and she heard the rustle of the tent flap. She could hear Papa muttering as he dressed before he came through the curtain that divided the tent. He shook her arm a little.

"Catalina, you must wake. Your major has been injured and might need your sewing skills."

She did not pretend to be asleep any longer. "What has happened, Papa?"

"He caught Dion listening outside Wellington's tent. They fought and Dion stabbed Knight, but he was still able to overcome Dion. I do not know how, but he is unconscious."

"Will he be hanged or shot?"

"I do not know. We must hurry."

He left her to dress and she quickly threw on the plain gown she had been wearing earlier because she could tie it at the sides. Maria was sleeping in another tent with other servants. It was a very fortunate thing at the moment, for she had an affection for Dion. Catalina gathered up her sewing kit and items she thought she might need, and hurried out of the tent with her father.

As they crossed the camp to where the British officers' tents were pitched, all was eerily quiet. The camp fires still smoked a little and a few embers still glowed. Dew had already begun to settle and the air was crisp. Other than the occasional animal crying out in the distance, the only sounds were their boots crunching across the ground and the river flowing along beside the camp. She wrapped her shawl around her tightly and shivered with fear as well as cold, for she was afraid of how she might find Major Knight.

A guard opened the tent for them and they ducked inside. Bound hand and foot, Dion was laying on the floor, eyes closed and groaning. It took great strength of will for her not to spit in his face.

"This way, my lady," Wellington said, directing her to the rear behind a curtain. Major Knight was lying on Wellington's own cot, watching her warily. He was propped up and a little pale, but appeared fully alert.

"You did not mention you were also a surgeon," he quipped.

"I am not, but I am the best you have for now." She walked closer and placed her sewing kit on the bed beside his bandaged leg. His leg and what remained of his breeches were stained heavily with dark crimson from the blood loss. "How deep is it?"

"I have not removed the bandage to see. It feels wretched, but any cut does."

A batman brought in a basin of steaming water and Wellington searched through a trunk and handed her a bottle of spirits. The same batman placed a stool behind her and she sank down on to it. Opening her small sewing kit, she placed everything out in a neat row and threaded a needle.

"Beckerman will assist you," Wellington remarked before escaping to the front of the tent where her father and Dion waited.

Wellington's knowing Beckerman brought strips of cloth for bandages, then he stood beside her ready to assist.

"Shall we view the damage?" Catalina looked Knight in the eye, hoping he did not see how nervous she was. She had stitched many minor wounds, but she was very afraid of what she would find once the tourniquet was removed.

Knight's hand reached out and touched her arm and gave it an encouraging squeeze. The knot was tight and Beckerman reached forward and cut it before she had to ask. She began to wonder if he should not be the one doing this.

Fresh dark blood began to ooze from a deep crevice in his large, muscular thigh. Quickly, she covered it with a fleece cloth before taking some of the water and beginning to rinse it until it was clean enough to determine what needed to be done. It was a very deep cut and she would only be able to get one stitch in at a time before the wound filled again.

"Spirits, my lady?" the batman asked in a suggesting tone, holding out the bottle. Catalina was a bit taken aback by the gruff German accent.

"Would you like some before I begin?" she asked Major Knight.

"I've already had plenty." He slurred the words a little.

"I meant to cleanse the wound, my lady," the batman corrected.

She frowned.

"We clean wounds with spirits," Major Knight explained. "It seems to reduce infection." He shrugged. "Some Scottish doctor made that up, very likely, but who am I to question such madness?"

Catalina was skeptical, but she knew some healers used herbs and even fire to treat such lacerations. She stepped back and let the batman pour a strong-smelling liquid into the wound. Major Knight grabbed the edge of the cot and blew out several deep breaths, his face contorted with pain.

"Are you certain you do not need some more to drink?"

He nodded with his eyes closed. "Yes, get this over with, please."

She stepped forward with her needle and thread. Beckerman pulled away the fleece with which he had been applying pressure. She could see very far down to where a vessel was throbbing at the bottom of the gaping hole. "I do not know a great deal, but I do believe you were very lucky."

"Tell me that in a few weeks when I am still alive," he drawled.

Very well; he did not appreciate knowing how close he had been to severing an artery. Without another word, she placed a deep stitch, pulling the muscle together, and tied the knot quickly before she could no longer see what she was doing. She trimmed the thread and Beckerman was waiting with the fleece to put pressure on the wound again. After a few more deep stitches, the skin closed and she was able to place some superficial ones on top.

"Not too tight, my lady," the batman advised. "Any deep infection needs to leak out."

She had never sewn a deep laceration before and had no idea what was best. "If you do not think there is any danger of its re-opening, I will do as you say."

"The deep stitches matter the most."

"You know a great deal. Perhaps you should consider being a surgeon," she remarked as she placed the last stitch. Major Knight was lying so still she might have thought him asleep except for the rigid posture he had maintained to withstand the pain.

Beckerman held up his other hand to show his disfigured fingers. "I used to help a surgeon, but I cannot make certain movements anymore."

"I am most grateful for your assistance," she said, smiling up at him.

He gave her an embarrassed nod and then began to clean up the disorder she had made before bandaging the wound.

She stepped away, her hand rubbing her sore back. She had not even realized she had been standing. Major Knight had opened his eyes and was watching her closely.

When the batman withdrew to take the soiled linens and dirty water away, she stepped forward when Knight held his hand out to her.

"Thank you," he said. "I wish I had been able to manage this less violently."

"I had not thought him even capable of such duplicity. I do not understand how he could do this to us."

Major Knight reached up his hand and smoothed out the creases between her brow, causing her to smile.

"I do not like to see you frown."

"I do not like to see you hurt." She placed her own hand on his brow. He was perspiring from the exertion. She would have passed out at the first stitch. "What do you think will happen?"

"I would not want to be Dion now. He will be wishing I had killed him when they finish with him. But they will try to keep this quiet so it does not cause unrest amongst the soldiers or the allies."

She twisted her lips in another frown. She was too tired to think of what would happen on the morrow.

He smoothed out her frown again. "Go back to bed. I will see you in the morning—and thank you for sewing me up."

CHAPTER SIX

FELIX'S LEG THROBBED like the devil throughout the night, and despite the copious amounts of spirits they had given him to dull the pain, he did not sleep well. For one, he had never expected Dion to show himself so quickly. Perhaps the man had felt he had no choice, given Felix's new friendliness with Lady Catalina, Wellington's arrival and the army's march north. Wellington had known something was afoot and thus had felt considerable urgency to discover it before it was too late. On the other hand, there would be decisions to be made about Dion's injury and Felix's own. They would be unable to travel normally, so would they be left behind or some sort of story fabricated?

The curtain opened and Beckerman looked in. "Good morning, sir. Glad to see you awake. How is your leg this morning?"

"I have not tried to move it yet, but it throbs like the very devil."

Beckerman gave a swift nod as if that were no more than he had expected. "I'll change the bandage, and then we had best see if you can put the weight on it."

Felix had not taken a good look at the wound last night. He had found from experience it was best not to until the surgeon had finished.

Beckerman unwound the bandage, and the simple movement of bending his knee caused Felix's muscles to contract with a shock of pain.

"Smarts good, dunnit? Not too much drainin'. I'd say the lady did a fair job of it."

Felix looked down and the laceration looked paltry compared to the sensations beneath it.

"It looks rather tidy," Felix agreed.

"Cut right through the muscle, it did. A hair more and ye would not be here this mornin', sir."

Felix did not need to be reminded. He had become rusty in his convalescence and Dion had surprised him. Felix had certainly underestimated the lieutenant's abilities.

Beckerman finished cleaning the incision and freshly bandaging it. Then he helped Felix to dress.

"There will be no riding for you today, sir," Beckerman said as he began packing up what remained in that part of the tent.

"Have any decisions been made about our captive?"

Beckerman made a sound of disgust in the back of his throat. "Not a word from him yet. He is pretending to be injured and concussed in the head."

Felix gave a nod as if it were no more than he expected. To be fair, he reflected, Dion probably *was* concussed, but there was no telling this gruff German that.

"Do we travel with the camp or does the commander have other plans for us?"

"The last I was told, they were to put you and the traitor at the back of the baggage train with some excuses about eating a bad piece of fish."

Involuntarily, Felix cringed. That had happened more often then he would like to recall. It was a plausible excuse.

"Ja." Beckerman nodded sympathetically. "Maybe eight or so hours in a carriage with you will get him to talking."

"If I do not lose my mind first," Felix muttered.

The batman had finished with all but the cot Felix was sitting on. Now, the moment of truth, he mused. Beckerman came and helped Felix to his feet, holding him up under the bad leg. A rush of pressure went straight to the wound and it felt as though a colony of ants had decided to sting him all in one place.

"Easy now, the blood left your head. Do you think you can walk?" Beckerman asked. "The carriage is not far from here."

"I will get there. This is not my first meeting with an injury."

The sergeant helped him to the front of the tent and then Felix hobbled the last few steps on his own. Anyone watching might think him ill, but hopefully would not guess the true nature of what had happened to him. He clutched one hand to his stomach in added effect.

Dion was already in the carriage, hands and feet bound. He was looking away from the door. It was going to be a very long day, Felix sighed to himself, his injury notwithstanding. He climbed in gingerly and pulled his leg up on the squab. He leaned his head back and caught his breath.

Dion turned his head and glared, followed by a look of satisfaction.

Colonel Hill put his head inside the door.

"Good morning, sir," Felix said.

"Beckerman reported you were doing well, but I wanted to see for myself. I regret having to punish you with him all day, but our choices are limited. Is there anything I can get you before we roll on?"

"Perhaps some food to settle my stomach?" He gave a wry smile.

"I will see to it. I will visit you when we stop again."

Felix just wanted to get the day over with. The sooner they began moving, the better. Curving mountain passes with a queasy stomach might torture Dion more than anything else Felix had up his sleeve to extract secrets.

Outside, female voices were chattering. The two men were to travel with the wagons at the rearguard which contained the camp followers.

The door opened again and Lady Catalina's face appeared, smiling at him. Goodness, was everyone going to check how they did before the carriage could leave?

"Put the basket there," she directed her maid, and then began to climb into the carriage.

No, please, no. Please do not let happen what I think is happening.

It was happening. Lady Catalina climbed into the carriage, looking entirely too cheerful and well rested. It would be as bad as being locked up for hours with Eugenia in a merry mood, except he could not lash out at this lady he barely knew as he could a younger sister.

She paused before sitting down and wrinkled her face as she surveyed the interior of the conveyance.

"Maria, I think you will have to ride up on the box. It is rather crowded in here." The maid cast a look of displeasure at Lady Catalina, but Felix was certain she missed the insolence.

"Yes, it is crowded, rather," Felix remarked. "You would probably be more comfortable on your mount."

"Very likely," she said agreeably, "but someone must play nursemaid. Dion cannot feed himself, after all." She looked back and forth between the two squabs, as if assessing where to sit. Felix did not move his leg down. She chose the corner opposite Dion. *Thank the heavens.*

At last, the carriage lurched forward. Lady Catalina removed her bonnet and began to make herself comfortable.

"I do not suppose you have the food in that basket I was promised?"

"Oh. yes. Sergeant Beckerman packed this for you. Apparently, rations are slim at the moment," she remarked as she looked with distaste into the basket before handing it to Felix.

There was a small loaf of bread, a few biscuits, and apples they had found growing on trees along the way. It was better than nothing.

"I have already broken my fast and Dion may eat if he decides to speak."

The lieutenant growled at her.

"In a foul mood this morning, I see, Dion. It makes you look even more guilty when you refuse to explain yourself."

"I have nothing to say to you." He nearly spat on her.

"Who said anything about me?" She waved her hand through the air, assuming the role of the silly society lady more than she had the first night Felix had met her. "But Papa, he treated you like a son."

Did the woman intend to drive them both to Bedlam with her incessant chatter? He leaned back and closed his eyes. If she could wrangle the truth from Dion, he would not have to employ more violent methods later. At least he had the good grace to wait until after they had been on the road a few minutes, but Lady Catalina was determined. Did the lieutenant realize what she was doing? Probably he did, but Felix was happy to let her wear away Dion's will. He himself was not feeling quite the thing this morning.

She rambled on and on about what his family would think of his betrayal, from his mother to his poor grandmother. Her father had been prepared to make great things of him in the army and make a heroic name for him, but now, he would be remembered as the lowest scum of the earth. Traitors were lower than the worst criminal, she declared. Even criminals had honor of sorts, but he had none.

She must have rambled on for two hours, Felix conjectured. He was impressed with her tenacity, despite himself. Hopefully, they would be stopping for a break soon, because there was not enough air in the small vehicle. Dion looked stoic at the moment, as if he had resigned himself to this female form of torture. Felix wondered when last the prisoner had eaten. Lady Catalina must have read his mind, for she pulled out some delicious looking pastries and began to eat them in the most unladylike fashion. Felix, who thought himself immune to anything, could barely keep from squirming as she made noises of pleasure and licked her fingers.

"You think you are clever, but you are nothing but a *micosa mimada* trying to make herself feel as though she has purpose. You are nothing to me," Dion snarled.

"I am glad our mutual distaste for each other is settled, then. We can move on to more memorable activities." She reached into her reticule and pulled out a small satchel of tools and slowly unrolled it. Felix was impressed in spite of wishes to the contrary. He had assumed the señorita's role to be little more than eyes and ears, which was what a great deal of spying amounted to. Nevertheless, there were more unpleasant tasks required, on occasion, to extract information, and she appeared ready and willing to do whatever she deemed necessary. Felix knew that she had a personal vendetta to settle with Dion, so he remained quiet in his part of the carriage and watched.

⇥⟫⟫✕⟨⟨⟨↤

HOPEFULLY, NO ONE could tell she was hoodwinking them. She had never done anything remotely resembling torture except, perhaps, to brush the knots out of her cat's fur. However, she remembered being a child and having to fetch her own branch from a tree, with which to be punished. It had been very effective.

Slowly and carefully, she took each instrument out and examined them, one by one. Dion was trying not to look. No doubt he was wondering if she had the courage to do anything or not. He had only seen one side of her.

Besides making him nervous, she had to remind herself why this would be necessary if he would not talk.

"Dion," she began, as though they were about to share a cup of tea, "if you would tell me why you were listening outside the commander's tent, I might be inclined to be more lenient."

He jeered at her. "Why does anyone listen?"

She clicked her tongue. "Shall I be more specific? Clearly I must be. Why were you listening where you were not supposed to be?"

"Do you think your father has not already asked me these questions? Why would I say anything to you if I would not to him?"

She took a pair of tweezers and reached over and plucked a hair from the back of his hand. He did not flinch. Perhaps she should pull harder next time.

"My father is more understanding than I am. You see, I believe there is far more to this. I think you are working for someone else. If you would be so kind as to give his name, we can stop this now."

He glared at her and said nothing, so she plucked a few more hairs out. "Being a torturer is not so hard," she remarked, feeling rather pleased with herself. "I should be quite good at it by the time we reach Vitoria." Her gaze strayed towards Major Knight; he was watching her with a great deal of amusement.

"It seems our Lieutenant Dion has become forgetful, Major Knight. Should we suggest some names?"

He proffered a lazy shrug. "It could not hurt to refresh his memory."

"I agree." She turned back to Dion. "One hair for one name? I think that is very reasonable of me. Gonzales?" she asked, watching him closely. "No?" She plucked another hair. The back of his hand was quite pink already. "De Castro? Garcia? Perez?" She continued on with every name she could think possible from their regiment. Then she surveyed her handiwork. "I suppose we should make the hands equal," she murmured, beginning on the other hand. "Your nails are quite shapely. It would be a shame to have to pull them off," she remarked offhandedly.

"Let us move on to another regiment. Molina? Silva? Santos? Borges? Castro?" Pluck, pluck, pluck, pluck, pluck. The hands were now equally bereft of hair and she had exhausted the list of likely people from the Spanish and Portuguese officers. "Hmm. Perhaps he is

French, Major Knight? Dion can be either, did you know?" She looked at Knight as though this were a commonplace matter.

"I am not surprised," he responded in a bored voice.

"The Basque country we come from borders with France. Perhaps his sympathies are with Napoleon and he believes in killing innocents because of titles and wealth. He believes in taking what is not his."

"The possibility is looking more likely every moment," the major agreed.

"What should we do with traitors, Major Knight?" she asked in an innocent voice.

"Draw and quarter them in front of the regiment?"

"That is too kind for a traitor, I think. Perhaps I can ask Papa to let me decide. I think solitary confinement with a mischief of hungry rats would be slower and more painful."

"We could fashion a pile, such as the Romans used. I hear it takes three days to die," Knight suggested.

"Is your reason for betraying your country worth it? If you are doing it for money, that might be understandable."

"You have no idea of what you speak," Dion growled.

"I am waiting to be enlightened," she retorted. "I think it must be the fingernails next, unless you have other ideas, Major Knight?"

The carriage was slowing to a halt, and she hoped they were stopping for a rest. She had talked nonstop for what felt like several hours and she was losing her nerve, truth be told.

"Do you think we will have time for coffee? I do so love a cup of coffee with a splash of cream and a hint of sugar. It feels heavenly on a dry throat, do you not think?" She knew coffee was Dion's favorite drink.

Beckerman opened the door and helped her to alight. She made a big show of stretching her arms and legs. Major Knight was also making an effort to get down from the carriage. She had not asked him how he was because she did not think he would appreciate Dion knowing how much he had injured him.

Beckerman then climbed in behind them and closed the door. "I will guard the traitor while you refresh yourselves," he said grimly.

Catalina held on to Major Knight and he gave a good performance of walking without much of a limp. They had stopped at a clearing overlooking a valley with a copse of trees for shade.

Once they were out of hearing of the carriage, the major spoke. "Do you intend to do this the entire way?"

"I think I will ride for the next leg of the journey. He can ponder on what I will do to him next." She shrugged. "It may take several days, but eventually he will tell us something."

"He did not flinch when you mentioned the Spanish and Portuguese officers. My guess is that he is planted by Bonaparte or he is doing it for money."

"The usual reasons," Catalina said, wrinkling her nose in disgust and waving her hand dismissively.

"My main objective for now is to discover who he is working with. I do not know how much he overheard before I caught him."

Catalina looked up at him. "Did you suspect someone was spying when you left me?"

He shook his head. "No. I always walk the perimeter of the camp before I retire."

"It was coincidental, then. It is a shame we did not see him pass information on to someone else."

"Yes, this is not ideal, but it seldom ever is. I could not risk losing him. It was dark and he could have easily slipped away from me."

"I do not blame you, señor. I would have done the same, she remarked. "There has to be someone who is passing messages for him. He never leaves my father's side long enough to do it himself."

"The only names you have not suggested are English," Major Knight pointed out.

"Very true. Perhaps you may draw something out of him on the next leg of the journey."

She left him at the edge of the trees and went off with her maid to find her own privacy, wondering what else she could do, in all seriousness. Dion was never going to confess to her, but hopefully she had helped to wear him down a little.

CHAPTER SEVEN

F ELIX HALF SLEPT the next leg of the journey, and he thought Dion did as well. Sometimes silence was a more powerful, disconcerting form of torture than talking. Quiet allowed your mind to wander to deep, dark crevices that you were not aware existed, which disturbed your mental state and led to near derangement. Let Dion stew about what was coming.

When the cavalcade stopped again, Lieutenant Colonel Roberts came for a visit and looked in on the prisoner, but he did not stay long. Then Lady Catalina rejoined them.

Dion had not said a word for the last few hours, but he groaned with displeasure at the sight of her.

Felix chuckled. "It seems your form of torture is most effective, Señorita."

She raised her eyebrows at him and took a seat, settling her skirts around her. Dion shuffled to the side to get further away from her. He was definitely becoming irritated and testy, which was a good sign.

Sounds of activity rose from the chatter around them; the sounds of horses and wagons being loaded in preparation to set off again. They had left Villanueva behind and the road was taking them over the Mountain of Oca. It was already a rough, stony road and further on would be steep and narrow. Felix did not much relish being the last vehicle, but he knew it was necessary.

Such a narrow thoroughfare would doubtless have places where the passing of only one horse or mule at a time would be permissible. He grimaced. The artillery would have a hard time of it, that was for certain, and would inevitably delay their own progress. One by one, they heard the wagons and carts in front of them begin to pull forward. This was to be the last leg of the day before they crossed the River Ebro and then began the descent to Vitoria. To judge from the maps, the route down the mountain would be equally as torturous. Once at Vitoria, Wellington hoped to make a decisive push against the French army by surrounding them. It only awaited the intelligence that that was the best place.

Felix was growing impatient; he never enjoyed riding inside, but being the last vehicle, their carriage was inevitably the slowest and he was ready to be done with this day. Part of him wondered what Lady Catalina had in store for her next show and he felt himself smile. Then the carriage shifted from the movement of someone jumping down from the box seat.

He and Lady Catalina exchanged frowns. There was more movement and he was not sure if someone jumped on or jumped off.

"What is happening?" Catalina asked.

"The driver is probably tightening the traces," he answered, privately not convinced.

"Probably," she said, still frowning. Clearly deciding to look out anyway, she stood up and opened the panel in the roof. "Where is Maria?" she demanded. "And who are you?"

"Nothing to worry about, miss. We are just changing drivers to give yours a rest," he replied in excellent Spanish.

Felix heard the crack of a whip and the carriage lurched forward while Lady Catalina was still standing. She strained to regain her balance and Felix reached up to steady her.

"How dare he!"

"Who is he?" Felix asked.

"I have never seen him before and my maid is no longer there. I do not like this at all."

Neither did Felix, but he tried to appear calm.

"What uniform was the driver wearing?"

Catalina appeared to think. "I would say it was English."

Felix nodded. It probably was as simple as resting the other driver, but why would the maid be gone?

They both settled back for the journey, but Felix could not be easy. They began by going at a snail's pace, but then the vehicle's speed picked up noticeably just as they began to navigate the winding passes. The driver took the bends at reckless speeds and, alarmingly, it felt as though they were tipping on to two wheels whenever they rounded a sharp turn.

Catalina began to look very green and Dion's face took on a look of terror, his eyes wide. Felix felt mild regret for the man, being bound, but let it pass. Dion deserved to be terrified, but he and Lady Catalina did not.

"Do you know anything about this?" he asked Dion.

The lieutenant shook his head vehemently.

"I strongly suspect that whoever you were gathering secrets for is now trying to rid himself of all of us." Felix scooted toward the window and looked out to see the steep cliffs plunging straight down into a deep ravine. The summits of bleak, rocky mountains reared above them, white caps of snow glistening in the June sun, while goats and sheep grazed tiny belts of grass above deep chasms. Swallowing deeply, he sat back quickly to quell his lurching stomach. Something was not right.

Did the driver intend to sacrifice himself in order to kill the rest of them? If the pace was not slowed quickly, they would all plunge to their deaths.

"What is happening?" Lady Catalina asked. "I think our driver is drunk!"

"Stop him!" Dion shouted frantically.

Felix was not certain what he could do, but he began to push himself up, ignoring the pain. Trying to climb out of a moving carriage was a feat he was not certain a trained Astley's performer could accomplish on a level field. In this perilous situation, with a bad leg, he had a slim chance at best.

Lady Catalina groaned. "Never mind, I will do it," she said, muttering about the unfairness of having to wear skirts. She opened the door and he got a glimpse of barren, dusty rocks speeding by. As she clung to the side, he heard her begin to retch. He thought he recalled she had mentioned feeling sick with the motion when inside a carriage.

Somehow, she seemed to have gathered her composure, for she put her foot on the seat beside him and climbed on top of the carriage. If they lived, he would compliment her later, he decided appreciatively. The conveyance was not the best sprung and rattled from side to side, lurching over loose stones in its path. If he allowed himself time to consider, he would not do it. Swallowing again, he followed behind his courageous charge, determined to help. Even if she was able to subdue the driver, would she be able to control the horses?

Felix held on to the side, the carriage body shaking beneath his fingers; his feet still on the doorstep, he watched Lady Catalina doing the same where she knelt on the roof. Seeing her safe for the moment, he stole a glance ahead.

They were on a straight stretch of road for the moment, though the drop down was decidedly steep and rugged. He tried not to think about it as he heaved himself up onto the carriage alongside the lady.

The driver, a nondescript individual wearing an infantry uniform, shot a frightened look over his shoulder just then and noticing them, began to panic. He started to climb from the box onto one of the horse's backs. Felix shook his head. That was instant suicide.

Nothing about this drama had a happy ending written upon it, though, and they needed to find a way to stop the hurtling carriage and quickly.

"For God's sake, man, don't be a fool. Pull them up!" Felix shouted in English, but either the man was ignoring him or did not hear over the noise.

At any moment, he thought, when the horses saw the man trying to jump on them they were going to bolt, and then they would all be smashed to pieces in the bottom of the ravine.

The driver jumped, and the horses immediately shied. The carriage lurched.

Somehow, the man managed to land on the back of one of the wheelers and was sawing at the traces with a knife.

The carriage veered from side to side. Felix inched forward towards the box, clutching tightly to the rim of the body lest he be thrown, and Lady Catalina did the same. "Try to grab the reins!" he shouted over the roar in his ears. The narrow lines of leather were flapping loosely over the foot-board. One heavy jerk and they would be down around the wheelers' legs...

Lady Catalina was more nimble than he and she somehow clambered on to the box and grabbed the reins as the villain succeeded in cutting one of the traces. Felix had not thought the double leather could have been so easily cut, unless they had been weakened beforehand.

As Felix watched in horror, it was one of those moments which happened in a second yet stopped time. He knew the carriage would skew at an angle and turn them over and throw them only God knew where.

"Jump!" he shouted to Lady Catalina as he threw himself off the side away from the steep cliff. The carriage lurched and lost its balance; the second trace snapped, the horses galloped on and the body of the vehicle tumbled over the side of the cliff. *Dear God, Dion is tied up!* Felix thought belatedly as his body landed with a thud against some scrub bushes. Jolts of pain shot through his injured leg.

"Catalina!" he shouted, looking around for her. She had landed a few feet in front of him and was lying very still. Too still. As he forced himself to crawl to her, he noticed the driver was vanishing into the distance with the horses, clinging like a monkey and managing to stay on. Felix would worry about that later.

Somehow, nothing else seemed to matter but Lady Catalina.

When he reached her, she was staring up at the sky in a stunned condition. "Señorita?" he asked before he touched her. She was gasping for breath. "My lady? Are you harmed?"

"It hurts to breathe," she answered through shallow breaths.

"Can you move your arms and legs?"

She responded by moving them slightly and Felix breathed a sigh of relief. It happened often to soldiers when they fell off a horse. They called it getting the wind knocked out of them. He was not certain Lady Catalina would appreciate the humor at the moment.

"Breathe slowly and it will pass. Trust me." She gave a slight nod and obeyed.

"What happened to the carriage?" she asked between gasps.

"You should not try to speak. I have not looked yet. It went over the side. If you are unharmed, I will try to find out."

"Go," she wheezed. "I will be well again in a moment."

As Felix pulled himself to his feet, every part of his body hurt. No matter how many times he had fallen from horses, he had never learned to do it properly. Although, actually, this time he did not seem to have broken any bones, so perhaps that was as proper as he could expect.

He limped over to the edge of the road and looked down. The carriage had landed some twenty feet below and was upside down on a ledge. Felix closed his eyes and said a quick prayer. Very likely Dion had been destined for a traitor's death, but Felix would have at least given him a fair trial.

As he pondered how to climb down to the carriage, Lady Catalina came to stand beside him, holding her arm.

"Do you think he is dead?" she asked.

"It will be a miracle if he has survived, but I intend to find out for certain. Have you broken your arm?"

"I fear I must have done. We have made a wonderful pair of spies, have we not?"

"We are alive. That must count for something. Especially as I believe we were all intended to die."

CATALINA KNEW IT was the truth, but it was still a shock to hear it.

"Do you intend to climb down there?" she asked doubtfully.

"As soon as I have put a splint on your arm."

"My arm can wait. I will look for a piece of wood while you go—if you think you are able with your injury?"

His only response was an ironic lift of an eyebrow.

Feeling her cheeks warm, Catalina watched nervously while Major Knight climbed downward despite his knife wound. In her opinion, he went much too quickly, and a time or two he slid on loose scree. She was certain he was going to fall down the entire side of the mountain. It was so steep, he had almost to run from limb to limb to catch himself.

Catalina held her breath as he crept the last few feet towards the carriage. It was precariously positioned on a ledge and looked as though it would only take a mild gust of wind to blow it on down the mountainside.

"Can you see anything?" she called down, growing impatient to know Dion's fate.

Major Knight cast an annoyed glance her way, to which she gave a little shrug in response, although he had turned away and did not even see.

She watched as he held on to some vegetation on the side of the mountain and went down on his knees to peer inside. It appeared he could not see well, for he held on to look inside the door, which had broken off. The carriage hitched precariously and he leaned back while it settled. Then he moved cautiously forward to look inside again. What he saw must have been shocking, for he turned his head away quickly, as though composing himself, and then looked around.

Catalina's own stomach convulsed sympathetically, which was not so far-fetched after her earlier queasiness. She gave thanks that she was not the one to have found Dion. Sadness and fear caused her to tremble. If it was true that they had all been intended to perish – that the driver had been ordered by someone to see that they had an accident—then they would likely try again... unless Dion had been their main object and she and Major Knight were merely incidental casualties. Much though she wished it might be so, she found that possibility difficult to believe.

A movement below jerked her from her reverie. Major Knight was reaching into the carriage, the idiot. It swayed, and she gasped. He crawled backwards from the wreckage holding a couple of haversacks and the basket of food she had brought him earlier. It seemed so long ago.

He looked all around the carriage and down where it would go if it fell further. She turned away to hide her eyes. She could not look as he began to climb upward. When she heard his exertions nearby, she turned back around and took some of his burdens from him as he pulled himself up on to the road. Breathing heavily and now covered in dirt and sweat, he limped away from the precipitous drop.

Catalina did not know what to say; she was still trembling with fright. Now that Knight had once more reached safety, the horror of their situation began to occur to her. Her broken arm throbbed with pain and they were alone on a desolate mountain road. It would be several hours before anyone realized they were missing and come looking for them. Soon it would be dark and no one would venture out this way, in such dangerous conditions, without a moon.

A comforting arm wrapped around her, pulling her from her disturbing thoughts.

Heedless of the familiarity she settled into his arms, simply grateful she was not alone.

"What do we do now?" she asked with her head against his chest, comforted by the beat of his heart against her ear.

"Your arm. I must splint your arm." He reached over, took up the basket and broke it apart, fashioning a flat, hard surface to place beneath it for stability.

He touched the bottom of her petticoat. "May I?"

"Please do," she answered wryly. "When we danced in the palace ballroom, I had no notion that one day, when you touched my skirt, it would be for such an unromantic reason."

"And I had not thought to be touching your skirts at all," he answered in an equally dry tone as he ripped the bottom strip from the linen petticoat and tore it into strips. "This will hurt," he warned as he placed her forearm on the piece of wood and straightened it from her hand to her elbow.

She gritted her teeth, but managed to refrain from screaming. He wrapped it with the lengths of petticoat and tied them firmly.

"You have done this before," she remarked.

"More times than I would like to think about," he agreed. "Is your pain improved?"

"Now that the first agony of straightening has subsided and I think about it, I believe it is. Thank you."

He laughed. "We certainly make a pair, do we not? We have completely bungled ourselves and our task."

"Yes," she agreed with a chuckle, sobering immediately when she thought of where they were, what had happened and how far they would have to walk to catch up with the rest of the train.

"I should have realized what was happening when they changed drivers. It is not even a clever ruse. I suppose I thought your being with us was protection from such tricks."

"Not if they know of the true nature of my role with my father. It did not occur to me such villainy would be attempted while traveling with the entire camp."

"Except we were at the very end—an easy target." He held out his hand. "They are becoming desperate."

"I cannot believe the driver agreed to do such a thing, but obviously it was his intention all along."

"That, or to jump when the carriage rolled off the cliff."

Catalina sighed heavily. "I expect we should begin walking. The caravan will stop for the night soon and perhaps we may gain some ground before they notice we are gone."

"I do not know how fast—or far—I can walk this night. I fear my incision has split open." He tilted his head towards the offending thigh, which, she now noticed, was bleeding through his bandage onto his trousers.

Catalina frowned. "My sewing kit is with my trunks in the wagon."

"I believe more of your petticoat might have to be sacrificed, Señorita." He sounded amused.

"Then it is a good thing you are not tempted by me," she snapped.

He ripped another good length of linen and wrapped it tightly around his leg.

"Hopefully it is only the outer layer of sutures and this will stop the bleeding."

"What do we do now?" she asked as she looked about them.

"We must make camp for the night and pray they send searchers for us quickly. I suspect your maid will realize first."

"If only my maid were so astute."

Major Knight pulled himself to his feet and began to walk along the road, looking, Catalina assumed, for a place to make camp. She stood up and followed him, carrying the haversacks in her uninjured hand. She wondered what there might be in them of use.

After walking a few hundred feet, she saw he had found a stream and a small cave-like hollow in the side of the mountain. She also noticed he was gathering sticks along the way, presumably to build a fire. Hopefully it would serve to guide any rescuers towards them and keep predators away.

She walked to the stream and splashed water in her face. Tidying herself as best she could, she tried not to think about being all alone with a virtual stranger. It was not that she was afraid of him harming her, but when it was discovered they had been stranded alone together, she did not know what might be the outcome. Naturally, she had never been completely alone with a man, let alone in such a situation, but she did understand men quite well having followed the drum for so long.

Major Knight had a fire started by the time she walked back to their makeshift camp. He had even set out a few of his rations of bread and apples for a small dinner. Now she understood why he had brought the haversacks. The rations would not last long. With good fortune, however, they would be rescued soon. Catalina did not know the details of Wellington's intended attack, but she knew something large was being planned. The commander and his officers would not be pleased with having to spare men for a rescue mission. Catalina sat near the fire, enjoying its warmth. Major Knight poked at the logs and branches, seeming lost in his thoughts. She stared into the glowing flames for a few minutes before speaking.

"Was Dion badly mangled?" she finally found the courage to ask.

He shook his head. "Dion was not in the carriage."

CHAPTER EIGHT

FELIX COULD FEEL Lady Catalina tense. "Dion was not in the carriage?" she asked slowly and quietly. "Do you think he has fallen out or escaped?"

"I could not say. He was bound, and I do not believe in coincidences. I believe the driver planned for the carriage to wreck, but I could not say if Dion managed to come out of his bindings or if he flew from the carriage when it struck the ground."

"So he might be waiting to kill us while we sleep," she said calmly.

"I will take watch while you sleep."

"That is hardly fair. Your injury is far worse than mine. At least I can walk," she argued.

"Then we shall take turns. I will wake you in a few hours." He had no intention of doing so, but it seemed to pacify her.

"Very well. Should we put the fire out? It signals exactly where we are."

"No, *because* it signals where we are. Let Dion come if he is alive and able. I strongly doubt he survived that fall without severe injuries."

The lady seemed somewhat reassured by his words, but Felix was concerned. He doubted a sorcerer could have escaped that carriage under the circumstances, but he could only hazard guesses at this point. He said a silent prayer that Mendoza would quickly realize his daughter and carriage were missing and send out a party to search for them.

"How far behind do you think we are?" Lady Catalina asked.

Felix was wondering the same thing himself. "We have been halted for close to two hours. Perhaps they could have been ten miles ahead if they made good time. I know the final push towards Vitoria was to be on the morrow."

"Is that where Wellington wishes to rout the French?" she asked as she settled one of the haversacks on the ground to make a pillow and began to untie her bonnet. She struggled with one hand, but having succeeded, pulled the pins from her hair, releasing a long cascade of silken black hair.

Felix was mesmerized but looked away, trying to recall what she had asked him. Oh yes, the French. He did not see any harm in telling her the plan now.

"He has divided the allied forces into four parts and intends to surround the French there."

Lady Catalina nodded her head as she combed her hair with her fingers. "I assumed he was planning something clever like that. Indeed, I an anxious for this war to be over."

"As am I."

She looked as though she was trying to plait her hair with one hand, so he moved behind her and took over the task.

"Sometimes it is useful to have a younger sister," he muttered, by way of explanation, trying to think of her as a sister, but failing. Her scent of roses still lingered faintly and he was unsettled by how natural it felt to be doing such a thing for the lady. Despite their tenuous start, they had settled into a comfortable amity.

"Who do you think Dion was working for? Nothing makes sense when I think back. I can picture him talking to almost every officer in every battalion!" she blurted out.

"You will run yourself mad approaching the problem like that. You must look for patterns." He took a ribbon from her and tied off the end of the plait.

"When did your first discover information was being leaked?" she turned to ask.

"Six months past, I believe. I have only just returned to Spain, so cannot tell you the exact moment."

The lady lay back and closed her eyes. Felix thought she was asleep. "Six months ago we were at Palencia. Dion was given leave, I assumed to visit family. If I am honest, I was glad to be rid of him and did not pay too much attention."

"We may ask your father about it tomorrow. You should try to sleep."

"My mind is loath to be quiet when there is a problem to solve," she said wearily.

"Give your mind permission to rest. Sometimes the best solutions happen in your sleep."

She inhaled deeply, then her breathing gradually changed to a slow, rhythmic cadence.

Felix began to ponder their next course of action, determined not to allow himself to think of the woman lying next to him. He firmly believed Mendoza would soon be on his way back to search for them, but knew he must be prepared for the worst. He would wake Lady Catalina at dawn and they would begin to walk towards the next camp. Hopefully, there would be a small village at no great distance where they could find help.

When the first lightning of the sky happened, Felix was ready to start walking. There had been no hint of any other sign of life bar the few animals he had heard in the distance. Lady Catalina had nuzzled close to him for warmth as the fire had died out and the chill of the night had settled over the valley below. They were above a layer of cloud, which gave him the sense of being separated from the rest of the world.

Felix gently nudged Lady Catalina over and brought himself slowly to his feet, trying to ignore the pain and stiffness. Perhaps it would have been better to continue on last night before the soreness of their injuries had had time to settle into their bones, but they had both been exhausted.

He stood tall and stretched his arms to the sky, hoping a little movement would help his willingness to begin the day. He walked away to survey the surroundings, hoping to see some other sign of life – smoke from chimneys or lights off in the distance. The clouds made that impossible. He knelt down to splash his face and clean his leg in the stream and then went back to wake Lady Catalina. She was already sitting upright, though looking deliciously rumpled with her hair askew and her eyes full of sleep.

"Good morning," he said when she looked at him.

"For a moment, I thought you had left me," she said with the petulance of a small child.

He raised one brow and gave her the haughty Knighton look, which always amused him when his brother employed it.

"You really do think highly of me."

She gave a little shrug and he noticed she was holding her arm. "How do you feel this morning?"

"As though I jumped out of a carriage and then slept on a rock," she muttered. "I imagine I feel much the same as you."

He held out his hand and helped her to her feet.

"The water is quite refreshing," he remarked, looking down into her wide eyes while still holding her close. For an instant he allowed himself to be weak and held her there. The simplicity of the morning was his favorite time. He had known from their first meeting he would prefer her like this. She was not immune to him, either, but it would be a mistake to take advantage of this situation.

He stepped back and let her go, chiding himself for allowing a lapse in control of his emotions. He—they—had a job to do.

"We had better be on our way. With any luck, we will find a village somewhere along the road."

"My, you are optimistic this morning. I know of no villages on the mountain pass, but perhaps we might meet a farmer."

She turned and walked off to the stream to wash while Felix packed up the bags and cleaned up the site.

CATALINA WALKED DOWN to the stream, trying not to think of the aches and pains in her body, and also trying not to think about what had just happened with Major Knight. Not only had she sensed a change in him, but she could feel a weakness in herself. It had felt perfectly natural to be held in his arms. She had needed him last night and had clung to him for comfort and safety. Never before would she have thought herself so weak. It was shameful. Kneeling down, she splashed her face with the water that, at this hour, felt like ice. It was a stark reminder of what was yet to come that day. As she returned to the small camp, she determined to keep her emotions in check and spend her time trying to solve the mystery of Dion.

Major Knight was ready to begin walking as soon as she rejoined him. They scrambled through the shrub back down to the road and resumed the journey again. One foot in front of the other, she told herself. Never had she taken for granted the foot soldiers who walked everywhere, but she could now sympathize. At first, it was not so bad, but after hours of tramping along with blisters on one's feet, it could be numbing to the soul. Catalina knew many people would disagree with her entirely, but she had the most respect for those soldiers who could march in such discomfort day in and day out.

"You look very serious," he said, matching his stride to hers. His legs were much longer, and she wondered if he must be doing it intentionally. Although, she mused, his leg *was* injured and perhaps he could not stride as normal.

"There is a great deal on my mind," she replied. "How is your leg?"

"The bleeding seems to have stopped. I believe I was fortunate and only the superficial sutures were opened."

"I should have made them tighter." She frowned.

"Then I could well have been dealing with infection by now. Who could have predicted such a fate for us?" He shrugged.

"Not I," she agreed." I for one am glad we were not murdered in our sleep."

"Yes, the plot thickens. I cannot think what could have happened to Dion. I do not think he could have escaped without help."

Catalina did not know either. They lapsed into silence for a while, the only sound the path crunching beneath their boots as they fell into a rhythm. They continued to climb for a while before Major Knight stopped at a clearing beneath some stunted trees where there were some large boulders on which to sit.

"This spot looks like it was made for a rest."

"I am afraid I will not get up again if I stop," she said cautiously. Nevertheless, she sat down and relaxed with the bliss of such a simple thing. Her arm was throbbing even though she had tried not to let it swing, and she could feel it swelling with displeasure. Major Knight held out his canteen to her and the cool water tasted like the nectar of God.

"Water never tasted so good?" Major Knight asked as he watched her.

"Indeed." She handed it back to him and he drank with equal appreciation.

As she gazed down the mountain at the path they had climbed, the cloud lifted from the valley and revealed the sun above the horizon.

"Most people never get to see something like this," he remarked.

"No, there are blessings to be found in nature that only the few who exert themselves discover. I only wish the circumstances were less dire, that I might fully appreciate them."

He laughed. She looked up to view this rare sight and immediately had to ignore the effect it had on her. There were crinkles around his eyes and the harshness was erased. She smiled back, then forced herself to look away.

He rummaged through one of the sacks and, after a few moments, offered her a piece of bread that he had torn in two.

"Thin pickings this morning, I am afraid, but I have hope that we will soon be found."

"I wish I shared your optimism."

"Perhaps I would not be so confident were you not with me," he replied.

"How far do you think we have come?" she asked, avoiding the obvious meaning behind his words.

"Two or three miles, perhaps. If you look in that direction, I believe there is a sign of life in the distance."

"Our camp?" she asked hopefully.

"Or a small village."

"I believe it is!" she agreed after squinting hard and seeing something in the distance. "Perhaps it is just an optical illusion, but it is quite astounding how my spirits have lifted. I believe I can go on now." She laughed.

They gathered the packs and walked on again, soon growing hot and dusty with the warmth of the sun directly on them. Once more, they settled into a monotonous rhythm; Catalina was lost in her thoughts and it seemed the major was too.

"I hear something," Major Knight said some time later, abruptly halting and holding out his arms for her to do the same.

"Horses!" Catalina agreed, feeling ridiculous amounts of excitement.

"We should wait in those trees at the side of the path," he directed, "in case of brigands."

"There are several," Catalina remarked as the hoof beats grew louder, but it was still several minutes before they could see anything.

"Thank God!" Major Knight exclaimed when half a dozen riders came into view.

"Papa!" Catalina cried, recognizing her father leading the group.

Major Knight stepped forward to the road and waved.

Catalina threw herself into her father's arms the moment he stopped his horse and dismounted.

He hugged her and frantically kissed her head. "I knew you could not be dead! I knew I would feel it in my heart had I lost you."

"It was horrible, Papa!"

"The driver arrived in camp with only the horses and said there had been an accident and all of you were dead." He shook his head. "It has been the longest night of my life."

"Thank you for not believing him." Catalina shook her head and her father crushed her against him. She winced in pain when he squashed her arm between them.

"You are hurt! I should have asked this first, yet I was so relieved to see you alive! Do you know what it does to a father to think he has foolishly risked his daughter's life?"

"I am well enough, Papa. I am so grateful Major Knight was with me."

Her father had not even noticed the major. He looked at him and gave him a grateful nod. "I thank you for protecting my daughter," he said humbly.

"She gives me too much credit. She took care of herself."

Catalina shook her head. "He is too modest. He kept watch while I slept."

"And Dion perished?" her father asked in a choked voice. He was evidently still very hurt by his lieutenant's betrayal.

Knight held out a hand, as if searching for the right words. "I suspect Dion was thrown from the carriage, but I did not search for the body."

Her father gave a brusque nod. "You are also hurt. Come, let us return to camp and you may tell me the story on the way." They had brought three horses, but of course, Dion was not with them. "How far back along the road was the wreck?" her father asked.

"Between four and five miles, is my best guess," Knight replied. "There is a sharp turn which the carriage could not negotiate. It fell about twenty feet and landed on a slight ledge."

Her father turned to the men who had come with him. "Go and search the area for Dion, but do not put your own lives at risk," he ordered.

"You are able to ride?" he asked them both.

"I will ride with more pleasure than I can express," Catalina agreed emphatically.

She was lifted on to Luna and Major Knight mounted his sleek white Andalusian. They rode slowly, just the three of them since she could not manage more with her broken arm. She and the Englishman told her father the fantastical story of their adventure the day before as they went. It was more a tale of horror, Catalina reflected to herself as she listened to Major Knight recount what had happened.

"And where did you spend the night?" her father asked in a mildly accusatory tone.

"Papa!" Catalina scolded. "Major Knight protected me; you should be grateful to him. We are both injured. I assure you, nothing but survival and sleep were on our minds!" Catalina hoped her cheeks were not red from having to say such a thing, and thereby betray her true thoughts besides.

"Forgive me. The fears of a doting father, you know—I do, most sincerely, beg your pardon," he said to the major, who cast an amused glance at her.

"There is nothing to forgive, sir. I am certain I would be the same with my own daughter, if I had one."

They rode for a few minutes in silence. "Were you able to discover anything from Dion?" he asked them both.

"Very little. He seemed as shocked by the events as we were," Knight answered.

"I have gone over every possible moment in my mind," her father admitted. "I can think of nothing out of the ordinary."

"As have I, Papa. The only small thing I remember is him speaking with the English Lieutenant Colonel Roberts. He stopped at the carriage just before the last part of the journey when the drivers changed over. However, that could have been simple and genuine responsibility for the prisoner's wellbeing," she said, reasoning as she spoke.

"Perhaps," her father said, but she could see he was unconvinced.

Major Knight said nothing.

CHAPTER NINE

THEY REACHED THE camp without further mishap and Felix was surprised to see the commander and Colonel Hill waiting for them. The rest of the caravan had already moved on, but they dismounted for a rest and a small meal was waiting for them.

Wellington gave him a look that seemed to express a great deal of relief and curiosity. It was almost as though he had known they would arrive for the meal. Wellington had an eerie sixth sense about things and Felix was too grateful to question it.

"Good to see you both alive and whole," Wellington said. "Come and eat. I am certain there is a great deal of news to impart."

The five of them sat at a small table and shared a meal of grouse, pease, olives and potatoes with some *chacolí* wine that was native to the region.

Felix gave his report to his superiors while General Mendoza and Lady Catalina listened quietly.

"I do not like this one bit," Wellington commented after hearing the tale.

"We must hope my men will return with Dion. That would eliminate one variable," Mendoza said.

"We have the driver of the carriage in confinement, but he will not speak," Colonel Hill remarked.

"Have you spoken to Lieutenant Colonel Roberts?" Felix asked.

"He looked in on Dion before we took off and the drivers swapped. Perhaps he might have noticed something.'

Wellington and Hill glanced at each other curiously.

They knew something, Felix was certain. Something they did not want to say in front of the general and his daughter.

"We are moving ahead with our plans. Everleigh and Owens have returned and reported that Joseph is fleeing north, back to the bosom of his brother, along with his troops. My plan should work," Wellington remarked.

"With luck this delay will not disrupt anything," Felix said.

"It could not be helped. If this is the only hiccup in the plan, then I consider us fortunate," he answered. "I understand you broke your arm, my lady?"

"I did, but the major was very competent in splinting it," Lady Catalina answered. She smiled at Felix. "We are even on our medical services to each other. Hopefully we will have no further need of them."

"I do not like this at all, querida, perhaps it is time for you to return to Villa Blanca," General Mendoza said quietly, obvious distress writ upon his features.

"I will see this to the end, Papa," Lady Catalina replied, as Felix would have expected. He knew this was personal for her, which made it even more dangerous. Yet there would be no talking her out of it, he knew. If her father would not order her home, Felix would be wasting his own breath. He had enough experience with stubborn females to concede that fact.

Felix looked at Wellington, who was wearing an expression he knew well. It meant he was plotting something. Felix wished he had been sent with Everleigh and Owens instead. Reconnoitering seemed vastly simple compared to this.

"What do you suggest happens now?" Mendoza asked.

"I was just reflecting upon that myself," Wellington admitted.

"What have you considered?" Hill asked.

"Whether it would be to our advantage to let everyone believe Knight and Lady Catalina perished."

Felix understood the reasoning, but it would mean they would be separated together from the rest of the party until the rat was discovered.

"How would that be beneficial?" Mendoza asked.

"It could make our perpetrator relax a little. That was a very risky chance he took with the carriage accident," Wellington explained.

"Most of the camp is aware of the accident," Mendoza said, frowning.

"But very few know they are alive. We sent everyone else ahead," Hill answered.

Felix could tell that Mendoza realized the ramifications. His face was very expressive.

"Where would they go? It is bad enough they spent last evening alone together. If that became widely known in society, Catalina would be ruined."

"It does not matter, Papa." She reached over and squeezed her father's hand. "We must catch the traitor. What is my reputation when the sovereignty of Spain is at stake?"

Felix was impressed despite himself. Not many ladies would be so dismissive of their good name. He had misjudged her at the beginning, he had to concede to himself.

"I would like to keep them close," Wellington said, coming back to the earlier question. "Perhaps in my own billeting. I appreciate it is not an ideal situation for a lady, but this must be kept as quiet as possible."

Mendoza did not look pleased, but he said no more.

"This will only work if you trust the men who rode out with you earlier."

"I do. At least I trust them as much as anyone. They have been with me a very long time. Longer than Dion," Mendoza replied.

Felix understood how the man must feel. It was easy to see everyone as a threat when trust had been breached.

"Shall we travel together for a while until we reach the edge of the camp? That will allow us time to think some more upon this plan. Whoever is responsible has been told you are dead, but it is always prudent to be cautious. If you are discovered then we will form another plan."

They finished the meal and packed up to ride on.

Felix felt much better after a rest and a meal, and that they were no longer alone while injured. The uncertainty of the plan disturbed him, but that was nothing unusual when at war. At least they had some information, even if they did not have Dion to pry information from. He did have the lieutenant's haversack, and he would like to explore the man's belongings.

"Now you are the one deep in thought," Lady Catalina said as she walked towards him, leading her gray Andalusian mare.

"I was thinking how to proceed. We will be spies in truth."

"Why, in disguise, of course. I was pondering how best to accomplish this, and have asked permission to make a diversion to Villa Blanca."

"Your home?"

"It is not so far from where the commander intends to camp. It will be much easier to find proper costumes there."

Felix gave a nod and helped her to mount her horse. There was reason in what she said.

He mounted his own painfully and rode over next to Wellington on his new mount, Copenhagen. "A word, with your permission, sir?" he asked.

"Of course," Wellington acknowledged as they began to canter north. "Mendoza told me of Lady Catalina's plan. I think it is an excellent one."

"And once disguised?" Felix asked.

"I will have Everleigh or Owens bring you instructions once I see the French position and determine how to act. I suspect the four of you will be most useful as eyes and ears. At least we are in friendly territory, but make certain you are not caught when not in uniform."

"I do not need to be warned," Felix replied. The grim reminder of his time in captivity was etched forever on his memory.

"You are succeeding in your task with the lady? If she is too much of a liability, I can put a stop to this."

"My initial reservations about her have been found to be erroneous. She has shown herself to be competent."

"Excellent. I had my own reservations, since she is Mendoza's daughter, but it is deuced helpful to have someone from the Spanish camp on the inside. She is more pleasant to look at than Owens, to be sure!" Wellington laughed.

Felix tried not to scowl at his commanding officer.

"Do not tell me you are immune, Knight! Or have you lost your touch?" He shook his head. "I have survived countless battles, and I am about to be flayed alive by one of my majors!"

Felix had to repress a twist of his lips at that remark and thought it best to swiftly change the subject.

"Are there any particular areas or persons you wish us to concentrate our efforts on, sir?"

Wellington did not answer for at least a mile. "I have Everleigh and Owens watching the Spanish camp. I fear our man will be too suspicious of Mendoza just now. Much though it pains me, I believe we must watch some of our own men. I will confess there are some I have been keeping an eye on. In fact, I had asked Knighton for information to be gathered on some of them, just in case, but I have not received any dispatches from him."

"He said not a word of suspicion about anyone to me," Felix replied.

"Perhaps there was nothing there for him to find. But I intend to rout this nuisance quickly and whoever is leaking information, for whatever purpose, will have to make a move soon. We will catch them. I can abide almost anything but a traitor, regardless of the reason."

Felix could not agree more. "Now that we know Dion was leaking information from the Spanish camp, do you suspect anything more from there?"

"At this moment I suspect everyone and everything. It is what has kept me alive this long."

CATALINA AND MAJOR Knight left the comfort of her father's and Wellington's protection and branched off on the road to her home. *Home*, she sighed inwardly. At least she had the assurance of sleeping in her own bed that night, even if it was only a temporary reprieve. She could somehow sense that Major Knight would rather not go with her. No doubt he still felt like her caretaker, but she thought he had gained a little respect for her, even if begrudgingly. Nevertheless, he still treated her respectfully and she could not complain. Her father, she reflected, would never have agreed to her going alone if her aunt did not reside at Villa Blanca, although he probably hoped Catalina would decide to stay there and not return.

With every step they took—and drew closer to the estate—she grew more excited. Perhaps it was her imagination, but she thought she could even detect a hint of sea salt in the air. They began passing more and more vineyards, which were in full bloom this late in the spring and filled her nostrils with the sweet fragrance of home. Summer was only a week or so away – Catalina had lost track of time altogether. She pulled up her mare at the top of the valley in order to survey everything below. Major Knight reined in next to her and did not even ask why she had stopped. It was a compulsion of hers and he seemed to understand.

"This is your home?"

She gave a nod and pointed to a wide expanse of vineyards and farmland. The crystal blue waters of the Mediterranean sparkled in the distance, and the familiar white stone mansion with a bright red tiled roof stood watching over everything around it.

"I see why you are fond of it. It is certainly one of the most beautiful places I have seen."

She smiled. "Let us pray we can stop the French before it is destroyed. Many have not been so fortunate."

"No," he said so softly she barely heard it.

"It has been a long day since we awoke in that small cave of rock. Now the sun is setting. It is not often I see the sun rise and set in the same day."

"Quite a day it has been, indeed," he added.

Luna knew this path well and she needed no urging when Catalina allowed her to walk on. There was something in the air—a smell, a feeling, when you were home. Perhaps it was nostalgia, but Catalina did not think she could have appreciated it if she had never left home. The household would not be expecting them, but it would still be a luxury to be there compared to any lodging they had had in the past year. As they passed through the gates, all the familiar sights brought warmth to her heart. Even the gate was enough to make her giddy. Fig trees lined the road and the garden was in full bloom with bright Bougainvillea.

She slid from her horse in front of the house before Major Knight expected it and could come to assist. He quickly followed.

"This is Villa Blanca, my lord," she said with pure happiness in her heart, allowing herself to forget, for a moment, why they were there.

"My lord?" he asked with an amused, sideways glance.

"We are not officers at the moment, are we?"

A surprised groom came to take their horses, and they walked stiffly up the steps to the front entrance.

"My lady!" Zubiri, the butler, came running to greet them when it came to his notice someone had walked through the front door.

"Good evening, Zubiri. His lordship and I will be spending the night here... if a light supper and a room for him could be prepared? We might remain longer; that depends on the commander's wishes. Please inform the servants that no one is to speak of our presence here."

"I will ensure that is understood, my lady."

"How is my aunt?"

"She sleeps a great deal, but is well. She has already taken a tray in her room."

"Of course. I will show his lordship to the *azul* room, if you will have some hot water sent up. The sheets may be aired and the room prepared while we dine."

"Yes, my lady."

Catalina directed Major Knight to follow her up a winding stone staircase with an intricately designed iron railing. Familiar statues and paintings greeted her, along with the scent of fresh Etxeko Biskotxoa which was Aunt Esmeralda's favorite treat.

"This is a lovely home," Major Knight said from behind her. She had almost forgotten he was there, she was so lost in the pleasure of familiar surroundings.

"You must have grown up in a grand house yourself, being the son of a duke."

"Indeed I did, but I cannot say I am not grateful to have escaped the inheritance of it all."

"I can understand that. It is a great responsibility."

She stopped before a large, carved wooden door and opened it to a suite of rooms. "I hope you will find it satisfactory."

"It does not take much to make me comfortable," Major Knight remarked and their eyes met. Her thoughts turned to where they had spent the previous night, and she was wondering if he was thinking the same when she remembered he had not slept at all. "You must be exhausted. Dinner will be ready shortly and then you may retire if you wish. Do not feel the need to entertain me."

Catalina almost laughed out loud at her words, but he had been a gentleman even when they were in adversity, and old habits of polite behavior were hard to break.

A door opened and the sound of paws clicking across the marble came to her ears, followed by the butler shouting, "No Toro! Heel, Toro!"

Catalina should reprimand her beast, but he was already climbing the stairs and bounding towards her. It had been too long.

Toro was taller than she was when he stood on his hind legs, and the instant he reached her, he put his front paws on her shoulders and licked her face. His tail wagged as though she had been away forever. It felt as if she had been.

A winded Zubiri came up and stopped at the top of the stairs to catch his breath. "Forgive me, my lady."

"He has a mind of his own, Zubiri. I have been gone far too long."

"I cannot tell how he knows, but he came charging in from the fields, he did. Shall I send him off?"

"He would not go if you tried. Thank you, Zubiri." Catalina laughed as the butler left and Toro fell to the floor, his paws in the air. She began the obligatory belly rub without thinking. When she looked up, Major Knight was watching the whole scene with an amused expression.

"He is not much of a guard dog," he remarked. "He has not even noticed me."

"He senses you are safe."

"Am I?"

"Just try to hurt me when he is nearby." Their gazes locked, and his eyes darkened. It was the first time Catalina had detected any hint of desire in him. Toro grew impatient with her lack of attention and finally stood up to acknowledge Major Knight.

He held out his hand. Toro sniffed it for a moment and then butted it with his head to indicate he wanted to be stroked.

"Pleased to meet you, handsome fellow." He was a giant, brindled mastiff, and very friendly.

Toro's hind leg shook with pleasure as Major Knight scratched the best places, and won him over, as if there had been any doubts. Toro had not displayed the least sign of wariness about the major. That should reassure her, but Major Knight unsettled her more than any man before.

Several servants appeared, carrying cans of hot water for baths and Toro whimpered outside Major Knight's door when he went inside.

"Traitor," Catalina whispered affectionately to her dog as she went inside her own room. He lay down between their chambers as if guarding them both.

The bath felt heavenly. Although it would be better for a good scrubbing, she dared not put her broken arm under the water, so that part of her had to remain uncleansed. Afterwards, she dressed simply in one of her old, comfortable muslin gowns that she could fasten for herself. Besides, she mused in vindication, she loved them too much to throw them away.

She brushed and arranged her hair as best she could, and then went to the adjoining room to show Major Knight the way down to dinner.

Zubiri had set up a repast of Tigres, Talo and Porrusalda on the back terrace, overlooking the valley. The little corn cakes, mussels and soup were simple but comforting. It was Catalina's favorite place in the house and she was grateful the old retainer had thought to put them there. Somehow, sitting formally in a room alone with Major Knight was too intimate.

It was a warm evening with a soft breeze, a nice contrast to the cold mountain air from the night before. Catalina should probably be embarrassed by her informality, but Major Knight had seen her thus on the mountain. She had caught an appreciative gaze in his eyes when he had first seen her, so she tried to dismiss any bashfulness.

"This is most pleasant," he remarked, once they were seated before their meal which had been laid out on a small table with folding leaves. "It is hard to reconcile this with what is soon to come.

"Do you think this will truly be the end?"

"Do we not always hope each battle is the last? I wish we knew who our man was. I fear it is someone very close to the top."

"It has to be someone high enough for Dion to have thought it worth his while to give secrets away. He was always looking for ways to better himself—if that is the right phrase."

"Improve his lot, perhaps," Knight suggested.

She emptied her glass, and he took the jug and refilled it with some mild, refreshing *chacolí* wine.

"I cannot remember a meal tasting so good," he remarked, a contented look on his face as he watched a golden pupavac land on the balustrade next to its mate, and spread its black and white striped tail wide.

Catalina wished life could be as simple as it was for those birds.

"I suppose we should look for some disguises," she said, regretful of the need to leave the moment of serenity.

"I daresay we should. I do not expect we will tarry here long."

They left the table and she led him upstairs to the attics. It had been years since she had come up here to play, dressing up in the old clothes stored in the various trunks. Never would she have thought then that the next time would be with a man—and an English gentleman at that.

CHAPTER TEN

FELIX COULD NOT remember the last time he had been up in an attic. He was certain it must have been when he was a child, and he and his siblings used to hide in the vast lofts of The Grange. This one was surprisingly neat, with rows of trunks on one side, furniture to the other, and paintings and decorations of sorts on another. The sun had fully set, and each of them carried an oil lamp to light their way.

Lady Catalina set hers down and looked around. "I have not been up here since my mother died," she said with a touch of sorrow in her voice. "I used to come up here and rummage through the trunks to see what outrageous costumes I could create."

"My sister used to do the same, although she has yet to realize they are costumes and not to be worn for everyday affairs." He smiled at the thought of Eugenia.

"You love your sister," Lady Catalina observed, stirring him from his thoughts.

"I do. We are the youngest and I spent the most time with her. She is an original, to be sure. I think you would like her."

"I am certain of it," Lady Catalina agreed as she began to open trunks. Dust motes flew through the air and he noticed she had a cobweb stuck in her hair.

Felix hoped they could leave soon, because tonight he had suddenly felt the pull of domestic bliss which must have enchanted his brothers.

Unaware, thankfully, of the traitorous direction of his thoughts, Lady Catalina was bending over a trunk and digging through it.

"I know they are here somewhere," she muttered.

Felix tried to look at the ceiling instead of her luscious bottom up in the air. "What are you looking for?" he asked, moving to study a still life of fruit.

"My father's and my grandfather's old garments. I think it best if I dress as a groom, and we can disguise you as a vagrant."

Felix raised his brows. "Somehow I doubt you have an abundance of old, tattered clothing."

"Of course not," she said with impatience. "But there are clothes that we can make appear thus."

He doubted any disguise would make her look like a man, but at least people would have to look twice.

"What about this?" she asked, as she pulled out a hideous costume from at least two-hundred years ago. He kept his face impassive.

"No? I was only jesting you," she said with a mischievous grin.

Being here was most definitely not wise. Lady Catalina and her society side—a diamond of the first water or belle of the ball—he could resist most emphatically. Catalina like this... hair down, dressed simply, being her natural self... was irresistible. He found himself moving closer and standing by her side, his body flatly ignoring his mind's direction to remain still and indifferent.

She went diving for treasure once again, and Felix moved to the small window to look out. Not that there was anything to see, but he most definitely needed to cool his blood if there was any cool air to be had.

"*Magnifico!* Do not turn around," she warned. "I shall step behind the paintings to change my dress."

Did the woman not know that was the worst thing to say to a

starving man? *There is a raw steak here, waiting for your delectation, but you cannot have it?* He could hear the sounds of her changing and ordered his mind to think of the most unromantic things he could. At least, he reflected sourly, that was one positive thing he had learned during his imprisonment. He concentrated on the dark, cold cell in which, sorely injured, he had spent three months, not knowing what fate would befall him.

"Major Knight? Felix?" He turned. Lady Catalina was standing beside him, looking up at him with tenderness and concern in her eyes as she searched his face. "You look as though you had suddenly taken a trip to Hell."

He forced himself back to the present, abruptly cognizant he would give his life to protect her from personal knowledge of such places.

"I was thinking of something in my past." He forced a smile to his face.

Her head was tilted, still looking up at him as though she did not believe his smile. She would not be easy to deceive.

Stepping back, she placed a hat on her head and circled before him. "Will I pass for a servant boy?"

How could Felix tell her truthfully what she looked like? His own thoughts were wayward and his voice was hoarse when he answered, "No."

She frowned and looked down at herself. "Oh. I see." Her cheeks flushed when she realized what was the matter.

With praiseworthy determination, Felix tried to pretend it was Eugenia standing before him. It helped a little.

"I believe I can take care of the problem." She scrambled back behind the row of stacked pictures and changed back into her gown, looking more disheveled then she had before. He swallowed hard.

"Now we must find something for you, my lord. Is there any particular disguise you wish to assume?"

"I only need some different clothing and powder for my hair. I do a rather convincing old man," he answered, using male arrogance to cover his discomfort.

Catalina pursed her lips and narrowed her gaze in clear disbelief, then shrugged. "Very well. We need only to go to my father's dressing room for that." Toro was waiting for them at the bottom of the narrow stairs, his tail thumping like a loud drum when he saw them descending the bare wooden steps. He stood, stretched his large, brindled body and then followed, treading like a horse.

Felix sat in a large chair in the adjoining sitting room while Lady Catalina rummaged through her father's clothing. The room felt more like that of an old king than a general, with dark, heavy colors and thick velvet draperies and bed hangings.

Catalina emerged, arms full of clothing, and placed them on the couch in front of him. "I am certain you can find something to make you look old in here," she announced. "Father cares little for fashion and is frugal in addition. Some of these items must be twenty or thirty years old." Toro came over to sniff everything as if they were a long-lost treasure.

Catalina had to pry something from Toro's mouth. "Give me that, you beast," she commanded, then held the item up for inspection. It was a large, loose jacket of an indiscriminate tan, and she found a pair of long, loose-fitting trousers. "I think this will do nicely. I remember my grandfather wearing this to inspect the fields. It covers your arms, but is not too warm for summer. He had a hat he always wore with it," she said, otherwise completely ignoring Felix sitting there as she marched back into the dressing room, the dog following close behind. Felix could hear her rummaging in cupboards and drawers, and Toro's happy grunts.

Taking the trousers and coat, Felix went into the room next to the dressing room, which was the sleeping chamber. There was a tall screen painted with intricate birds, and Felix went behind it to change.

When he went back into the sitting room to wait for Lady Catalina, she emerged with a large-brimmed hat such as a gardener would wear to shield his neck.

She smiled, looking proud of herself. *"Triunfo!* I knew it was here." She walked towards him and he obediently bent his head down for her to place the hat there. When he straightened, she pursed her luscious-looking lips and tilted her head, studying him critically. "You will never pass for *un viejo.*"

Felix smiled at her. "I need some powder."

She looked skeptical, but she went back into the dressing room and came out with a box. "Father still wears powder to Court." She held out the box to Felix.

He gave her a knowing look, then proceeded to transform himself, aging his appearance three decades with the powder. When he placed the hat back on his head and turned around, he stooped his posture and took several steps with a different gait. Toro growled.

Felix looked over at Lady Catalina and lifted a brow enquiringly.

"I am all astonishment! I did not think it was possible."

"People see what they expect to, my lady," he said in a gravelly voice, shuffling over to bow before her and place a kiss on her hand. He was taken aback by the warmth he saw in her gaze when he looked up at her.

She clasped his hand and pulled him to her, his hat flying off in the process.

There were so many reasons why this was not a good idea, but his brain refused to be reasoned with. Her hand wound its way around his neck and she boldly placed her lips to his. *Resistance is futile*, the wretched devil of a conscience whispered in his ear as he kissed her back. For now, he gave into the passion of the moment.

Toro began barking and for a fleeting instant, Felix thought the dog was trying to protect his lady. Then Felix heard a knock on the door and released Catalina. She turned away, presumably to hide her face, so Felix answered the door. Zubiri stood there, his face impassive yet an unmistakeable accusatory gleam in his eyes. He held out a sealed letter.

"This just came for you, my lord. The messenger awaits your answer downstairs."

"Thank you, Zubiri. I will be down directly."

Felix went back into the other room to put his normal clothes on and brush some of the powder from his hair. Catalina was still waiting for him when he finished, every trace of passion erased from her face.

"Did you read the note?"

"Not yet. I was about to do so."

She shook her head as though a proper spy would have looked at the note first. He broke the seal and read it.

"What does it say?" she asked impatiently.

"It is from my brother. He has information for me."

"Is that good news or bad?"

"I have no idea, but it looks as though I will be journeying into Bilbao tomorrow."

⟫⟩✶⟨⟪

MAJOR KNIGHT SET out the next morning to meet his brother in Bilbao, garbed in his disguise. Catalina supposed he could have gone in uniform, but perhaps he did not wish to draw attention. How had the brother known how to find him? He must have tracked Wellington's movements and then the messenger had been sent on from there.

Catalina was left to have a morning of leisure – she had forgotten what it was like. She was not at all certain that she *did* like it, in fact. Aunt Esmeralda had smiled when she saw Catalina, but it quickly became apparent she did not recognize her. They shared coffee and pastries, but her aunt fell asleep in her chair as soon as she had finished. The maid shook her head.

"She sleeps for much of the day now, my lady," she said, tucking a blanket about Esmeralda's knees.

Catalina left, not knowing what to do with herself. Her broken arm inhibited her, other than to take a bath or read a book, which she could not concentrate on. She was fretful, wondering what Major Knight was discovering, and she was ready for their next task. When one was used to being busy, it was difficult to settle into nothing. It was easy to say you longed for boredom, but when you had it, it was unsettling—and tedious.

Toro butted her hand with his head, as if on cue. "You want to go for a walk, do you? Very well. Waiting here does me no good."

She changed into some sturdy half-boots and put on a bonnet. It had been over a year since she had been home. Life went on and the estate was well managed without either herself or her father needing to be there. It was humbling to realize she was not needed here.

She strolled through the vineyards and down to the river, Toro bounding happily about her. This same river ran towards Vitoria and where the next battle was likely to be. It was too close to home for comfort, and she prayed Wellington would be able to put an end to the conflict with this battle.

Hot and thirsty, she returned to the house a couple of hours later. She pulled off her bonnet and Toro went immediately into the drawing room. Catalina noted the butler's guilty look with curiosity.

"There are visitors, my lady."

"Indeed?" She was not properly attired to receive anyone, but Toro was already investigating the newcomers. "I had better go at once and meet them. Please send in a tray of lemonade. I am sorely parched!"

She hurried after Toro, wondering why her butler had ignored the order to keep their presence a secret. As soon as she entered the drawing room, she understood.

Captain Everleigh and Captain Owens stood up to greet her. Both men bowed.

"I hope you do not mind our intrusion, my lady. We bullied your butler into admitting us," Owens teased.

"Please be seated. May I offer you refreshment? Tea or spirits?"

Zubiri entered with a tray of lemonade. Both of the men's eyes lit up. "I would rather have lemonade," Owens confessed. "It is a rare treat these days."

"Of course," Catalina replied, fully amused by Owens's childlike nature. She would never have guessed he was one of England's sharpest spies, but perhaps that was why he was so effective.

She passed both of them a glass and drank hers faster than was ladylike. "May I assume you have news?"

"We have orders, but where is Knight?"

"He received a message from his brother to meet him in Bilbao, so he rode out early this morning. I could not say when he will return. It is over twenty miles. You are welcome to stay here as long as you need to. I understand if you do not wish to tell me the orders without Major Knight being present, but if there are any preparations to be made, perhaps you can advise me in that direction?"

Owens and Everleigh exchanged glances. "I see no reason to withhold anything from you, Senorita. Wellington's orders included your ladyship," Everleigh reasoned.

"Was anything discovered of Dion?" she asked, curiosity getting the better of her.

The men exchanged glances again.

"You may stop that. My sensibilities are not so delicate that you need protect them."

"The men returned to the camp last evening. Dion was not found. The terrain was very unfriendly for searching, so it does not necessarily mean he escaped death."

"Or from the carriage prior to the accident," put in Owens.

"And it is still the belief that we all perished?" Catalina asked.

"Indeed," continued Everleigh. "Your father is keeping himself aloof and is most convincing as he pretends to grieve."

"Some of his grief will be genuine. He was very attached to Dion and very hurt by his betrayal," she explained.

Zubiri knocked on the door and opened it, bringing in a tray of meats, cheeses and fruits for them.

"Thank you, Zubiri," Catalina said, having not realized how hungry she was herself.

"You are a god amongst men, Zubiri," Captain Owens praised as his eyes devoured the tray of beautiful food.

Catalina laughed. "We do not often see such delicacies in camp, Zubiri," she explained.

"Rations are extremely thin at the moment. The French ransacked Burgos and took almost everything," Everleigh added.

"I am pleased we have such things to offer, sir," the butler replied. "Is there anything else I might have Cook prepare for you?"

"This will do for now," Captain Everleigh replied. "Our thanks to you and Cook."

Zubiri looked pleased and bowed before he left the room.

Catalina waved her hand over the tray. "Please enjoy. I have been here longer than you and I am no longer ravenous, "she laughed.

"I think I am secretly wishing Knight stays away a long time," Owens jested as he ate another piece of cheese.

"It is not secret if you say it aloud," Everleigh said dryly.

Catalina sat quietly, watching and listening to the two banter back and forth. It was a welcome relief from the tedium of waiting for news, but her mind would keep wondering about Dion and she could not be at peace regarding him.

Zubiri re-entered, bringing café con leche and a tray of Etxeko Biskotxoa, her aunt Esmeralda's favorite dessert, a shortbread crust pastry with an almond cream filling.

"Is there a tier above a god, Zubiri?" Owens asked. "Because you have achieved it, my friend!"

Catalina could have sworn Zubiri actually blushed, and she was taken aback for a moment.

"Cook wishes to know if you will stay for dinner?" Zubiri asked with a slight twitch of his lips. Catalina had not realized how much this war had affected the household as well. The servants had not catered for any entertainment in a very long time.

"We would be honored to dine here," Captain Everleigh said, "if the Lady Catalina agrees."

Hiding her amusement at this interchange, Catalina nodded her consent. Zubiri bowed, then left again.

The two gentlemen each had a dessert. Smacking their lips in appreciation, they leaned back in their chairs in contentment.

"I could die happy at this moment," Owens said, gazing at the ceiling.

"You must tell me the plan before you go to Heaven, then," Catalina quipped.

"Have we not done so?" Owens lifted his head and cocked one jaunty eyebrow upward.

She shook her head. "You have only told me of Dion and my father."

"No siesta for me yet," Owens answered and sat back upright.

Everleigh set his glass down and cleared his throat. "There is more to tell. The driver who had been in confinement was found hanged."

Catalina did not know why, but hearing that news made her whole body feel chilled. "Was it by his own hand?"

"My suspicion is no," Everleigh replied quietly. "It was made to look as though it was a suicide."

Catalina's mind raced. Although her instinct told her this went far deeper than Dion and the Spanish contingent, she had no suggestions to offer otherwise. "And what of our new task?"

"We have a list of people to follow, but if my suspicions are correct, Knight will return with a more detailed list and we may narrow our suspects."

"May I see this list?"

Owens and Everleigh exchanged glances again.

"What is it?" she asked, though in her heart she knew. "My father is on the list," she said, not bothering to phrase it as a question.

CHAPTER ELEVEN

F ELIX RODE TO a small café that Lady Catalina had recommended to meet his brother, Edmund. He wore his disguise in order to see how effective it was. With a full beard that he had not shaved since prison, and dressed in his commoner's clothing, peasant's hat pulled low, it ought to be—and he had done this often enough that he was not worried. Edmund should be in no danger from the French at this distance from the encampment.

Bright red and purple flowers poured from windowsills and seemed to crawl up every wall in the coastal town. He traversed the steep, narrow paths and streets, winding through the white stone terrace houses that were small but tidy. He left his horse at a posting inn a few streets from the café and walked in a stooped fashion to practice.

There was no one else there when he arrived, several minutes early, and he sat down to wait with a rich cup of coffee. Many thoughts had swirled through his head as he had ridden there this morning, until a few things had become clear to him. The kiss between Catalina and him should not have happened. She had initiated it, but he had not resisted – in fact, quite the opposite. It did not mean it was a good idea. There was no future for them and he would have to make certain she understood that.

There was a reason spies were told not to become involved with their colleagues... although this was a highly unusual situation. Catalina was not precisely a colleague, yet he had been ordered to work with her, to protect her. If the accident had not occurred, Felix could have kept his feelings at a distance. However, there was no denying that Lady Catalina was a beautiful, attractive woman, and to him that was more seductive than practiced wiles would ever be. Nevertheless, his mind must remain sharp without any distractions, he cautioned himself severely. How was he to accomplish that with her always in his pocket? She was also used to his way of life, and understood him like no protected society lady in England ever would. Part of him would like to snatch her up and take her to England, where she would be protected from this, but Felix still resented his brother's efforts to do the same to him, and he knew better than to let his mind wander down that path.

The only thing which had worked so far was to think of Eugenia. He smiled down into his coffee cup when he thought of his little sister. He almost wished he could be there to see whomever fell into leg shackles with her! When he had left, their old neighbor, Tinsley, had been squiring Eugenia about to protect her from her most damaging inclinations. He shook his head and looked out over the sea, becoming lost in his thoughts once again until he heard the waiter directing a couple to a nearby table. His heart gave a squeeze of affection at the sight of Edmund, and even Isabella. She was perfect for him.

When Felix had left England, he had not known what the outcome of Isabella's situation would be, but he had sensed Edmund's and her rightness for each other. They smelled of April and May, or some such silly saying the old dowagers liked to use.

They must have married as he had suspected they would. Both were glowing with happiness, and he felt a small twinge of jealousy in his heart. What a ridiculous feeling! And to think how he had shunned their domesticity only a few, short weeks ago...

He watched them order coffee and pastries and genuinely enjoy each other's company. They seemed not to even notice him, but perhaps Edmund was only being cautious.

After a few minutes, Felix coughed—in his best imitation of an old, consumptive man—and saw the hint of a smile on Edmund's face. So his brother had realized the peasant was him. Isabella looked over at him pityingly, no hint of recognition in her expression. Good.

"The poor man. He sounds consumptive," Isabella said, full of concern.

Edmund began to rise, but Felix signaled for him to stay where he was. It took a great deal of strength for Felix not to go to his brother and embrace him. Not here, he reminded himself.

After they had sipped their coffee and consumed their pastries, Edmund removed the packet sent by Rowley and, as they rose to leave, slipped it carefully beneath the napkin on the table.

He watched them leave, feeling pulled by some unholy force to go after them. As soon as it was safe to do so, Felix stood and left coins beside his cup before retrieving the packet from Edmund's table. Moving as quickly as he dared, he caught sight of them as they strolled arm in arm down the street and followed at a safe distance until he was certain no one was watching him. Spies were everywhere, noticing every little thing and dismissing millions of unconscious items every day. It was highly unlikely that anyone had followed Lady Catalina and him to Villa Blanca, and likewise him on to Bilbao, but one did not stay alive by simply following probabilities. This was his family, and he would never forgive himself if he caused them harm.

Edmund and Isabella clearly admired this beautiful coastal town as they walked leisurely through the ancient stone streets, where terraced gardens spread fragrance and a palette of color, making it a romantic's dream on this sunny day. In another life, he would have enjoyed walking this path with Catalina, not a care in the world but savoring each other's company. What was happening to him?

Edmund and Isabella turned down a narrow alley and he knew it was time to make his move. He was upon them before they knew aught of his presence. Granted, they hardly seemed to realize there was anyone in the world but them, at the moment, but Isabella squealed when Felix touched their shoulders.

"Hush, it is only me," he said quietly.

He gathered Edmund into his arms for a deep embrace and then gave Isabella a shorter one with a kiss on each cheek. He pulled the packet of letters he had written for his siblings from his coat and pressed them into his brother's hands.

"Thank you," he said to them. "It is reckless of me to expose you so, but I suppose I am selfish."

"Do not apologize," Isabella said, grasping his arm in reassurance.

"You are well?" Edmund asked, his eyes searching with concern.

"I am," Felix replied honestly.

Edmund gave a nod, as though he were satisfied.

"I gather congratulations are in order?" he asked them both.

They smiled at each other, and once again Felix felt a deep pang of envy inside. "I am very pleased for you. Will you return directly to England?"

"Only if you require us to," Edmund replied.

"Not at the moment. Enjoy your travels. Everywhere but north should be safe enough at the moment. Now, I must not tarry. I should not have sought you out."

"I am very glad you did. I cannot tell you how much strength of will it took to walk away from you at the café." Edmund's voice trembled. He was the most tenderhearted of the family, yet the strongest in many subtle ways.

Felix hugged his brother fiercely, expressing his mutual feeling. Words were not his forte, but he knew his brother understood. He kissed Isabella on the cheek once again and turned to leave.

"Go with God," Edmund said, just where Felix could hear. He turned to offer one last smile before resuming his character when he turned back onto the main street and doing his best not to give in to his overwhelming compulsion to weep.

Perhaps he had been knocked in the head when he had jumped from the carriage. He was becoming morose with longings for domestic bliss. How grateful he was for the twenty-mile ride back to Villa Blanca!

⇶⇷

CATALINA ENJOYED CAPTAIN Everleigh's and Captain Owens's company—they were charming and flirtatious and helped to distract her a little from the endless waiting period—yet, if she were truthful, she had been listening for the sound of hoof beats all day long. After years of following the drum, Catalina had thought herself an expert in the art of dissimulation, but today had proven her completely wrong. Over and over she had caught herself thinking about the passionate kiss she had shared with Major Knight and wishing it could happen again. Other gentleman had tried to kiss her before, but she had felt absolutely nothing. When you could think of dead fish while someone was kissing you, it was not an experience you wished to repeat. However, she had felt an overwhelming need—no, compulsion—to kiss him and the force of it had swept her away from reality. It had been heaven and hell in one moment. Becoming lost in passion was something she had never thought would happen to her. The devil of it was, she wanted it to happen again. It was consuming her thoughts and dulling her wits. She had known Major Knight was dangerous, and now she felt the tip of the blade piercing her heart, yet was powerless to prevent it.

Never would she confess to anyone how the drum of hoof beats on the drive sounded like music to her ears. Her heart leaped for joy and some strange sense of wellbeing filled her body. Even though, in her mind, she realized it was infatuation, she longed for more. Toro heard them when she did and scrambled to his feet. Trotting to the door, he barked loudly.

"Our Jack of Hearts has arrived," Everleigh announced.

"Impeccable timing," Owens murmured, since they were just about to go in to dine.

"Zubiri, we will put back dinner to give Major Knight time to wash off the dirt of his journey," she told the butler as he opened the door to let Toro out. Accompanied by the two captains, she followed as the beast ran towards the stables.

Catalina watched as Toro nearly pushed Major Knight to the ground with his effusive welcome.

"Down!" Major Knight commanded with a smile. This order duly adhered to, he then proceeded to fondle the beast enough for his immediate satisfaction. Catalina stood back as his two friends greeted him and called her dog to her side. She hoped her pleasure at his reappearance did not show on her face. Even in his ridiculous disguise, he was the most handsome man she had ever met.

They began walking towards the house, but Major Knight met her gaze and bowed.

"Welcome back, sir. I trust your brother was well?"

They all fell in to step as they returned to the villa. "Yes, indeed. He had his new wife with him."

"And you received what you needed from him?" Everleigh asked.

They entered the house before he answered. "Yes, but I have yet to read it fully."

He would say no more, but from what he left unsaid, Catalina assumed it needed to be deciphered.

"We have put dinner back so you may wash. I hope you have an appetite, because Cook has been to a great deal of trouble to please the Englishmen."

Owens rubbed his hands together with anticipation. "Hurry, old chap. My mouth is watering already."

Knight chuckled. "You need not wait for me, I will be down short-ly," he said, before taking himself off to his apartments.

"I daresay we may take our seats," Catalina suggested.

Zubiri filled their glasses with one of their own Tempranillo wines and brought in a tray of figs, cheese and almonds for them to have while they waited.

Indeed, it was not long until Major Knight returned, attired in fresh clothing and with his hair damp and slicked back from a quick wash. She had taken the liberty of having his clothing washed while he was away, and he had put it back on.

A footman brought in some gazpacho de mango and served it to them. Once the other courses had been brought in, Catalina dismissed the servants and she and her guests dined alfresco so that they could speak freely.

"We will have no more interruptions," she said, "but I think it best if we speak in English."

The gentlemen nodded their agreement and Major Knight took out a paper from his coat and unfolded it.

He handed it to Captain Everleigh. "I did a preliminary decipher-ing, but you are most welcome to check my work."

Everleigh scanned through the words, a deep crease forming be-tween his brows, marring his dark, handsome features.

"It is much as we expected," Everleigh remarked, "but I would like to examine it further after dinner."

Catalina said nothing, assuming the information involved English concerns.

Once the list was put away, Owens spoke. "When we left camp this morning, Wellington was about to cross the Ebro. He received word of French movement towards Vitoria, so it looks as though his strategy is coming together as planned."

"We have to keep that information from leaking, first," Catalina added. "How many days do we have left?"

"It is a two-day march, now that Wellington has rejoined the troops. I do not expect it will be much longer than that if the element of surprise is to be kept on our side."

"And we are to become the shadows of the suspected men?" Catalina asked.

"Precisely."

"And the list from your brother narrows down possible traitors?"

"It is a list of men Wellington wished to have investigated," Knight answered.

"So he already suspected them?"

"The commander misses nothing. He takes his responsibility to his troops to heart. Those on his immediate staff he must trust implicitly. No one is there without being investigated or passing a test. It was how he knew exactly where the leak was coming from," Everleigh explained carefully.

"So this list will be of the men who could have had such knowledge, but of those, is there one who might have a reason to betray their country?" Owens expounded further.

"Wellington will lay some traps and hopefully it will be as simple as that."

"And these troops will make it obvious?" She hated the feeling that she was having to draw information from them.

"We can only hope. Owens and I will take two of the names and you and Knight the other two," Everleigh replied.

"When do we leave?" Catalina asked.

"It would be best to be in place before the troops begin their movement. I suggest we snatch a few hours' rest and then leave before dawn."

"Then we had better have dessert, if it is to be our last meal here for a while. It would not be a Spanish meal without dessert and café." Catalina rang a small hand bell, indicating it was safe for the servants to return.

"Music to my ears, my lady," Owens said in a sing-song voice.

The three men were relaxed and charming, and Catalina found herself dreaming of a future... one with a specific face, which she had no business to be thinking of at this moment. It was gratifying to be treated as an equal – not as an ignorant female, but one with whom they let their guard down and spoke freely; one with whom they exchanged ideas.

Darkness fell and then the clock struck ten. It was obvious the gentlemen all heard it almost as an ominous toll, for as one they began to push back their chairs from the table. By the serious expressions on their handsome faces, they knew it was time to prepare for the morrow and take what rest they may. Catalina was sure her face must reflect the same.

Owens, Everleigh and Knight all took her hand and kissed her cheek gallantly before going up the stairs to their chambers. Catalina went to tell the senior servants she and the gentlemen would be leaving during the night and to ask if they would please pack as much food for them as possible. Catalina did not know how they were to live if not a part of the camp. She had never done such a thing. Frankly, this next task was the stuff of Gothic novels, she thought, while at the same time excitement pulsed through her veins. She only hoped her body would cooperate and rest during the night, for who knew when they would have the luxury of such sleeping accommodations again. *Perhaps never if Napoleon won.*

She began to lay out her disguises for the morrow. Camouflage would be her trick to success. No one must suspect she was a lady. She held her broken arm, praying it would not be a liability. Riding was difficult but doable, but many things were not, such as plaiting her hair. As she combed through the tangles, she smiled when she remembered Major Knight performing the task for her.

It was time to set romantic thoughts of him aside, she chided herself. There was no room for any wayward thoughts just now. She crawled into her bed and put out her taper. Bowing her head, she prayed this war would be over quickly, so that her country and her heart could escape without irreparable damage.

CHAPTER TWELVE

T HEY LEFT VILLA Blanca under the cover of darkness. Lady
Catalina had not uttered a word of complaint and, furthermore,
had had the forethought to ask the cook to prepare provisions for
them. The horses were even saddled and waiting for them at the front
door at the appointed time. Again, the lady had surprised him with her
resolute efficiency. He had expected to do all these things himself. The
four of them exchanged sleepy good mornings and bid thanks and
farewell to the senior servants, who had risen to see them on their
journey. Toro had to be held back, not wanting to be left behind again.
Felix understood—he wanted to follow the lady as well.

They mounted and set off. Felix was grateful for the bit of leisurely
time for his leg to heal. It still hurt like the devil when he moved, but it
was healing nonetheless.

Little was spoken for they rode hard when they reached the open
road. Everleigh and Owens took the lead, since they knew the exact
location they were going to, having left the camp and scouted their
prospects on the way to Villa Blanca. Felix and Lady Catalina followed,
riding far enough behind to keep the main cloud of dust out of their
faces. The road was not wide enough to ride four abreast even at this
hour of the very early morning.

He finally allowed himself to glance sideways at her, trying to
think of her as Eugenia or as a boy. It was difficult not to notice her

strong, shapely legs as she rode. He had to admit she had done a fair job of disguising herself, but he still knew it was her. He shuddered to think how she must have bound certain parts of her anatomy in order to be successful.

She noticed him looking at her. "Will I do?"

"I believe so."

"Confess, you did not think I could succeed."

"No," he corrected, "I still held out hope, but was skeptical."

She laughed. "It took help from one of the maids. I do not know if I will be able to disguise my hair so cleverly by myself," she replied, then adding, as if to herself, "It might need to be cut, but it will grow back again."

Felix contained his urge to command her never to cut a hair from her head, but he knew it might prove essential for her survival.

"I hope that will not be necessary. I will assist as much as I am able." He watched her transfer her reins to one hand and tuck the other against her stomach. "How is your arm feeling, by the way?"

"Having two days to rest has been a blessing," she answered at once. "I do not want to hold anyone back. It is difficult to realize I am not whole. I am used to being rather agile."

Felix had witnessed her abilities. "I never did compliment you on that daring climb from the carriage and the ensuing jump."

"In skirts," she reminded him.

"In skirts," he conceded. "At least you have no such inhibitions now. Pray your abilities will not be required this time."

They stopped twice to water the horses and Owens and Everleigh pulled up at a small farmhouse west of the encampment. They dismounted, and Felix and Lady Catalina followed their lead.

"This is about a mile from the encampment. We have already spoken to the family and made arrangements to use their barn for our horses, and the hayloft for sleep if necessary, in exchange for a warning if the fighting is expected to come in this direction. And, of course, some coin to pay for feed." Quietly, they led their horses down a path to a wooden outbuilding; Captain Everleigh opened the door and let them all inside.

Fresh hay and water had been placed in the empty stalls. It seemed the farmer was prepared for them. Two job horses looked up with mild interest, but quickly went back to their own hay.

Felix wondered if Catalina had ever slept in a barn before. They found billeting when able, but often slept in tents when on the march. This adventure would continue to test her mettle.

"Pack as lightly as you can and leave the rest here. If something happens, meet back here later. Owens and I will do our best to stay together, and you two should do the same," Everleigh said.

Soon they set off on foot, only a small bag of rations, two knives, and a pistol for each of them. Felix had a spy glass which had, in the past, often saved him from exposure.

The mile-long walk went by quickly, the sounds and smells of the large encampment reaching them long before their feet reached the perimeter. Everleigh and Owens gave them a nod as they separated from them.

"Who is on the list?"

Felix sighed heavily. It pained him to admit to the presence on the list of the Englishmen they suspected.

"Roberts and Hill," he said softly into her ear.

A look of shock crossed her face. "The first I suspected, but the second? It makes no sense to me."

"Nor to me, and I do not want to believe it, but apparently there is enough evidence not to dismiss him out of hand."

"But he runs the British Intelligence operation," she said, obviously trying to comprehend what he had told her. Felix understood her shock. If she felt this way, his feelings were much deeper, having worked for the man for years. It had taken a long, hard ride to compose himself. Owens and Everleigh had been equally shocked.

"He knows we are alive. He knows everything."

"Yes, but he does not know Wellington suspects him. He will lay the trap himself and you and I will have to find the proof."

"I have mixed feelings," she said, frowning adorably. "I wish to vindicate my father, but I do not wish for Hill to be guilty."

"My sentiments exactly," Felix agreed.

"And Dion." She threw her hands up in the air. "Will he be watching us watching him?"

Felix could not help but smile at her. Such passion would be deeply frowned upon in an English ballroom.

"What did I say?"

"It is not so much what you said but how you said it. If you speak with your hands like that, you will never pass for a servant boy." Felix felt an immediate urge to kiss her, but he restrained himself. This most definitely was not the time, and if they were seen, there would be worse consequences.

"Come. We must discover where the command tents are. Typically, they are placed in a particular order, but now that they have rejoined all of the contingencies, it will be a bigger undertaking to watch every movement."

"We will need to search his belongings," Lady Catalina remarked.

"Yes," Felix agreed. "There will only be a small opportunity to do so, if at all. Everything will be in code and he must not know anyone has been in there."

"What, specifically, would we be searching for? Have you any idea?" she asked as they walked around the perimeter of the camp.

Felix shook his head. He had been over everything in his mind ad nauseam. "Wellington and Hill go back longer than anyone else out here. They attended school together in their youth. Both have a long family history of loyalty to the Crown. Why would he betray his country or his oldest friend?"

"Perhaps he does not wish England and the allies to fail, but Wellington himself," she suggested.

"Jealousy," Felix whispered. Such base emotions had not occurred to him in connection with Hill and Wellington. He did not wish to believe it, but it *was* one of the deadly sins, and Hill was as human as the rest of them. Felix should not be blinded by his personal feelings or wishes. Yet, something did not feel right.

⟫⟫⟫⟨⟨⟨⟨

CATALINA COULD TELL Major Knight was struggling with thoughts of his superior betraying his country for such evil reasons. She had felt much the same about Dion. Were the two connected or was it a coincidence? Major Knight had said he did not believe in coincidences, so they must look for the connection. Perhaps it would explain much.

It took them several hours to map out the encampment. Hill and Wellington's tents were well surrounded and unless there was to be a meeting or dinner, there was too much activity for them to conduct a search.

Once an hour the two of them returned to their starting point to exchange information.

"It is too risky to do anything by daylight. We may reposition ourselves closer to the tents, now that we have found them, but I do not expect any blatant exchanges of information in daylight. We must wait for nightfall and hope the tents are empty long enough for us to take a look," Knight said when next they met. "I have found the perfect place from which to watch, however."

Catalina followed him as they repositioned their lookout to where there was a slight elevation overlooking the camp. Well hidden by brush and olive trees, Major Knight settled them to wait, as comfortably as was possible, beneath the shade of the tree.

From their vantage point, the encampment looked like a city of tents. The allied army had amassed to over 120,000 men, plus the women, children and animals who accompanied them. Smoke rose from the hundreds of fires, and the smells of cooking tempted her growling stomach. Sounds of children's laughter could be heard in the distance, and groups of soldiers walked toward the river to fish or perhaps to hunt.

"You are certain we cannot be seen? Your Colonel Hill will know we are out here."

"Yes, but recall he does not know he is a suspect," Knight answered in a low voice.

"I still cannot like it. I feel like a duck waiting for the fox to pounce on me. Do you not feel the sensation of being watched?"

Major Knight put down his spyglass and looked around cautiously. "I do not, but I never discount anyone else's feelings on the matter. When did this feeling start?" he whispered.

"Since we came to our new position, but it only became very strong a few minutes ago," she replied.

"Very slowly, I want you to lie down on the ground."

Catalina obeyed, with as little movement as possible. She watched as Major Knight checked to make certain nothing bright or reflective was standing out, and tilted his head down lower to cover the light of his face.

Catalina quieted her mind to listen for sounds. It was quite astonishing, what you could hear when you allowed yourself to listen. Insects chirped and birds sang, and very often listening would give you clues, if you paid attention. It was difficult to ignore Major Knight's lithe body next to her, but she did her best to keep still and keep her mind on her surroundings.

They heard a rustling in the bushes at the same time, for he placed his hand on her arm and gave a gentle squeeze.

The hairs on the back of her neck stood to attention, and she felt her heartbeat quicken with anticipation. He positioned his eye-glass carefully and began to survey the area around them.

A disturbed branch made another rustling sound and Major Knight took hold of his pistol as she put her hand on the butt of a knife.

Both of them held still—she knew he did not wish to give away their position. They did not have the evidence they needed to convict anyone.

She felt him move his spyglass to his eyes, and she could sense the relief flood through him.

"What have you found?" she asked.

He took the glass from his face and placed it in front of her eye, trying to point her in the right direction.

It took her a moment, but she spotted a doe and two fawns. "How beautiful," she whispered. It was a good reminder to proceed with caution, however. He uncocked his pistol and placed it back in its holster.

Catalina awoke with a start and realized she was once again resting on Major Knight. She really needed to stop doing that. She glanced up to see him smiling down at her.

"I fell asleep," she said stupidly.

"Yes," he agreed, looking entirely amused. "I took a short rest myself," he added.

Catalina sat up, careful not to put any weight on her arm. She was exhausted and most likely disheveled, and their true work was just beginning. It would be a few difficult days until the battle was over.

"We should eat and prepare to go back down to the camp. We must situate ourselves close to the tents and take any chances we have. You will be my lookout."

Catalina was grateful she had asked her cook to prepare them some food. It hardly compared with the fare from the night before but pinxtos, topped with goat cheese and olives, was still welcome to her hungry body.

Major Knight stood gingerly and began to transform himself once again. By the time he was finished, he could have been taken for a batman or foot soldier. He caught her watching him.

"I could hardly be an old man in this camp," he explained, as he put his arms through an old red uniform coat that he pulled from his bag.

"I suppose not." She stood up as well and righted her clothing; the too-large trousers and coat had twisted a little. At least there was less to rearrange in men's clothing. She reached up to feel her hair and realized it had escaped the tight confines the maid had placed it in that morning. She glanced at Major Knight, who was trying not to laugh.

"That is most helpful," she retorted.

"I know, but you are too adorable for words," he said, completely disarming her.

"I could stab your other leg and I do not think you would find that adorable," she snapped.

"Indeed not, but you would never do it. Come here," he said and when she complied, began to pin her hair back down to disguise it.

They were both dirty and tired; she should be repulsed by his smell of sweat and leather, but she forced herself not to inhale deeply of his scent. She closed her eyes and enjoyed his touch, which was surprisingly gentle.

"You will do. With a hat," he added.

"Thank you," she said dryly as she placed her hat low upon her head.

They began to make their way back down through the trees and brush, reaching the edge of the camp in a quarter of an hour.

"Hopefully they will be dining with Wellington and we may search with some leisure," Knight said low in her ear.

"I do not think that is the correct word, Señor."

He chuckled quietly, but sobered as they grew close and started walking amongst the tents.

Darkness had finally fallen and they both heard the ringing of the bell to signal dinner. He pulled her to his side and back into the shadows as someone emerged from the tent.

Colonel Hill walked in the other direction, settling his tricorn hat atop his head, not bothering to look behind him.

Catalina moved forward but Major Knight held her back. "His batman," he whispered. They waited a few more minutes and, sure enough, the servant emerged. After his footsteps could no longer be heard, Knight moved forward.

"I will whistle if I see someone," she said as he passed.

He gave a nod and then disappeared into the shadows.

CHAPTER THIRTEEN

ELIX ALREADY HAD his story in place if Hill happened to return to his tent for some reason. He would simply explain that he was waiting to consult with him. The simplest stories were usually the most believable, in his experience.

Nevertheless, he crept quietly into the tent, lifting the canvas only enough to slip behind. Once his eyes had adjusted to the darkness, he pulled a taper from his pocket and lit it with a flint and steel.

Felix knew he had to be quick, but thorough. Having worked for the man for some time now, he knew there was a limited amount of information actually written down, but it would be foolish not to take the opportunity of looking.

No matter how many times he had done this, it was impossible to completely still his body. There was always a fear, mixed with the thrill of being caught. Every sense was on high alert, every feeling magnified. His heart pounded in his ears, his breaths were shallow, and his body beaded with perspiration as he looked about to assess his task.

Hill would not expect to be searched at this juncture, in the middle of their encampment, so Felix hoped the Colonel had not been too careful.

Beginning on the left side of the tent, Felix searched methodically so as not to miss anything. The batman had a pallet and a large duffel bag with his belongings and a haversack. He would not begin there, doubting even the servant knew of his man's perfidy. Hill was too cunning for that.

Next, Felix searched under Hill's cot, as well as through his blankets and pillow, finding nothing. He moved to his trunks, searching for false bottoms and hidden linings. There were some personal keepsakes and letters, but nothing to indicate treason. Lastly, there was a small folding table, used as a desk when traveling. Across it lay several dispatches, which was nothing unusual, although it looked as if he were writing them himself. Felix frowned. Normally the aides de camp and secretaries acted in the place of scribes and wrote these records as dictations. Felix scanned each one, detailing Wellington's plan for the upcoming plan to defeat Bonaparte.

Even if Hill felt secure in this camp, why were these documents in plain view?

Felix read each one more carefully, memorizing phrases and looking for coded messages. He could detect none, which was even more strange. Perhaps he had not yet had the chance to cipher them?

He could feel, in his bones, that these papers held what they were looking for—or coded commands to someone to do something nefarious. However, there was nothing truly wrong about Colonel Hill being in possession of these dispatches. Could it be that he was copying the contents to share with the enemy?

Carefully making certain everything was just as he left it, Felix blew out his taper and cautiously left the tent.

Lady Catalina was where he had left her.

"Did you discover anything?" she whispered.

"I am not sure," he answered truthfully. "Were there any movements from Roberts' tent?"

"None. I have been watching all of them, and I believe they have all left for dinner."

Felix gave a nod. "I had better try my luck there as well. There may not be another opportunity." Dinner itself was not a lavish affair in camp, but some would linger for the time to relax and be social. Wellington encouraged the camaraderie in order to make this life and the battles as bearable as possible. Felix could only hope Wellington knew he would be searching and detain these men as long as possible.

He repeated his method of entry into the second tent, knowing he might have less time than the first. Felix knew much less about Roberts, since he had joined Wellington's staff during Felix's time in prison. Roberts seemed amiable enough, but there was nothing to either recommend or disconcert about the man.

There was no table with dispatches in here, so he spent more time on Roberts' trunks. They also contained personal papers and letters, but at the very bottom, there was a packet of love letters, written in French. There was nothing particularly incriminating about that, but they warranted further perusal.

At the back of the tent, footsteps rustled in the grass, just as though they were on the other side of the canvas. Lady Catalina was off to the side. Felix quickly shoved the letters back into place, covered them with clothing and set the latch back on the closed trunk. He blew out his taper as he crept back to the flap.

He heard more footsteps and stilled in place; heart pounding loudly in his ears, he kept his back against the fabric wall. All senses on alert, he placed one hand on the dagger in his waistcoat and waited, listening intently as he tried to decipher the sounds he heard. The footsteps stopped for a moment and he wondered why Lady Catalina had not sounded an alarm when someone was so close.

FOR A BRIEF moment, he wondered if she had heard the steps on the opposite side of the tent, but he could not ponder for long. Hopefully she had had the sense to get out of sight. The footsteps began again and paused at the entrance of the tent, he was sure. Why the hesitation? Someone returning to their own tent would go straight in. Unless they had seen Lady Catalina…

He had no more time to think about her; someone was entering the tent. Felix debated whether he could slide out behind them through the opening and make his escape, but something made him pause.

The intruder did not move, as though they sensed his presence. Employing all his faculties, he searched for some clue as to who the person was. The figure was too tall for Lady Catalina; besides which, she would have announced herself.

Was this someone else searching? An eerie sense of familiarity came over him and he had scarcely seconds in which to decide what to do. The recollection of what had happened the last time he had tangled with this villain still throbbing in his thigh. *How did you slip past Catalina,* he wondered, *and did you know she was there?*

Panic for her welfare infused his veins and he leaped forward in an attempt to capture the dastard.

Together, they fell through the tent opening, hitting the ground with a loud thump and a simultaneous grunt. There was just enough light upon the man for him to see Dion's face.

A slight movement out of the corner of his eye momentarily distracted Felix. Seizing his chance, Dion growled and dug in his toes, gaining enough purchase to throw Felix onto his back. Groaning as the man landed heavily upon him, Felix quickly drew back his dagger and plunged it into the blackguard's arm. Roaring in pain, Dion released Felix and grabbed at the knife, pulling it free. Instead of continuing to fight, he scrambled to his feet and ran away into the night.

Felix cursed and pulled himself to his feet. Just then, a moan sounded from his right. Rushing to the prone body on the ground, he rolled the slight form over and tried to search her face.

"Catalina!" he whispered urgently.

A few muffled sounds came from her throat, but she was not completely conscious. Debating what to do, he gathered her into his arms and carried her away from the camp. It was almost a mile to the farm and he had no horse, but he dared not keep her out in the elements all night. It would compromise the undertaking if he were to seek out Dr. Broughton or Wellington. He must find a way to send a message to the commander to apprise him of what he had discovered.

If he could find an unsuspecting soldier, he could send a message. He prayed Dion had run far away and was not waiting to return in order to cause Catalina further harm. He moved her to a more sheltered spot in the shadows of an Inula bush and hurried back towards a line of tents. There was a sergeant walking the perimeter and he hailed him.

Rightfully suspicious, the sergeant put his hand on his sword.

"Stand easy, Sergeant. I need your assistance."

The soldier relaxed a little at Felix's aristocratic diction in the King's English, which he had emphasized on purpose. "I need you to take a message to Lord Wellington immediately. The message is for his ears only and no one else's. Is that understood, Sergeant?

"Yes, sir!"

"Do not repeat it, even to any of his aides de camp or other staff. Tell only Wellington." Felix stressed the instruction. It was his best hope for now and Lady Catalina. "The phoenix flies west a mile with a wounded sparrow, to the nest."

Felix left the Sergeant and hurried back to Catalina. She was limp when he gathered her into his arms. He began walking back towards the farm, trying to think of getting her help instead of the pain in his leg. Fortunately, she was petite and light, or he might not have been able to carry her a mile.

It was impossible not to flinch at every sound, having seen Dion again. The look on the man's face, though only a brief glimpse, had been as one possessed. Felix had little doubt that Dion's intent had been to kill Catalina. How long had he been stalking them? Why was he at Roberts' tent? Was he also searching or was he there to meet and report? One thing was certain in Felix's mind—Dion was not working alone and it was imperative they find his comrade before they were both killed.

CATALINA HURT EVERYWHERE. Her head throbbed as if someone were beating it with a sledgehammer. What had happened? Thoughts flooded through her head as she tried to remember where she was and what she had been doing. Images of being at home and walking through the vineyards with Toro played in her mind, followed by vague pictures of tents, British soldiers, and deer. It did not smell like home, she realized, when odors of animal dung and hay wafted to her sensitive nose.

"My lady? Catalina?" a mildly familiar voice said.

Catalina moaned. She needed to open her eyes, but it hurt like the devil.

"That's the way, my lady, wake up." A cool, wet cloth swept across her brow.

Catalina squinted with one eye partially open. Faces swarmed before her blurred vision and she felt the overwhelming urge to retch.

"Wait! A basin!" the voice said, loud enough to make her wince.

Gentle hands rolled her sideways and she emptied her stomach into the proffered basin. A wet cloth then wiped her mouth as someone held her hair back from her face.

She rolled back over and groaned; it felt as though the room was spinning about her. Her bed was a blanket on the floor, over a pile of soft hay.

"Have a sip of water, my lady," the familiar voice said. Felix. Major Knight.

"What happened?" she asked, finally opening both eyes and concentrating her gaze until his face converged from two into one.

"Dion must have crept up behind you while I was searching. I heard footsteps at the rear of the tent, but was unable to warn you."

She closed her eyes to think, which was not pleasant. Ah. She remembered. "I did hear him, but he was faster than I. Just as I raised my whistle, he hit me on the head and pressed on my neck until I passed out. He knew my habits, but how did he know 'twas I?"

"I believe he saw us earlier. That eerie feeling you had..."

"Yes. The deer distracted us from further investigation—from realizing somebody was near."

"It was more comfortable to believe it was the deer causing the sensations. Do you have any other injuries? Your head did not appear severely harmed, as far as I could tell. He did not break your head, at least," he remarked. Suddenly, Catalina realized he had probably examined her from head to toe. She felt her cheeks heat with embarrassment.

Closing her eyes, she took a mental survey of her body. "It is a shame I have no wound to prove my pain," she answered dryly. "I feel as though I have been thrown from my horse." It was the best way she could explain her various hurts.

He gave a nod of understanding. "You fell to the ground, in addition to being hit on the head."

She looked around, noticing her surroundings for the first time. "We are in the hayloft of the barn? I do not remember returning here." Then it occurred to her what must have transpired. "Surely you did not carry me all that way—and up the ladder?"

"It was but a mile," he answered dismissively.

They heard the door open below. The latch rattled and, from the stamp of boots, it sounded as though more than one person entered. Everleigh and Owens? Anyone with malicious intent would have endeavored to move silently.

Footfalls thudded on the ladder and the rungs creaked. They were climbing the ladder! Catalina released a slow breath as Owens's face appeared, first with a smile then a frown as he surveyed the scene.

"My lady! What happened?"

Everleigh appeared behind Owens and then they moved out of the way for Lord Wellington himself.

Major Knight stood immediately and saluted. "Thank you for coming, sir."

"I did not trust anyone else to relay the news for me. I am pleased to see you awake, my lady," Wellington said as he approached her with his hat in his hand against his chest. "How severely are you harmed?"

"I believe I will recover, sir, but I was unconscious until a few minutes ago. It seems Major Knight carried me all the way here."

Wellington inclined his head to Knight and exchanged glances which seemed to convey some mutual understanding.

Owens and Everleigh brought some wooden crates over from the far side of the loft and placed them near her as makeshift chairs. Once seated, Wellington motioned to Knight to tell the story.

Catalina had not heard his discoveries, so she was also interested to hear the news.

"Our timing was fortunate. I was able to search both Hill's and Roberts' tents while Lady Catalina stayed on lookout. Unfortunately, Dion must have been looking for us, because he sneaked up behind her and hit her over the head. He must have been watching us."

"I also felt him squeezing the veins on my neck," she added.

"A very efficient technique to make certain you passed out," Wellington remarked.

"Indeed," she agreed. "I had been taught about it, but can testify to its effectiveness. Otherwise, I do not believe there is any lasting damage."

"I am relieved to hear it. I needed to see you for myself before I informed your father."

"¡Porque no!" she exclaimed. "Do not speak a word of this to him! Besides, it will compromise the operation."

The men looked at her strangely.

"I believe my father to be innocent, but I would like to see him proven to be so that there is no doubt."

"Understandable, my lady. What else did you find, Knight?" Wellington asked.

"As I said, very little. Besides Dion entering Roberts' tent, there were love letters written in French, but I was interrupted before I could ascertain their contents to determine if they were coded."

Wellington frowned but continued to listen.

"The only thing that struck me as odd in Hill's tent was that his desk was covered in dispatches."

"Out in the open?" Wellington sounded appalled.

"Precisely, but without the knowledge of your exact plans, I could not say if they were false or not. Perhaps he was trying to lure our perpetrator himself," Knight suggested.

"Do you think you could remember what you read?"

"Not word for word, but the locations, yes."

"Excellent. I will have those from you before I leave." He turned to Owens and Everleigh. "And was your evening successful?"

"It was as dull as ditchwater," Owens replied.

"We searched both Mendoza and Molina, but there was nothing at all. Not so much as a hint of anything," added Everleigh.

Catalina had been unaware of Molina being under suspicion. He had been one of her most serious suitors.

"It made me feel rather sorry for them," Owens admitted.

Catalina tried to stay neutral on the subject of her father, although she knew, even trying to look objectively, that it could not be done. However, it did not mean that Dion had not planted something.

"You are notably quiet, my lady," Wellington said to her, stirring her from her thoughts.

"I have a little to add. I am trying to remain unbiased about my father, but I cannot help but think Dion might feel betrayed and try somehow to place something in order to implicate Father. It would be almost impossible to prove his innocence if that were the case."

"I had wondered if the information I had was not intended to mislead me. I am being overly cautious, perhaps, but I have over 100,000 lives to protect," Wellington said gently.

"I understand, my lord. I would do the same."

"I know you do, my lady, which is why you are still here and why your father has not been removed from command."

She turned her gaze slightly towards the captains. "If my father has anything worth hiding, it would be in a pocket within the lining of his hat. The problem is, he is rarely without it."

"Is Lieutenant Dion aware of this?" Everleigh asked.

"It is possible, although I am unaware of Father using it, merely that it exists."

"It is worth looking at," Owens said.

"I should be the one to look," Catalina said, knowing the impossibility of anyone else being able to do so.

"Your order is to rest," Major Knight said, eyeing her sternly.

"Tomorrow, I want the two of you to look over the French positioning and see what you can learn," Wellington said to Owens and Everleigh. "If all is as I wish, we will strike the day after."

"Yes, sir," they answered.

"Walk out with me, Knight, and you can give me those names." Wellington moved forward from his crate to kneel before Catalina. "I am very glad you are unhurt, but I would like you to stay here tomorrow to recover. As you said, it is likely that Dion feels betrayed and he may not stop until he kills you or your father."

Catalina tried to nod as she fought back tears. She did not wish to show weakness, but she was in pain and Wellington was right. Dion probably had meant to kill her.

CHAPTER FOURTEEN

WELLINGTON AND FELIX both remained quiet until they were outside the barn. Felix saw Beckerman across the farmyard with the horses, allowing them to graze and drink from a trough. He also had no doubt that Beckerman was keeping a careful watch of the perimeter.

Felix waited for his commander to speak.

"Tell me what you read, although I believe I have already decided to make some changes. That way, if Hill is sending out his own dispatches, it will be obvious." Wellington swallowed hard. Felix would not wish for his position for anything in the world. "Of course, there might be a simple explanation," Wellington added.

Except, Felix reflected, they both knew it was highly irregular. They kept everything in one location and it was guarded by two men at all times.

"I assume you will not confront him?"

"No. I do not wish for him to know I am watching him. He is one of my oldest friends, you know. I hope there is nothing to this."

Felix nodded, though he had no idea if Wellington could see him in the darkness.

"I had best be going. I have much to deliberate upon, but I believe it might be best to march from here instead." He shook Felix's hand. "Take good care of Lady Catalina. She will need you." With those cryptic words, Wellington took his horse from Beckerman, mounted and, with his batman following, rode away.

Felix stood watching the stars for a few minutes before returning to the loft. It was time to bed down for the night, for who knew what tomorrow would bring. Possibilities were beginning to narrow down in his mind but first, there was Lady Catalina to attend to. For a good while that night, he had begun to wonder if she would ever wake. The thought of a world without her vitality was too much to bear. Thankfully, her wits had been about her when she had come to—even if dulled a little by the pain. He had seen a few men take blows to the head and be alive in body but gone in spirit. Thank God she was not one of those. He knew, in his heart, he would have to deal with his feelings at some point, and Wellington's caution kept echoing in his thoughts. First, however, the traitor must be caught and Napoleon defeated. He had tyrannized Russia and Europe for too long, and would never be content with peace.

Lady Catalina was already asleep by the time he climbed back up to the loft. Owens and Everleigh had made themselves snug beds of hay covered with blankets and were preparing for sleep. The three of them exchanged glances of understanding. They had worked together many times, and knew that tomorrow was likely to be a critical day. As he prepared his own bed and lay down to sleep, he prayed that Lady Catalina would obey the orders from the commander to rest. If he had to worry about her, he was afraid he would miss something critical. Closing his eyes, he tried to recall the dispatches in his mind's eye, looking for a code.

The nagging feeling that he was missing something would not go away.

THE NEXT MORNING, Felix expected Lady Catalina to be up and prepared to go searching with him to cast about for more intelligence, but she was seemingly willing to cooperate with Wellington's orders.

To be precise, she was rather blue-devilled.

Owens and Everleigh kneeled beside her before they set out to scout the French position.

"You will be careful?" she asked them.

"Always," Everleigh reassured her.

Owens grinned. "Careful is not the word I would choose, my lady, but lucky."

She looked heavenward and crossed herself. "Your poor mother, if she only knew."

"She knows. Why do you think I was sent into the army, if not that she might worry generally instead of over each of my specific mishaps?" He laughed, and Lady Catalina shook her head.

"Be off with you, then. Now I will lie here all day and worry about you."

"Today, just for you, I will make it my solemn vow to be careful," he said valiantly, placing a hand on his heart. He bent over and smacked a loud kiss on her cheek before they took their leave.

"The rogue," she muttered as their footsteps descended on the ladder.

"An appropriate term," Felix agreed.

"And where are you going?" she asked.

He hesitated. He had already spoken with the farmer's wife to make certain Lady Catalina would be looked in on and fed during the day, but he did not want to say his goal was to search General Mendoza's hat.

She looked at him in a searching way, still beautiful, but pale and in pain, to judge from the creases between her eyes.

"The only time you will find Papa without his hat today is during siesta—if he is able to take one. His batman will often leave during that time."

"Why are you telling me this?"

She held out her hand; kneeling beside her, he grasped it.

"It is where you were going, is it not?"

He gave a reluctant nod. "I did not wish to worry you."

She barked a laugh of disbelief and then winced with pain. "¡Imposible! Of course I will worry! I will do nothing but worry! But I know it must be done for my father's sake as well as the war's. My biggest fear is that the *diablo*, Dion, will have hidden something incriminating and my father will not realize it."

He squeezed her hand. "The truth will out. We are already suspicious and I promise you I will fight for his innocence." Without thinking, he leaned forward and kissed her gently on the lips.

"Thank you, Felix," she said as a tear rolled down her cheek. She brushed back a lock of his hair and he was nearly undone. He rose to his feet and turned to leave before he could betray himself and his country further.

He climbed down the ladder and began the walk to the camp, hoping and praying that he would find nothing on Mendoza that would implicate him beyond belief. However, he vowed he would take care of Lady Catalina regardless of the outcome.

It was going to be a sweltering day. Already there were no clouds in the sky, and he was perspiring by the time he reached the edge of the encampment.

He searched through his haversack then changed into the old uniform coat again so as to blend in, and made his way towards where the Spanish battalions were situated. Thankfully, he was less known after his time in prison, but he could not be too careful. Mendoza himself would know Felix.

Unexpectedly, companies of soldiers were engaged in drills and the artillery wagons were being loaded with cannon and shot. There was always a certain hum of anticipation in the camp immediately before a battle. It was busy, yet almost eerily quiet.

He crept around the periphery with care, looking for the perfect spot for surveillance. Mendoza's tent was well surrounded and precisely where Lady Catalina had said it would be. There was no convenient perch on which to station himself as he and Lady Catalina had had to view the British tents. He needed it more today—and he needed a great deal more luck, as Owens had aptly termed it. There was neither darkness nor natural cover with which to shield himself, not that that had been successful.

He wished he had asked Lady Catalina more about her father's habits, but it had been difficult enough to reveal that his task for the day was to investigate Mendoza. Skirting the outer edge of the tents, he watched the Spaniards drill for a while, hoping to discover the man himself there reviewing his troops. After watching for half an hour, Felix could not see Mendoza anywhere, so he slipped along the lines to the man's tent, determined on the course of being a messenger if anyone inquired.

He turned from his hiding spot to look straight into the face of General Mendoza.

"Knight?" he asked softly. "Is that you?"

Felix held back a curse. Luck seemed to have abandoned him of late.

"Is something amiss with Catalina?"

Felix hesitated. He did not want to lie to the man.

Mendoza sensed his hesitation. "Come with me and tell me everything."

"I cannot risk being seen. If anyone else recognizes me, Wellington will have my head."

"Yes, I understand. Keep your head down and follow me."

Mendoza escorted Felix to his tent. Felix felt guilty for taking advantage in this way, but at least he would not be sneaking about to achieve admission. There was nothing unusual about a British soldier visiting the Spanish battalions, so long as he maintained his disguise. He walked a little differently and made himself as nondescript as possible.

Mendoza held back the flap to his tent and ushered Felix inside. The scent of roses was so strong, that Felix felt a desperation for this man and his daughter to be innocent.

The general indicated for Felix to sit down and joined him in another chair. "Tell me," he insisted.

Felix did not know how much to disclose. Was it wise to let him know Dion lived? He felt as though he were playing with fire and one way or the other someone would be hurt.

"Your daughter is resting this morning. She took a blow to the head last evening, but seems to have nothing more than a headache today."

Mendoza leaned back and closed his eyes as if praying.

Felix could not believe a guilty man would allow his daughter to continue spying in such circumstances. She would know his secrets. Nonetheless, they must be thorough.

"How did this happen?" he asked after a moment, the question Felix had dreaded.

"Dion," Felix answered, having already decided to judge this man innocent, yet hoping he had not made a fatal decision for his country.

GENTLEMEN WERE SO easy to dupe. As soon as Major Knight left, Catalina jumped out of bed and hurried down the steps after him. She had not undressed the night before, and the only thing necessary was to re-pin her hair. She had awakened and done that before any of the men stirred. Her head was pounding and the earth spinning, but this was urgent, and her future depended on it. There would be time for self-indulgence later. She crossed herself, praying it would be so.

Following along behind, she trailed Major Knight to the edge of the camp. She watched him change his coat again, shamelessly admiring the breadth of his physique.

Then she continued to watch as he skirted the Spanish camp. He stopped to watch the troops drill; perhaps he was looking for her father there. It was a wise move, but she took her chance and went to her father's tent. His hat was where he would keep something he was intentionally keeping private, but she feared Dion would place something accusatory in a more obvious place.

Her blood boiled when she thought of that *canalla* ingratiating himself with her papa for the last two years! What a way to repay his generosity! Some people could never be satisfied, and some people hated the aristocracy and thought it was their right to steal from them, like the English fable of Robin Hood she had heard told around the campfires. Of course, never did she want anyone to be poor and starving, and she believed it was their Christian duty to help those in need, but stealing was not right either.

Luckily, no one was about her father's tent, and if he was in there, then she would be pleased to see him. In all likelihood he was at the drill, reviewing his troops. He took great pride in the Spanish army being equal to any other, and would want to ensure they were ready. It was why she could not believe him guilty of anything more than trusting Dion.

Thankfully, when she lifted the flap and slipped beneath it, no one else was inside. Hastily, she went for her father's most private hiding places. She had not lied about the hat, and she would dearly love to check it, but Dion would be hard-pressed to have access to that as well, unless he had hidden something before he was caught.

She was surprised her father had left his tent unguarded, with Dion on the loose; although, of course, Papa thought his lieutenant dead. Catalina saw little point in keeping Major Knight's and her own survival a secret any longer. Dion knew and therefore whomever he worked for knew—*if* he was working for someone else.

There was nothing unusual in her father's trunks. Most of his private papers were kept at Villa Blanca. He did not think it necessary to carry much with him. Catalina kept the copy of his will in her belongings instead.

There were lists of all his troops, divided into battalions and regiments, along with their home addresses. There were other lists of supplies and other such information, but nothing out of the ordinary. She frowned. She wanted to prove beyond doubt that he was innocent, but she did not know what she could do.

She went to her father's bed and knelt to search beneath the bedding, then lifted his pillow. There was a miniature of herself and one of her mother. How different things had been when her mother had been alive! But now was not the time for sad reminiscence. She had to find the condemning evidence before Major Knight did. She believed he wished them well, but he had a duty to his country. She would feel the same were their positions reversed... and yet she knew in her heart that her papa was not capable of treason.

She put everything back where she had found it then stood and looked around the tent. If she were Dion, where would she conceal something?

Major Knight had mentioned dispatches on Colonel Hill's desk, and she thought back to that night she had first met the major. It seemed so long ago.

The knock on the head must have affected her more than she thought. She had to finish searching and be away from there before someone returned. She was not ready to explain herself to Papa, after all.

She found her father's traveling desk beneath his cot and slid it out. There were only paper, pens and ink underneath the wooden lid, but she knew there was another hidden panel below this one. She found the catch and released it, careful not to disturb anything. Papa was very particular and would know if anything was out of place.

There were several papers in someone else's hand. Quickly she scanned them, debating whether they would incriminate him in any way. It looked as though they were the plans for the battle on the morrow. But had not one of them told her the Spanish contingent would be the last to know? Her memories were muddled somewhat, but something told her that these should not be here. Would her father know if he was being duped? Was he being framed?

Footsteps crunched ominously on the ground outside and she made a quick decision. Shakily stuffing the papers inside her shirt, she wriggled beneath the cot, taking the little desk with her. Her hope was then to slide under the edge of the tent, but it was too well staked down.

She uttered unladylike words to herself and fruitlessly wished that it was dark. It was a myth that spies only operated in the dark of night.

A pair of polished black riding boots entered the tent, followed by another pair. Catalina gulped and scooted back as far as she could to make herself as one with the edge of the tent. She heard her father's voice, speaking to... Major Knight? Had he compromised his position to speak with him? What was happening?

She ordered the blood pounding in her ears to be quiet so that she could listen. This was not at all what she had expected him to be doing today.

Major Knight must have been seen by her father and been asked about her. The major was doing a fair job of prevaricating without fully lying.

They sat down, and Catalina maneuvered her head to try to see what was going forward. Would her father reach for his desk?

Her papa's boots were so very close to her face. She wished she could present herself and give him a hug. She closed her eyes, trying to listen while endeavouring to ignore the persistent pounding in her head.

Her father dropped his hat on the ground, and Major Knight bent to pick it up. Was the man blessed by the gods? Catalina held her breath when she saw him coolly reach inside and check the pocket before handing it back to her father, all the while keeping his eyes from his task. Did her father even realize what was happening? His voice indicated he was distracted.

"How did this happen?"

Major Knight hesitated and then answered, "Dion."

Catalina could not believe her ears. What made him admit such a thing? She was quite certain his commander and comrades would not approve. Had something occurred to convince him of her father's innocence, or had he done this for her? What a silly, wistful notion!

The very idea *that he would do such a thing,* she chastised herself, but hope began to blossom within.

"You are certain he is alive?" her father asked.

"I saw him myself."

Her father said some words she had never heard pass from his lips before. "Thank you for telling me this. If he harmed Catalina, then there is no telling what he might do. Do you have any idea who he is passing information to?"

"We have some ideas, but no hard evidence."

"I must return to my men," her father said, sounding weary. "Please give Catalina my love. I am depending on you to take care of her," her father said, standing up again. They shook hands as though something significant passed between them. Catalina felt tears welling up in her eyes. Her papa respected this man.

"I will go before you and warn you if anyone is about. If you hear nothing, assume it is clear for you to leave."

"Thank you, sir."

Catalina saw her father leave the tent and his footsteps grew quiet as he walked away, making no warning sound.

She relaxed, ready to escape, when Major Knight's face appeared in front of her. "You may come out now, you little termagant."

She almost jumped out of her skin. "How did you know I was there?" she asked, crawling from her hiding-place.

"I did not until you poked your head out to see what was happening." He held out his hand to help her to her feet.

"Did you find anything in his hat?"

"I did not," he admitted, sounding irritated.

"We must go."

"*You* must go," he corrected.

"There is nothing here," she told him hastily.

He eyed her suspiciously and pulled her to his hard body. The papers beneath her shirt crackled with loud accusation.

"Hand them over willingly or I will retrieve them myself." His expression said he meant it.

She glared at him, annoyed with herself as well. "Once we reach safety," she amended. "We must get out of here while it is safe to do so."

He did not reply, but instead took both her hands and led her from the tent, thence traversing the encampment until they were well away from the sea of white canvas and safely hidden among a stand of berberis bushes.

He looked at her expectantly and she grudgingly pulled the papers from her shirt. "These were in his desk. Papa would never have kept something important there." She closed her eyes as he read the documents.

"These are the ones I saw on Hill's desk last night. I must give them to Wellington." She felt his hand under her chin and she opened her eyes to stare into his dark gaze. "Do you trust me?"

"I want to," she whispered.

CHAPTER FIFTEEN

F ELIX HATED THE disappointment he saw in Catalina's face, but he could not risk the allied forces losing this battle because of one man. They walked on together until they reached the British side of the encampment.

"Go," she choked out, knowing it needed to be done.

"Will you return to the farm?"

"I came to do what I needed to. I will go back."

"Be careful. Dion is still out there."

She gave a nod as she barreled herself into his arms. He embraced her back knowing what she must be suffering, and the strange mixture of emotions that accompanied goodbyes before war.

He pulled himself away and prayed Dion would not follow her in the open daylight. He continued to hide his face as he made his way to Wilmington's tent, knowing that Hill would likely be there.

He passed a few other soldiers who grunted their acknowledgment to what they thought was their equal in rank. Good. He had not been recognized.

Stopping at the edge of the command tent, he debated how to find Wellington alone.

"You are becoming sloppy, Knight," a voice said behind him. He turned with his hand on his sword, then let out a rush of air when he saw Everleigh standing there.

"What is the matter? Can I help?" Everleigh asked.

"I found something I need to go to Wellington, but it is risky to stroll openly into the tent at the moment."

"Is it something I can pass on for you?"

"It depends on who is in there."

Everleigh gave an understanding nod. "I will go in and see." He looked around. "Wait for me beneath the tree up there. He pointed to where he and Lady Catalina had surveyed the camp the day before. "I will signal to you if it is safe to come back."

Everleigh went inside and Felix made his way back up to their perch, half wondering if Catalina would be there watching even now.

Alas, she was not. He suspected her pain was great and had only come this morning in order to vindicate her father.

Felix waited some time – long enough to read the dispatches in total. He wanted to be completely familiar with them before he turned them over. That suspicion was nagging at him again when he read them. It was a very plausible attack on the French if Everleigh and Owens found them positioned along the Zadorra. It allowed for Jourdan and Bonaparte's armies to be completely surrounded and thoroughly routed as long as everyone held their positions. It was risky splitting the force up, but could finally be the final nail in Bonaparte's coffin after his losses in Russia.

Everleigh arrived with Wellington. "I assume this is something good, Knight."

Felix handed him the dispatches. "I believe these are the ones I saw on Hill's desk last evening."

Wellington was surveying them critically. "And where were they found today?"

"Lady Catalina found them in her father's desk."

Wellington looked up sharply at that pronouncement.

"She did not obey orders to stay abed. I found her in his tent."

"And you trust this is all she found?"

"I do. However, she believes Dion planted them."

"And what do you think?" he asked.

"I am inclined to agree. I was in the tent with Mendoza himself. He had no indications of hiding anything. In fact, he left me in there alone."

Wellington seemed to nod to himself, if that was possible. "And were you able to search his hat?"

"Unbelievably, I was. He dropped it on the floor, giving me a perfect opportunity. He was very distracted upon learning of his daughter's injury."

"I had not yet had a chance to tell him."

"I must confess, sir, that I told him Dion was responsible when he asked how she was hurt."

Wellington looked at him long and hard. It was difficult not to squirm under the scrutiny.

"I am inclined to agree with you about Dion's guilt, though I am not certain how wise it was to divulge to a suspect." He went back to reading the dispatches, leaving Felix to wonder if that was the only reprimand he would receive. Felix felt much better having confessed his sin.

When Wellington finished, he tucked the papers beneath his crossed arms and looked off over the camp. "These are very cleverly done. I can only detect one mistake, which would leave the Spanish column vulnerable for slaughter. I do believe it absolves Mendoza and that these were, in fact, planted. However, does that prove Hill guilty?"

"It seems unlikely that he is innocent, sir," Everleigh replied.

Wellington shook his head. "There is only one thing to do. I must put Hill's regiment in place of the Spanish one."

Felix and Everleigh exchanged glances.

"I will not announce it until tomorrow morning when we march. It will be too late for him to warn anyone off. I will escort them myself. Now let us hope that I have not been outmaneuvered by my own people."

Felix was pleased for Catalina that her father was innocent, but he absolutely hated that Hill appeared to be the traitor. How Wellington must be feeling, ordering one of his oldest friends to the front line, similar to David with Uriah the Hittite. Except Wellington was not at fault and Hill was. It was entirely different, his conscience tried to reason, but what if he had been set up just as Mendoza had? If only there was a way to be certain, but Hill had left the tents with the dispatches still out in the open. The only other possibility was Hill's batman.

"What do we know of Hill's man?" Felix asked, just as Wellington and Everleigh were about to depart.

Wellington frowned. "I will have to ask Beckerman. I do not even know the man's name, come to think of it."

"Now that you mention it, I do not believe I do either," Everleigh added.

"Look into it when we return, Captain," Wellington said. "An unlikely culprit, but we must check every possibility. Now I must return. There's much to do before the morrow."

They went their separate ways, Felix returning to the farm trying to think of what else he could do. He was not terribly useful in the daylight, especially not in the English side of the camp where he was more likely to be recognized. He walked back to the farm, ready to eat and perhaps talk things over with Lady Catalina. Knowing that her father was free of suspicion, it would be easier to discuss the situation with her without that burden between them.

It occurred to Felix that he did not know what Lady Catalina would do during the battle. Did she normally wait with the women at the camp? To his knowledge, her main avenue for information came from charming gentlemen. That thought made him growl out loud, so distasteful was the thought of her flirting with other men that he had to stop himself from his possessive thoughts. Truly, he did not want to think what was next after the battle. Would he ever see her again? If Wellington succeeded, they would no longer occupy Spain and the Spanish force would probably remain behind.

The realization made him feel desolate, and guilty, for he should be elated by the prospect. In a mere few weeks, the petite Spanish señorita had wormed her way into his heart. The thought of leaving her was untenable. Visions of her and Eugenia creating mischief together kept intruding into his dreams as well as dark haired toddlers climbing into his lap for a story. Stupid, unwelcome thoughts. He dismissed them hastily and continued on his way to the barn.

When he climbed the ladder, he could feel his anticipation grow. What would it be like to come home to her every day? To be her partner?

He caught a glimpse of her asleep on the pallet, a tabby cat curled up in the bend of her knees. Now adding jealousy of a cat to his growing list of faults, he looked down upon the face which was so angelic in repose. He smiled wryly. She was a perfect mix of angel and devil, and he wanted to keep her. Only he did not know how.

THE NEXT MORNING, everyone was up before dawn preparing to ride out for a battle. Owens, Everleigh, and Knight all donned their uniform coats in stoic silence, unlike their usual mornings. Catalina was used to her father's ways, but it was somehow more real—more unsettling—to see these three men in such a way. It was a stark recall back to reality from the past few days she'd spent with them. In some ways, she envied them being able to put on a uniform and go fight. It was insufferable to be left behind waiting and wondering what had become of them. She had no such intention of sitting there idly at the farm all day, but she was not sure what she could do to help.

Many soldiers would die that day, and Catalina prayed fervently that her loved ones would be safe, including these three men who had become dear to her.

Besides the looming battle was the question of treason. Would there be surprises they had not foreseen or had failed to detect? Some things still did not sit right with any of them about Colonel Hill—especially the connection with Dion. It did not make sense. But if Hill was not involved, then someone had gone to a great deal of trouble to set him up.

Catalina, for one, was still very uneasy about Dion being out there somewhere meaning them harm.

While the men finished preparing for battle, Catalina gathered some of their provisions of fruit, bread, and cheese for their sacks and filled their canteens with water. It was definitely best to stay busy and not think about what lay ahead. She descended the ladder with them as they went to prepare their horses.

Major Knight lagged behind with her. "Dare I ask what you plan to do today?"

"I do not know," she admitted truthfully. "I want to do something. Perhaps I will go to the camp and see what I can discover."

"Will they not be shocked to see you alive?"

"Probably, but I can use that to my advantage. Maybe they will know something we missed. I will send word, but it may be too late."

"I do not like you being on your own." He frowned with endearing concern.

"It is not ideal, but I know there is some connection we have missed and Dion is still out there waiting to strike. I know it."

"You think your father is in danger?"

She waved her hands. "I do not know. I do not understand if he was trying to frame Papa or simply use him for cover. It seems strange that he would be working with your Colonel Hill."

"True. We have found no connection."

Catalina sighed heavily. "And you ride out with a regiment?"

"We run dispatches for Wellington or whatever he sees fit to task us with."

She gave a distracted nod. It was never easy to send her father away into battle, knowing he was a prime target. Somehow it was different this time. She was not sure why.

When they were ready to ride away, Catalina dutifully kissed each one of their cheeks and wished them God's protection.

She held back her tears until they were beyond hearing and continued to watch until they passed from site. The tabby cat was winding around her ankles and she picked it up and snuggled with it. "You knew I needed comfort," she said with a harsh laugh through her tears. She needed much more than comfort.

Catalina decided to become herself again and ride into the camp. She only had one dress in her small bag and it needed to be pressed. She took it to the house, and begged the assistance of a maid to help her dress and style her hair. If she was to return from the dead, she did not wish to look like she was.

By the time she reached the edge of the camp, the soldiers had already departed to form their columns for the battle some twenty miles away.

They would be able to hear when it began and despite what the women and children occupied themselves with when the men left, they would all be worried sick until it was over and the casualties listed. The walking wounded would make their way back, and many would busy themselves tending to injuries. Catalina often did, but first, time was critical to see if there was any last chance to find the missing piece to solve this mystery.

Catalina left Luna in the makeshift paddock where extra horses were kept by the cavalry and officers.

There would be many questions asked when she showed her face, but her pride was hardly worth giving thought to the consequences.

A few gasps of surprise and exclamations greeted her when some of the Spanish women recognized her. Soon, many had gathered around and wanted to hear the story.

She had thought about it a great deal before she arrived, and decided there was no point in withholding the truth.

As she told the story, something drew her eyes to the edge of the crowd where she saw her maid Maria, wide-eyed with a mixture of surprise and anger on her face. Catalina had given little thought to the maid since she left her that moment before everything changed. She smiled and gave a little wave to Maria, though it was some time before she could escape the curious crowd that had gathered around her. It was not every day that the general's daughter returned from the dead. She evaded questions of a personal nature that might impugn her honor, and when asked about Lieutenant Dion who had been a great favorite with the ladies, Catalina seized her opportunity.

"Lieutenant Dion did not die in the accident. We have been looking everywhere for him—'tis why we are so far behind. My father's men searched and never found his body, and then we heard reports he was seen near here two days ago."

There was a collective gasp from the gathering.

"Where could he be? Why would he not announce himself?" various women asked.

"That is exactly what we wish to know." Catalina made a face that pointed out suspicion without overtly accusing him of anything. "We believe someone is hiding him here in the camp. If you see him, please let myself or my father know. We only want to help him."

"Where have you been, my lady?" a voice shouted.

"I was taken to my home to recover. My arm was broken." she held up the offending limb so they could see her splint.

The first rifle shot echoed in the distance, causing all of them to still and many cross themselves in silent prayer.

A peppering of shots followed; it was always thus. Once the dam was broken, the battle rushed with fury.

The women began to disburse, and Catalina went to look for Maria. Instead of waiting for her lady, the maid was hurrying away. Catalina frowned and then her footsteps hurried after. Why did she seem to be running away? Many questions flooded through her mind that she had never thought to ask before. Where was Maria staying in Catalina's absence? Had she found someone else to serve? Had she heard Catalina's remarks about Dion? Maria had always been no better than she ought to be around the lieutenant.

That led her to another train of thought. Dion's trunks—were they ever searched? Major Knight had remarked upon wanting to search them, but where had they gone?

Every tent looked the same, Catalina thought, frustrated as she lost sight of Maria's dark dress. Never before had she chased anyone through camp either, she argued with herself disparagingly.

She was near to running in a most unladylike fashion, wishing she was still in trousers, when she passed a familiar face of a camp follower. "Where is my maid Maria's tent?" she asked, trying to catch her breath.

"Three down and to the left," she answered, and Catalina gave a wave of thanks as she hurried on.

Cannons boomed ominously in the background and Catalina flinched with every shot fired. It was impossible not to worry every time anew, especially not knowing where her father's column was, or where the English were. She grasped her rosary as she reached Maria's tent.

"Maria?" she called as she lifted the flap. Normally, she would have waited, but the maid had been no more than a few steps ahead of her.

The maid wore a look of fury. Her eyes were narrowed, her jaw was clenched, as were her fists at her side. "What do you want?" she growled.

Catalina was taken aback. Never had she heard a cross word from the girl. "Has something happened, Maria? I thought you would be pleased to see me."

"Has something happened?" the girl asked harshly. "Everything has happened! You have ruined everything!"

"I?" Catalina was at a complete loss.

"You have taken up with English. You are a traitor and a whore!"

Catalina stepped forward and slapped Maria. "How dare you! Do you know what I have been through this past week? The English have taken care of me and are our allies. They are helping us reclaim our country from the unlawful king!"

Maria spat. "I prefer him to the disloyal English who think raping and killing innocent women their right!"

Catalina had never seen Maria in such a state. She was becoming hysterical. "What happened, Maria?" she asked softly, trying to calm her down.

Maria looked her in the eye for the first time Catalina could re-member. Cold fury glared at her. "They raped me and my sister at Ciudad Rodrigo. Leonora did not survive."

"I did not know, Maria."

Before Catalina could express sympathy, Maria spoke again in a voice devoid of expression. "That is why they deserve to die."

Catalina felt sick at all of the signs she had missed. Everything began to fall into place, and Maria was the missing piece. She had to reach the front line before it was too late.

CHAPTER SIXTEEN

S INCE EVERLEIGH AND Owens had discovered that the French were easy targets in the valley around Vitoria, the Allies' hopes of success were greatly increased—the French believing even Wellington would not attempt an attack over such dangerous terrain. Wellington and his staff sat atop their horses overlooking a plain, which was dissected by broad and deep dykes. The trees were in full leaf of bright green and provided any number of places of concealment. It would not be easy, but war was a time to take calculated risks, not play safe; indeed, dividing the army was a definite risk. Wellington knew this was a chance to cut off the French army, and had declared his intention of seizing it.

Felix was acutely aware that Dion was still at liberty with the intent to do harm. In addition, his instinct told him Hill was the one to watch, not Mendoza, but both men would be carefully guarded—more so than was usual in a battle. Felix and Wellington were to stay near Hill's regiment, while Owens and Everleigh were to position themselves with Graham's regiment, alongside the Spanish to the French rear. His two comrades gave a nod as they moved off, and Felix watched as the remainder of the army began to fight, away to the right.

Felix often felt guilty for not being down at the forefront of the fighting, but he knew his job was important, nonetheless. Reconnoitering and staying one step ahead of the enemy was often what won and lost battles.

As he watched the guns fire and cannon explode below, he could not help but think of Catalina. He hoped she was being wise— although he doubted she was giving much regard to her safety. She would do what she thought necessary. He wondered how she had been received by her people. Few of his fellows had been surprised to see Felix; his position involved danger and intrigue, and he had returned from imprisonment before.

His mind busy with these musings, Felix led his horse away from the fighting to stroll the perimeter. Unfortunately, the terrain, which they were using to their advantage, also left areas blind and vulnerable. If Dion truly wished to hide and be a marksman for Hill or anyone else to whom he answered, this would be the perfect spot. Currently, Hill was in the thick of his regiment as they advanced on the enemy.

A runner had just come forward and reported a bridge across the river to be undamaged and unguarded. Wellington had ordered the entire force that was not engaged in combat to cross. Wellington always seemed to have the luck of the devil, but if it meant this battle was the finale, then Felix did not care how it happened.

The air quickly filled with smoke and the acrid odor of gunpowder. Already, injured men were being brought to the medical tents erected for the purpose and those able were walking back to the camp.

He mounted and climbed a short rise to get a better view. At once, the hairs on the back of his neck stood at attention. Immediately, he dismounted from his horse, tied him to a tree and sought cover, stripping off his red coat to help him hide. He would not give Dion the advantage and he would not mistake his instinct for an animal. Usually, the animals made themselves scarce at the first noise of a firefight.

Perhaps he was imagining things, but he did not intend to be caught unawares for a third time. Dion certainly had the advantage in the situation. It still gnawed at Felix that he did not understand the motive or the connections.

He pulled out his spyglass and surveyed the area around him. He tried to think like one intent on destroying the Allies' plans. How would Dion react to Mendoza's regiment having been traded for Hill's? Without knowing his purpose, it was impossible to guess, but Felix would wager Dion was nearby.

Felix could detect nothing, and frustration filled his veins. Something was going to happen and he felt helpless to stop it. He watched from the heights above as the army crossed the fast-flowing river on the plain below. As soon as the French discovered the 3rd Division had crossed the bridge, they turned their cannon on them with heavy fire. It was difficult to watch, but they seemed to be holding their ground.

There looked to be a great number of casualties on either side. He watched a horse being shot from beneath its rider—the worst sort of tragedy in Felix's opinion – a man flying through the air when a shell exploded in front of him, infantry forming squares, bayonets raised, frantic reloading of muskets, pools of blood on the ground...

Unable to watch any longer, Felix drew his attention back to his surroundings, glad to feel the sensation of Dion's presence abating. Had he missed his chance? Reluctantly, he abandoned his hiding place and remounted to rejoin Wellington, who was commanding two columns of his own in addition to the entire army.

Owens rode over from the east to report, composed but his voice laced with urgency. "Graham and the Spanish have captured the road between Vitoria and Bayonne, and have taken the road to Bilbao."

"Excellent. We should soon have them surrounded!" Wellington remarked with rare effusiveness. "Pass the word on as you return. It should boost morale," he added, dismissing Owens, who saluted then wheeled his horse to return.

As they watched Owens depart, Wellington looked questioningly at Felix, but he shook his head.

"Nothing, sir. But I know he is near."

"I think you had better shadow Hill. It is the only thing we have to go on."

"I agree, sir."

"I must say, if Hill is up to trickery, then he is a bloody cold one. He showed not a flicker of emotion or surprise at the changes I made at the eleventh hour."

"So far, then, there is no indication of your new plans having been intercepted?"

"None at all. Things are better than I had hoped. Who would have expected them to leave the bridge unguarded? Was that oversight or sheer arrogance?" He shook his head.

"I will be off to join the 2nd, in that case," Felix remarked.

Wellington gave a nod of agreement, and Felix urged his mount down the slope and across the bridge towards where Molina's division and Hill's were fighting, running messages to both when necessary.

As the sun moved into the afternoon sky, Felix began to wonder if he had hurt Dion more badly than he had believed. It had been dark, and he had made contact with the fleshy part of the lieutenant's arm. He would not have expected the injury to be life-threatening, only disabling... however, they could not risk letting down their guard.

Looking up, he saw Everleigh approaching from the distance on his black gelding. Perhaps he had something of Dion to report. Almost anything seemed better than nothing at this point. He directed his mount towards Wellington to hear.

"Any news?" Felix asked hopefully.

"Nothing of our Spanish lieutenant, I am afraid," Everleigh replied. "Unfortunately, our pursuit of the French through the town has met with an unforeseen obstacle."

Wellington looked sharply at Everleigh.

"The baggage wagons have been abandoned, right in the middle of the road. There are hundreds of them. All the horses were taken and there is no way to move them."

Wellington cursed. "Then go around them!"

"I do not think you understand, sir. It is as though the entire kingdom's worth of goods was left in the way to obstruct our path."

"Send the cavalry in pursuit," Wellington ordered. "They can go around."

"Yes, sir!" Everleigh saluted and rode away.

"Unbelievable. We had well not lose a war to a baggage train, Knight," the Commander said, disbelief evident in his tone. He urged Copenhagen forward to follow, and Felix did the same to his own mount. Passing through an expanse of woodland, they came upon a village and found several wounded. The regiment had been "engaged and taken fourteen guns," General Picton reported.

"Then the Brigade, in column, sustained enemy fire for some time before dashing forward, and driving the enemy from their position. We won ten guns left behind in the rush." Continuing to report, he went on, "The entire French army broke up so precipitately that they left all their material of war on the field."

"Very good. Pursue them until dark," Wellington answered.

Picton turned his horse about and rode off to instruct his troops.

"We might as well take a look," Wellington said and followed, directing his own columns to pursue.

Felix realized that he had lost sight of Hill and began to wonder if they had imagined the plot all along. Out of the corner of his eye, he saw a white horse galloping in their direction and he turned about. Immediately, he drew his pistol and cocked it, shouting for the commander to get out of the way.

As the horse drew closer, the rider became clearly visible. Recognizing Lady Catalina, looking disheveled and... beaten?... he lowered his gun.

"Am I too late?" she gasped, pulling Luna to an abrupt halt.

"Too late for what? Nothing has happened except for a French retreat."

"Dion is trying to kill Hill."

>>>><<<<

MAJOR KNIGHT LOOKED more surprised by her appearance than at the news, from the way he was looking at her.

"I do not have time to explain," she said, exasperated. "Where is Colonel Hill?"

"He was just here. I was looking for him, in fact. I have had my eye on him."

"So he is still alive?" she asked hopefully.

"He was, half an hour past. Everleigh arrived just now to report and that is when I lost sight of Hill."

"We must find him quickly! Dion and Maria are seeking revenge," she said as they urged their horses forward. "They wish him dead."

"He is not involved with them? You are certain?"

"Yes. I did finally wring the truth from Maria. She was not at all pleased to see me. I cannot say if Dion told her we were alive or not, but from her response I suspect she perhaps thought I would return to Villa Blanca. Either way, she gave herself away this morning. She could not hide her displeasure and confessed all."

"It makes no sense. What do they have against Hill? He is not the man to ruffle feathers in the normal way of things."

"Ciudad Roderigo," she answered. The name was sufficient explanation. Everyone understood when they heard it. It had been a dark day for the allies. The English soldiers had snapped, despite their victory, upon seeing so many of their own dead. They had gone on a rampage of raping, pillaging and looting for hours before they were brought under control. Why they took it out on their Spanish comrades no one ever understood.

"But Hill? I cannot believe it of him," Major Knight said, disbelief evident on his face.

"I believe he is blamed for not controlling his men. 'Twas one of his divisions which lost control."

She could see the connections forming in his mind by the expressions that crossed his features.

"So, this plan was to make it appear that he was committing treason," he said slowly as he seemed to make sense of what she had said.

"A traitor dies without honor, the lowest of the low. He suffers complete public humiliation. Anything good they may have done in their life is wiped away by that act of betrayal."

"That certainly explains why the dispatches were changed, but whatever may be the outcome now that his plan has been foiled?" Knight asked, thinking aloud.

"I fear that Dion will try to find a way to publicly humiliate him—and then kill him. Dion has already lost his place and now his honor is at stake. He will attempt to rectify that before his own death. He knows there can be no possibility of living."

"He will be desperate," Major Knight said, his eyes roving around them as they approached the rear of Hill's advancing soldiers.

"A martyr for his cause. What are we looking for?" she asked, scanning the mass of red coats.

"I wish I knew. The French have abandoned their wagons just beyond the town, and the equipage is apparently proving a very effective method of delay."

"I can see that," Catalina remarked, pointing as she looked upon the chaos, visible in the distance. There were hundreds of wagons piled high with goods, which many of the soldiers had decided to loot, the temptation great. "It is Ciudad Rodrigo all over again," she whispered to herself. They set spur to their horses and pulled up nearer the mêlée to search the crowds for any sign of either Dion or Hill. "This is madness! How will we ever find him? If ever there were a perfect opportunity, this is it!"

"You look to the left, and I will look to the right, but stay away from the men," he answered calmly, his face taking on a look she had never seen. Certainly, she would not wish to face him in battle, she decided, riding in the direction he indicated.

Catalina tried Major Knight's methodical approach. She began in the center moving left, and tried to look at each face. Frankly, it was disgusting and she muttered a prayer that they might keep to looting. Dozens of soldiers were digging through the baggage wagons and shouting their finds to their comrades. Some were already drinking heavily from the jugs of wine and spirits found, and although there were a few trying to restore order, they were very ineffective.

Apparently, the looters considered the bottles of wine theirs too— if the raucous songs they sang, which made her ears burn, were any indication.

A loud shout rang out and a crowd began to form around a brawl? What was happening? She moved closer to look.

"*Muerte!*" Catalina exclaimed. "Major Knight!" she cried, trying to get his attention.

He must have seen what was happening at the same time, for he looked at her and inclined his head to indicate he was going to go behind the disturbance.

Dion was holding a knife under Colonel Hill's throat with a pistol in his other hand; at the same time he began shouting.

"You English disgust me! You are not fit to be on this earth! I am not surprised to find this... this *bastardo* again as your leader!" He said the last word in a mocking tone as he looked around at the sea of red coats. "He allows you to loot, and rape innocents, all in the name of victory. You will rot in hell for this day's work!"

Mouths open, the crowd of soldiers and spectators stood gaping at the scene, many of them too stunned or too intoxicated to do anything but jeer.

Catalina slowly moved her way through the rabble, afraid to dismount for fear of her own safety and of losing her beloved horse.

She drew closer, and could see the possessed look in Dion's eyes. Transferring the reins to her weak hand, she took the dagger from the sheath inside her coat. Never before had she killed a man, but she would do it if she had to. She must have courage, because she understood where Maria and Dion's hatred came from. Killing Colonel Hill would solve nothing; it would not bring back Maria's innocence or her sister's life. Colonel Hill himself had not done the deed.

Dion was still shouting. Catalina saw Major Knight trying to sneak up from behind the crazed lieutenant, but she could not tell if the Englishman would reach him in time or even have a clear shot. Dion was intent on humiliation; viciously, he began to cut away at Colonel Hill's uniform, mocking him as he did so.

Catalina waited, expecting the crowd to do something, but they stood like statues. She tried to maneuver Luna into a better position. No matter how many times one practiced something, one could never replicate the fear and trembling that happened when it mattered most. As he cut away handfuls of Hill's uniform from his body, Dion began to scream.

"Come on, you miserable cowards! Who wants a turn?"

Catalina took aim for her target as Dion sliced away another piece of fabric from his arm, cutting deep enough to make Hill bleed. She could wait no longer.

"For Maria! For Leonora!"

When Dion raised his knife high, as though to make the final kill, she threw her dagger. At the same instant she saw the flash of a pistol.

Afraid to look, she closed her eyes. Shouts of approbation echoed in her ears from the mob. Through the drumming of blood in her ears, she heard a rush of footsteps towards the scene, and put her face in her hands. She swallowed deeply, barely able to contain her bile at the realization of what she had done.

Suddenly, strong arms pulled her down from her horse and

wrapped themselves around her as she began to sob, her whole body shuddering with the emotion. His scent mixed with sweat and leather a comfort despite her body's violent reaction.

"Hush now, it is over. I have you," Major Knight whispered into her ear.

If only she could stop. She felt no control as she trembled and shook like a leaf in the wind.

"Dion is dead. You have saved Colonel Hill."

That news only made her weep louder.

"Catalina. Look at me." He took her face in both his hands and kissed her gently.

At last, she opened her eyes to stare into the dark depths of his.

"That's my brave girl. I have you."

She nodded absently, finding only a brief solace in his arms.

CHAPTER SEVENTEEN

F ELIX KNEW THE best thing to do was remove Catalina from the
scene. She was suffering from shock, and already several soldiers
were beginning to defile Dion's body. Wellington had arrived, and
Felix expected he would have everyone in line in short order. He did
not doubt a great deal had been plundered, but hopefully the indisci-
pline would end with that.

Somehow, he managed to help Catalina onto his mount, and then
lead their horses away from the scene towards where the Spanish
contingent and her father were reported to be. He wished he could
take her back to Villa Blanca and to safety, but it was not his place to
make that determination. He also had his duty to the army. Even
though it would seem they had soundly routed the French that day, he
had not heard of an abdication.

Catalina clung to him as they left the town and went north on the
road to Pamplona. It would be dark soon, and he expected to come
upon the camp at any moment. Catalina still had not spoken a word,
but her violent shaking had stopped. He hoped she had found some
comfort in his arms. While she had clearly been trained to use
weapons, he did not think she had ever used them to kill—and to kill
someone she knew, at that. Somehow, there was a difference when
shooting across a battlefield at a faceless person. It would take some
time for her to accept that she had acted from necessity, or else an

innocent man would have died.

They reached the edge of the camp, where the tents were being erected for the night. It would take hours before all the survivors arrived. They had not moved too far beyond Vitoria because the looting was still going on.

An army post battle was a difficult thing to explain to any not involved. Many individuals busied themselves with the wounded and many more assisted in cleaning up the carnage. Those who had survived did their best to drown out the memories of the day in some form or fashion. Some slept, some drank, and some had more unfortunate tendencies. Felix was conflicted about the outcome of the brush with Dion. Anyone who had lived to witness what occurred at Rodrigo, and likewise at Badajoz, could not explain away or justify what had happened. It was unconscionable and unfathomable, especially to one who had never experienced war. Toy soldiers and history books could not begin to scratch the surface of the reality.

Felix had stopped to ask for General Mendoza's division when he saw the man himself.

"*Mi querida!*" he cried when he saw his daughter limp in Felix's arms. He himself had not been able to ask her what had happened before she had arrived at the front. He had assumed she had fought with Maria, but she had not spoken of it, only of Maria's confession.

Upon seeing her father, she released Felix and slid down into her father's arms.

He crushed her to his chest and kissed all over her face, weeping openly. Felix dismounted and watched uncomfortably.

"What happened, Catalina?"

"I killed Dion," she answered with surprising calm. Felix was glad she had been able to compose herself.

General Mendoza looked at Felix for confirmation and he gave a slight nod.

"Come! Let us go inside, where you may explain everything."

Following behind with the horses, Felix handed them over to a soldier to be rubbed down and tended to. When the little group reached the tent, they found the general's trunks were just being unloaded.

They sat down on hastily unfolded chairs and Mendoza's man brought them wine. Felix paid little attention to anything but Catalina's face. She bore the signs of shock, recounting her horrific day as though detached from it like a mere spectator. As he suspected, Maria had attacked Catalina once she realized her mistress intended to warn Colonel Hill of the plot. By befriending the Englishman, Catalina, Dion and Maria had decided, was a traitor.

"It was hateful, Papa. She thought to brawl with me like some tavern wench. Fortunately, one of the camp followers came to my aid and between us we subdued her. Then, summoned by her screeching, one of the cooks came upon us and trussed her like a goose! He has her under guard until such time as you decide what to do with her."

Catalina went on to give her father an abridged account of the looting, and how they had found Dion with a pistol and a knife at Colonel Hill's throat.

Felix could see by the look in Mendoza's eyes that he also felt torn with regard to Dion's motive. Anyone with a conscience would feel for those whose loved ones had been raped and killed that day.

"What happened next?" Mendoza demanded. "Did Dion manage to kill Colonel Hill?"

Now came the point where Catalina had to tell her father she had killed Dion. She looked up at Felix with pleading eyes.

"No, Colonel Hill is safe," he interposed calmly. "He suffered some cuts with the knife, but I think he will recover. I fired my pistol and your daughter threw her knife. We were able to take Dion down before he killed the Colonel."

Mendoza nodded absently while he pulled his daughter into a hug.

Felix knew then it was time for him to go. His throat filled with emotion from all the things he wasn't able to say. He wanted to beg leave to take Catalina away from all of this and to find the beauty in life again. She would have many dark days ahead—he knew from experience. He could help her forget, but it was not his place to comfort her, and despite their shared attraction—and kisses—there had been no declarations. They had been working together. Partners. He loathed the word at the moment.

He rose to leave, planning to escape quietly. He had taken only one step when her soft voice stopped him.

"Please wait."

Felix could not resist her plea.

"May we have a few moments, Papa?" she asked.

General Mendoza nodded. "I will see if the doctor is available to look at you."

"I do not need the doctor, Papa. I have no injury to compare with those who fought today. Leave him to those in need."

"Very well. I will wait outside."

When the opening of the tent fell behind the general, Felix watched Catalina walk towards him. She wrapped her arms around his neck and took a deep breath.

"Will I see you again? It is hard to believe that, just like that…" She snapped her fingers. "It is over."

"I do not know what charge Wellington will have for me now," he answered honestly, not hiding the twinge of regret in his voice.

"Despite the outcome, I have enjoyed these days more than any I can remember. Thank you for protecting me and respecting me."

Felix almost laughed. He would not tell her how he had had to pretend she was Eugenia in order to do so. Without another word, she stood on tiptoe and placed a gentle kiss on his lips. Not one of romance, but one of goodbye.

When he left the tent, he wanted to be alone with his churning thoughts, but of course, Mendoza was waiting to speak with him.

"Walk with me," he said, half order, half question.

Felix fell into step beside the Spaniard.

"Is that truly what happened?"

"It is, although it was your daughter's knife that killed Dion. I had no idea she was so capable with a blade."

Mendoza closed his eyes. "I prayed she would never have to kill anyone. It is a curse to have a daughter be so beautiful, and at the same time intelligent and cunning."

"She is all of those things," Felix agreed.

"Could you help me convince her to return to Villa Blanca?" The general stopped, his tone almost pleading.

"By herself? Sir, forgive me, but I do not think being alone, after what she has experienced, would answer the purpose."

Mendoza sighed. "Perhaps not. She needs to be married; to be a wife and a mother, not an assassin!"

"She has a very strong will, and I suspect she will refuse to do your bidding."

"And if her good name is compromised? Will you be honorable?" Mendoza stared at him in a most uncomfortable fashion.

"She deserves better than I, sir. The Lady Catalina could have any man she wished."

"I strongly suspect it is you she wants," the general said dryly, not sounding entirely pleased about it.

"I would do anything for her," he replied, unable to withhold his emotion.

To Felix's great surprise, Mendoza grinned at him. Had he been baiting him the whole time?

"She is my heir, you know. She will be a duchess in her own right when I die. Would you care to be a duke?"

Felix would have laughed, had that idea not been so appalling. He could hear Rowley's laughter booming from here. Ignoring the quizzical gleam in Mendoza's eyes, Felix bowed and parted from the gentleman without offering a response.

By the time he sought to report at headquarters, most of the soldiers had joined the camp. He found Wellington in a state of fury. The commander was already writing a dispatch to the Earl of Bathurst, reporting that many of his men had succumbed to the temptation of loot and the intoxication of wine. He dictated the missive in scathing terms, calling the perpetrators the scum of the earth and declaring it was impossible to command a British army.

Felix looked at the other intelligence officers and aides de camp, who all remained quiet as the commander vented his spleen in the communication to the Secretary of War.

He went on to describe the aftermath of the battle which had kept the French from being completely routed that day.

"...an immense park of vehicles of every type, waiting to be plundered... vast quantities of ammunition and military equipment; hundreds of carriages and baggage-wagons loaded with plate, paintings and valuable property, a profusion of food and drink. Many spoils of war—all abandoned," he growled, looking up. "I have it from Captain Browne that regular soldiers' wives and camp followers were wearing muslins, three or four gowns one over the other, trimmed with fine lace, several pairs of earrings dangling, reticules, watches and fans also part of their costume." He glared at each of them in turn as though they were responsible. Wellington abhorred plundering, and this was no exception. "I sent the 18th Hussars to guard the wagons. Whatever is taken will all be returned!"

Felix could think only of Catalina.

REPORTS WERE CIRCULATING that the French were running back to France and that Wellington had hopes to cross the border into France soon. Somewhere, deep down, Catalina was glad, but it was topped with so many layers of pain and sadness, she did not know if she would ever feel happy again. When her father suggested she return home to Villa Blanca, since they were so close, she could not find it within her to object.

She was desolate. There was no other word to describe her feelings. As if it were not bad enough to have killed a man, she had to accept that it was unlikely she would ever see Major Knight again. Oh, she could continue to follow the drum and flirt with him, but there was no future for a Spanish duchess and an English gentleman. Doing so would only delay the inevitable.

She did not know what his future held, for they had never discussed it. There had been no promise of anything on either side. No doubt, to him their association was no more than a flirtation that had been a part of his allotted task.

Unfortunately, her heart had decided to give itself away and no other would do.

Her father escorted Catalina back to Villa Blanca since it was on their way north. He told her Wellington hoped to take Pamplona and San Sebastián to keep the French from returning.

In some ways, it was a blessing to be back home, she reflected, but it was difficult not to think of Major Knight with everything she did. In two short days, he had changed her memories of every part of her childhood home. Even Toro seemed to be looking for him to be with her.

For several days, she scarcely left her bed. It was as though her body insisted upon healing itself.

Then the nightmares began to intrude. Her mind twisted the cold reality of the weeks leading up to Dion's death with her worst fears, and she began to relive them in her sleep. Instead of being unable to wake, she soon began to dread sleep. Each night, she would scream herself awake to find she was staring into the pitch-black darkness, drenched in sweat as though fighting for her life.

The dreams varied. Sometimes she was at Dion's mercy, his knife to her throat as he'd done with Colonel Hill. Others, she was trapped in a well or pond, near drowning… cold water poured over her head and she gasped for air.

As she fought to gain her bearings, she realized this was not a dream. She was in bed and soaking wet.

Then a movement in the moonlight caught her attention.

"Aunt Esmeralda? Is that you?"

The noise of the ceramic pitcher being set down on the washing stand was followed by a noise of disgust. Her aunt glided from the room as though she were an apparition, yet closed the door behind her with a loud click.

What was happening to her? Catalina shook her head and climbed from her bed to change her bedding and clothes for a dry ones.

EVENTUALLY, TORO HELPED to pull her from her melancholy.

At first, she felt dissociated from her body and was barely able to go through the motions. Toro teased her to walk her through the vineyards, which were almost ready for the harvest, every day. Life was serene and beautiful at Villa Blanca—as though the battle had never happened. So much emotion was churning through her, though, she felt unable to express any of it. It was as if nothing had happened, yet it was impossible to fit back into her old way of life. Why could she not cry? Why could she not be angry?

Days passed into weeks, and the harvest was upon them. It had always been a favorite time of year for her, with the festivals and parties that accompanied it. She did not wish to entertain on her own, but ordered the festivals to be organized for the villagers and workers who looked forward to them every year.

The grapes were especially sweet that year and there was a good harvest. Catalina did not care.

The reality, that Major Knight would no longer be aught but a memory in her life, was beginning to sink in. At first, she longed for him to appear on the terrace at the rear of the house, and even, a time or two, fooled herself into thinking him there. She knew it was just a mirage—her mind playing tricks on her.

LETTERS ARRIVED FAITHFULLY from her father every few days, and he was hopeful he would be home for Christmas. "The Allies have successfully secured San Sebastian and Pamplona, and it seems as though Spain is free from French rule at last!" he wrote in early November.

"I hardly see General Wellington and your Major Knight. The English forces are centered in Pamplona and he allows us to guard the port. However, I have been considering perhaps a big celebration at Villa Blanca. What do you say to something grand, such as we used to do?"

"Wellington believes the French and Napoleon will abdicate soon, and he and I have discussed hosting a ball to boost morale. Villa Blanca is a good point between our two posts, and has been sitting empty for too long. I am certain I can count on you to make it grand. I am also certain you will be itching for something to do once the harvest is over."

Catalina folded the letter and began to wander around the garden. She was unsure how she felt about hosting a grand party for all the officers. She missed everyone, of course, and she was desperate to see Major Knight again—too desperate. Only now was she able to begin doing things without thinking of him every minute. Her resolve to be brave and forget him would dissolve the moment she saw him again. Very likely, she would throw herself at his feet and beg him never to leave, she mused in disgust. She would utterly disgrace herself.

At least she had time to consider. There was hardly a way she could deny her father and the soldiers such pleasure when they had so little to keep their spirits up, month after month and year after year in poor conditions.

She blew out a frustrated breath and looked around for Toro. Normally he was beside her, ready to go on their daily walk.

She made her way down to the stables, where he was often to be found, considering himself to be the equal of any horse. There she found him, hovering over a black retriever who had just given birth in an empty stall. Toro barked at her with urgency and she knelt down to see the puppies. Two were brindled and two were black like the mother. But there was one small, mixed puppy, black with patches of brindle, which was not moving.

The mother looked exhausted as the four fed, and Toro began barking more frantically. He was trying to get her to help! She gathered up the still puppy and began to rub it with a handful of straw. After a few minutes, she wrapped it up in a flannel she found on a nearby shelf and, hugging it to her, willed the tiny animal to breathe. She did not think she could deal with another death in her life at this moment.

Toro nudged at the small bundle as though he wanted her to do something. The concern he displayed was touching.

She heard a little squeak from between her hands and suddenly she felt a spark of hope within her breast. Kneeling down beside the mother, she carefully unswaddled the runt and held it to the mother's teat encouraging it to suckle. It would be the only way it could live.

"Toro! What be you at now?" The head groom came in to discover what Toro was barking about. "Buenas dias, Señorita," he said, greeting her. Noticing the puppies, he laughed. "Toro, you big devil. Now I understand why you have been running off."

"I have not been here to keep him occupied," Catalina remarked.

"He brought her here to protect her." The groom chuckled.

Catalina frowned. The pup was not suckling from his mother. The groom noticed. "It is best to let it go, my lady. Even if you spend every minute bottle feeding it, it probably has something wrong with it and will not live long anyway."

Catalina did not care. She could not bear to give up. "You are probably right, Jorge, but I will try, nevertheless. I need something besides myself to dwell on."

"As you wish," he said, with a sigh of regret. "I will fetch the nipples and some goat's milk and see if he will take it."

Catalina took the small pup back to her chambers, determined to help it live. In those few minutes, she had found a reason to look to the future with equanimity. Of a certainty, it had nothing to do with the possibility of seeing Major Knight again.

CHAPTER EIGHTEEN

"**Y**OU LOOK LIKE a cockerel without any hens," Wellington remarked as he looked up from reading the latest set of dispatches brought in.

"I will try to appear more lively, sir."

"I have never asked you to abstain from women. It is not healthy."

"No, sir, but when you cannot have the one you want, a substitute will not do."

"Why can you not have her?" Wellington asked.

"She is the daughter of a duke and Spanish to boot. What have I to offer her?"

"What has that to say to anything? You are the son of a duke."

Felix shook his head.

"She is already living the life you lead and if I am any judge, she wants you as much as you want her. I am certain you may come to some arrangement if she does not wish to live in England, nor you in Spain or vice versa. It is not so hard to take a ship home from here, near the coast." Currently they were billeting in a large manor house near Pamplona on the Spanish-French border while they regrouped before the army's final push into France.

Felix had played all of these arguments in his mind hundreds of times. If she had given him one sign that her attraction for him was more than a passing fancy, he might just throw caution to the wind.

But with her gone, it was as though the sun was not as bright over the camp.

"Wanting and having very rarely go together, sir." This was an odd conversation to be having with Wellington. Not that he was impersonal, but they were so close to removing Bonaparte from his self-proclaimed throne, there was a little time for social discourse or fun these days.

Wellington gave him a wry look. "If you are satisfied with that, then perhaps you should not accompany me to Villa Blanca."

"I beg your pardon? What business have you there?" Recollecting to whom he spoke, Felix hastily adjusted his tone. "I mean – that is, ah – is something wrong?"

Wellington looked amused. "Lady Catalina is well. You can erase that look from your face."

"It is only natural that I be concerned. We were partners for a time and shared experiences both dangerous and emotional," he defended himself.

Wellington laughed openly. "It just so happens that I have been corresponding with Mendoza. Villa Blanca is not above thirty miles from here and San Sebastian. It has come to my attention more than once recently that we have done nothing but work, and some leisure time would not go amiss."

Felix's wretched heart began to beat faster and something within him lifted—a heavy weight that had been holding him down during these past weeks.

"What did you have in mind, sir?"

"I had thought to take those who knew her well on a visit. Her father mentioned a ball or some such. Of course, I cannot remove every officer from the camp; the recent base behavior after Vitoria is still fresh in my mind."

It was still quite fresh in Felix's mind, for other reasons.

"Also, Colonel Hill did not have the opportunity to personally thank Lady Catalina. So you see, there are multiple reasons for this visit."

"And do not the other officers—and the men—also deserve to have a little fun?" Felix asked.

"Of course they do! That goes without saying. We shall hold festivities for them and not announce our purpose when we leave for a few days."

There was a knock on the door, followed by Everleigh and Owens entering the room with a recovered Colonel Hill. They were sharing a house which the grateful Spanish had insisted they occupy until they crossed the border into France.

"Has he agreed?" Everleigh asked as they took their seats around the room for their daily meeting. Soon, the other members of the staff would be arriving as well.

"Did everyone else already know of this?"

Owens snorted. "Everyone else suggested it, my friend. You are but a shadow of yourself these days."

"Are you complaining about my work?" Felix asked, offended.

"No one has any objections about your professional capabilities, lad," Wellington added hastily.

"Your personality could do with a little humor, however," Everleigh added dryly.

Felix put his head back over the chair and stared at the ceiling. "So everyone has been plotting against me."

Instead of bothering to deny it, there was a chorus of emphatic agreement, followed by a great deal of laughter.

"Why did no one say anything?"

"At first we felt it was best to let well alone."

"And now you wish to torture me?"

"Now we see it is more than a passing fancy. She is one of us, after all."

"It would never work." He shook his head. "I will do better to contain my grumpiness."

The rest of the staff came in and they began their meeting. Everyone gave their individual reports, and then Wellington delivered his. When he announced the upcoming trip to Villa Blanca, all knowing eyes bored into Felix; then a cheer went up when he announced his intention to hold a celebration for all soldiers.

Once the meeting was adjourned, Everleigh and Owens made a point of slapping Felix on the shoulder in good-natured camaraderie. He still grumbled. Being called out in a group, even though they were his closest friends, still rankled. He had always thought himself able to master his emotions, but never had anything cut so deeply before.

Felix stood up, intending to leave, but Wellington stopped him. "Stay a minute, Knight."

He could not begin to wonder what else needed to be said. Wellington had said quite enough before everyone else had joined them.

Felix sat back down in his chair and waited for Wellington to speak.

"My brother is the Ambassador for Spain, you know."

"I did know," Felix admitted.

"Much though I would hate to lose you, Henry needs a good staff and I cannot think of anyone better than you. You are quite comfortable with the language, and I thought perhaps it might be an attractive post for a certain lady?"

"You would do this so that I might marry Lady Catalina?" Felix could not believe his ears.

"You know I have a soft spot for a pretty lady, and she did us quite a service." He held up his hands. "I will say, I would not fancy becoming a matchmaker in the general order of things, but if I see a way in which matters might arrange themselves without disrupting the army, then why not make it so?"

Felix was astonished. Apparently his bewilderment showed on his face.

"Think about it. If the diplomatic service is not to your taste, then I am pleased to keep you on my staff."

Felix gave an absentminded thank you and salute before leaving. He had thought his feelings for Catalina would fade with time, but it had not happened. His feelings had only grown stronger and far more apparent. Nonetheless, was diplomacy the life he wanted? Was it the life she wanted? He knew it was a splendid opportunity being handed to him. Making the transition to the diplomatic service would enable him to still serve England, while saving Catalina from the harsh life of following the drum. It would also allow him to spend some time in England without removing her entirely from Spain.

It was an offer too good to be true—if Catalina would have him.

He was not so conceited or confident that just because she had offered him some affection, when they were alone and in a desperate situation, that her feelings ran as deep as his. She might laugh at him – but she might not – and he would never know unless he asked.

It seemed the thing to do was go to Villa Blanca and test the waters, so to speak. He would sleep on it before he gave Wellington his final decision, but he could already feel the change within his spirits, telling him that it was the right thing to do.

CATALINA WAS EXHAUSTED, in a satisfying way. The house had come to life again during preparations for the visitors, and little Midnight, the puppy, occupied the rest of her time, thus allowing her little left to dwell on her feelings of loss. The pup was finally eating, though Catalina had to wake every two hours during the night to feed him. The rest of the time, he was content to stay next to her in a makeshift sling similar to those she had seen some of the women wear to carry their babies when working in the fields.

She was utterly done up, but completely in love. She had named the little fellow Midnight as a small reminder of her time with the major of the same name and colour eyes.

"Will he come?" she wondered aloud. "Will it be strange to see him?" she asked the little pup as he slept close to her heart. She walked down to the stables several times a day to allow him to be near his mother and Toro, but Midnight still seemed to prefer Catalina.

For the third time that day, they made their trek down to the stables and, as usual, she hoped he would take to his mother. Toro stayed nearby, hovering protectively close and barking if any strangers came in there.

Catalina released Midnight from his wrap; Toro at once took the pup by his scruff and carried it to the mother. Catalina watched as the little one moved about. The larger siblings were feeding furiously and Midnight made a weak effort to root around.

"Look at that, Toro!" As she exclaimed, he wagged his tail at the excitement in her voice. She placed a little milk on his tongue to encourage him, and at last, he gently suckled.

Catalina thanked God for allowing the puppy to live, but she still suspected something might be wrong with him. No matter, she told herself sternly, she would take this victory today. Her heart lifted another little bit; slowly, the layers of depression she had been feeling were peeling away.

She sat down and stroked Toro as they watched the little pups eat. As she watched, she began to wonder what would happen when she saw Major Knight again. What if he was cold to her?

"No, he would never be that," she said to Toro, who took a moment to look at her inquisitively before putting his head back down. "However," she continued, "he might be indifferent or merely friendly, and that I do not know if I could bear." She sighed. "I suppose I should return to the house and see how the preparations are coming along."

She expected to have more than fifty officers and their wives staying at the Villa, with more billeting nearby. The housemaids were bustling about, airing the bedchambers, making up the beds with fresh linens and setting clean towels on every washing stand. Meanwhile, several more, and three under footmen, were employed in polishing the ballroom to a high shine, from the parquet dance floor to the large chandeliers. The smell of beeswax and lye soap seemed to fill the whole house.

In less than a week, her quiet life would be turned on its tail again. She did not know whether that was good or bad. As she stroked Toro, she tried to think of a theme that would be pleasing to the soldiers for a night in which they might forget the often dreadfulness of their duties. Since costumes would be too difficult to arrange for so many without recourse to cities and shops, that idea was out of the question. Perhaps she could have dominoes made and hand them out when the guests arrived, she pondered.

Shivering, although the day was clement, she glanced over her shoulder. It was strange; she had begun to have the eerie sensation that she was being watched again. Perhaps her spying faculties had completely failed her. It was impossible for anyone to be here, and the nightmare with Dion was over.

Well, mostly over, her inner voice corrected.

Unfortunately, she feared that episode would live on in her nightmares for the rest of her life.

"I must go now, Toro," she said, standing and shaking out her skirts. "I think I shall leave Midnight here for a little while, to see how he does."

With a little whine and a huff of indignation, Toro objected to her leaving, but he nevertheless stayed to watch over his new family. She returned to the house with a smile on her face, wondering how big the pups would turn out to be. The mother was half Toro's weight and size. Would they be a mixture or would some be large like him and some small like her? This miracle of life was fascinating and beyond imagination. Thinking of babies gave her a small twinge of regret.

It was time for her to marry and continue with her life. She knew the time had come, but she had delayed the decision with the excuse "when the war is over". Spain was free for now, it seemed, and Napoleon would hopefully be dethroned or at least be forced to stay in France.

Her father had not truly spoken to her about marriage or expectations, but it was one of the things understood when one was brought up as the heir to a duke. He must have some suspicions about her feelings for Major Knight, but would he object if he thought it more than mere flirtation? She had broken most rules of propriety with her entanglements with the Major. Previously, she had kept her spying skills secret and above reproach. Mostly, it had been a way to avoid the tedium of her existence.

It had not been her fault that everything had spun out of control, but by some good fortune she had not been ruined. However, she knew she was ruined for other men. Perhaps she could have a marriage of amicability, which was all one could really hope for in her position... yet in her heart, she knew it would never be enough.

Aunt Esmeralda was sitting in the garden, staring off into nothing. She had no children or grandchildren to keep her company or bring her joy in this stage of life. Perhaps Catalina should have stayed with her aunt instead of following the drum, but she had needed her father when her mother died. It had also seemed so much more exciting than staying at home and watching grapes grow.

She plucked a rose from a bush and brought it to her nose, inhaling deeply before sitting on the bench beside her aunt. The memories of that first evening, where she had been so determined to prove to Major Knight that she was a worthy adversary, came flooding back. She smiled sadly and handed the rose to Aunt Esmeralda, who still had enough wherewithal to smile at it and smell it.

Then she patted Catalina, unable to find any words, but it did not matter.

When her aunt's maid came to take her inside, Catalina decided to make sure preparations were progressing apace for the guests and so climbed the steps to the terrace, which had doors leading into the ballroom. It was set off from the back of the house like an orangery, with a balcony as its roof. The smell of fresh beeswax wafted from the room and she could hear the maids busy at work. She sat in one of the iron chairs where she and Major Knight had dined, all those weeks ago.

In her dreams, this is where she always saw him again, walking up from the stables. He would stop on the steps and smile at her and she would know. Without hesitation, she would run into his arms and he would kiss her. Not like a sister, not like a responsibility, but a devastating caress which portrayed the deep emotion he felt for her.

"What a peagoose I am!" she chastised herself, using the English term she had stolen. Closing her eyes, she shook her head. Warm tears fell down her cheeks and she let them. Truly, she had not allowed herself to weep and it seemed as though the dam had finally broken and every drop needed to run out.

A hand wiped the moisture from her cheek, startling her. She had heard no-one approach. It was necessary to blink away the next rush of tears to see his face.

In disbelief, she barked a derisive laugh and shook her head. "I am so weary of my mind playing tricks on me!" Shutting her eyes again, she leaned her head back to indulge in the fantasy, but... did she normally smell him in her dreams? She wrinkled her brow and then opened one eye to peep at the vision again.

The dark, handsome face and dark eyes were looking down into hers. She reached out to touch a smooth face. She had never seen him shaven.

"Are you real?"

"If I am not, do not wake me from my dream."

"I have done nothing *but* dream of you." Tension thrummed through her body at her boldness. He was here, by his own accord, and was looking at her as though he wanted to devour her. She wanted nothing more than to be his feast.

His lips came over hers, upside down, and it was awkward and sweet and... perfect. She could not help the smile that shaped her mouth beneath his.

He pulled back to look at her. "How was that?"

"Not precisely how I had envisioned it—not that I wish you to think I am complaining."

"Hmm. Perhaps we should try again." He came around the chair to face her, and kneeling down in front of her, took her face in his hands. He looked her in the eye before he pressed his lips gently to hers. He kissed her reverently, speaking a language of love and devotion, so different from the kisses they had shared before. Catalina felt cherished, and kissed him back with all the passion in her heart. What if this was her only chance to show him how she felt?

He made a noise at the back of his throat before pulling away and pressing their cheeks together.

"Have I awakened you, my love?"

"A little," she teased.

"Much though I would love to do this all day, your father is right behind me."

CHAPTER NINETEEN

I T HAD BEEN a long, hard ride here with General Mendoza, and Felix felt as though he had undergone the Spanish Inquisition. Hopefully, he would be judged worthy.

It had been Wellington's idea for them to ride on ahead together, to assist Lady Catalina with her preparations. He had also sent a note to the Spaniard informing him of his intention of placing Felix with his brother. Who would ever have guessed that Wellington could rival the matchmaking mamas in London?

Felix hardly cared where they lived, so long as they were together.

He told General Mendoza this, and while he thought he saw a hint of approval in the elder man's eyes, he had nevertheless quizzed him extensively about his family, his prospects, and how he intended to take care of the future Duchess of Riojas.

In the end, Mendoza said he would not interfere, but it was down to Felix to win her hand.

Now, at last, here he was with Catalina and she was more beautiful than he remembered. She looked thin and sad. He hoped he had not contributed to it. Her greeting on the terrace was all he could have hoped for, but it did not necessarily mean she was ready to give up all she held dear and marry him.

"How come you to be here so soon?" Catalina asked, after he had reluctantly stopped kissing her. He was not ready to be seen in such a situation by the general, thus forcing Catalina's hand. "Do not think I mean to complain, however."

"I am very glad to hear it, after that reception!" he quipped. Seeing her about to take him to task, he decided to answer her honestly. "I thought I could give you up. I was uncertain if your regard for me was equal to mine. We were working together and I believe we both felt attraction, but letting you go was the hardest thing I have ever had to do."

He dared to glance at her and saw her lips were trembling. Looking away again, he walked several paces down the terrace.

"As you are well aware, following the drum is not easy for a lady, especially once children come along. I had always vowed never to ask it of my wife. Moreover, as the fourth son, I had no thought of marrying, since I am hardly needed for the succession."

He took a few more steps and then stopped. Placing his hands on the balustrade, he looked down over the valley.

"I thrive on adventure. Would you believe, when I was home last, I actually shunned the domestic bliss my brothers had found?" he asked sardonically. "All of this was me, until I met you."

"Oh, Felix," she said softly, but he still could not look at her.

"When we first met, I prejudged you to be a vain, shallow beauty." He laughed again. "You quickly proved me wrong." Turning his head, he lifted one eyebrow, gazing at her with a passion he could not disguise. "Not about the beauty, mind you."

"Why, thank you, sir," she remarked dryly.

"However," he went on, staring once again at the landscape which had also claimed his heart, "we had a duty to perform, and often emotions are high. A few kisses shared in times of duress did not mean an everlasting love." He heard her emit a small squeak, but he still had to say what he had come to say.

"After you left, I felt empty," he said. "I barely cared what happened. Of course, I did not realize this, and I would have gone into battle and done my duty, but I did not understand. I felt hollow and frankly, was in a severe fit of the blue-devils."

He felt a hand on his back. When had she crept up on him? He turned to face her, and she had tears streaming down both cheeks.

"I felt the same. I did not rise from my bed for days. I knew part of it was from killing Dion, but I also knew I would never be the same without you."

"Catalina," he breathed, pulling her into his arms. He no longer cared how Mendoza found them. Knowing she reciprocated his feelings was enough.

"It will not be simple," he whispered into her ear as he held her close.

"It would be harder to be without you," she replied.

He closed his eyes and fought back his own, unmanly, tears. "I do not deserve this."

"Do not question why God has given us this gift."

"No," he agreed. "Do you have a fancy to be the wife of a diplomat? Wellington has graciously offered to give me to his brother, who is England's Ambassador to Spain."

"Felix, I have a great fancy to be yours, no matter where that may be. I am prepared to go to England or America or India, so long as I am with you."

"Have you considered, my dear? You shall be a duchess one day. You have a duty to your people." That had been drummed into Felix's head from the day he understood speech.

"One day, yes... but Papa is hardly in his dotage, and can hopefully return here as soon as Napoleon is gone. Besides, having a spouse experienced in ducal matters might be helpful to me."

"I know very little about running a dukedom."

"I imagine you know more than you think. Having been raised in one, I am sure many things will be second nature."

"I am certain we can contrive, but it is very important to me that you be certain also. Our time together was not exactly… normal."

She eyed him as though exasperated and shook her head. "I do not think anything you and I choose to do with our lives will ever be *normal,* as you say."

"I hope not, but I also do not think we will be chasing bandits when we are octogenarians."

"You never know," she answered with a saucy grin. "Or perhaps Papa will remarry and father a son to inherit the title."

"Things do not follow that course in England," Felix said with a shake of his head, thinking matters would be much simpler if either sex could inherit. "In all seriousness, we will now have a few days together and I would like to court you in the proper manner so you may be quite sure."

"After everything we have been through together, I cannot imagine changing my mind, although being courted in earnest sounds lovely."

A knock sounded on the end of the terrace and General Mendoza's head appeared around the end.

"Is it safe to come out?" he enquired.

Catalina laughed heartily. "Yes, Papa! Come, and I will ring for lunch to be served out here." She stood and embraced her father. "Thank you for bringing him to me."

The general smirked at her. "Do you realize how many letters I have received from the servants, who were most worried about you? Zubiri must have been very busy writing them. Even Esmeralda wrote."

"I cannot imagine what she said." Catalina's face wrinkled adorably.

"It was very short and sweet. It said only, 'Come home now'."

Catalina laughed, and it warmed Felix's heart.

"I do not suppose she told you she poured water over me in my bed one night."

"She did?" Mendoza looked astonished.

Catalina nodded. "It was not amusing at the time, but I was having a nightmare and I expect she wanted to quieten me. She does not speak, but I do not think all her wits have left her."

"I will remember to lock my door at night!" he said emphatically.

They all sat around the table and a footman served them a light meal of fruits, meats and cheeses.

"How I have missed this!" Mendoza remarked, rubbing his hands together with evident delight. "You are too thin, *mi querida*. I can tell you have not been eating. How anyone could not have an appetite for this, I cannot understand."

"I am eating better now, Papa. The first few weeks of being at home again were... difficult."

He reached over and squeezed her hand. Felix wanted to be the one to comfort her, but it was not the time. "Perhaps I should not have sent you here alone after all. Can you forgive me? I only wanted to protect you."

"I understand. It might not have been better to have stayed with the army. It does not matter now. And you brought him to me, so all is forgiven..." She took a sip of her wine and smiled as Toro came bounding up from the stables. He was carrying a black puppy by the scruff of its neck. Leaping up the steps to the terrace, he promptly deposited the creature in Catalina's lap.

"What in the world?" Mendoza asked as Catalina cradled the miniature beast.

"Toro is now a proud father. This little fellow was sickly and I believe I have nursed him back to life. It has kept me occupied this past week." Felix took the little runt from Catalina. He had always loved animals, and this little one nestled right against his chest. "I am happy to see he is taking to you," Catalina murmured. "I named him Midnight."

Felix was charmed. Mendoza was not.

"How delightful," her father muttered. "More Toros running about!"

>>><<<

CATALINA'S HEART MELTED into a puddle as she watched Felix make friends with Midnight. Not that she had had any reservations about him before, but any gentleman who could show affection towards the little runt in its current state was above reproach. Catalina knew better than many that looks were not everything.

"I sent a letter to Dion's family," her father remarked. "I tried not to go into the details."

"Does that mean his family believes he died an honorable death?" She tried not to sound as disgusted as she felt.

"What would be the good in telling them? In bringing them shame? They have lost their son."

"I daresay that is true. 'Tis not their burden to bear." She was glad she was not the one to have to write the letters informing families of their loss. Withdrawing her gaze from Felix, who was stroking the puppy's tiny body while Toro received caresses from his other hand, Catalina leaned back in her chair. For the first time since coming home, she felt content. There was really only one loose end that bothered her.

"What did you do with Maria, Papa?" The servant still bothered her deeply. They had not been close, but the maid had been with Catalina at her most vulnerable moments. The bond between a lady and her maid was supposed to be sacred. If Maria felt betrayed, Catalina did too.

"I let her go."

At those words, Catalina sat up again with a jerk, sharply turning her head to her father.

"I beg your pardon? I cannot have heard correctly."

He proffered a shrug. "You told me yourself she had been raped, my dear. Her feelings were understandable."

"Are you saying an eye for an eye is now acceptable?" she asked with disbelief.

"She has suffered greatly. Besides being violated, she has lost her sister and now Dion. I thought it might help her recover if she were sent back to her family."

"While I can sympathize with her plight, she attacked me and was involved in the plot to murder Colonel Hill."

"I understand, *mi querida...*" Although he spoke softly, she yet caught the note of wariness in his voice. "But I do not think Maria is capable of plotting and murdering on her own."

"No. She was, however, quite capable of attacking me!" She thrust back her chair, hastened to her feet and ran from the terrace.

The men let her go, thankfully. If she had stayed, she would have said many hateful things. It was harsh to judge her father and she knew she was being unfair—at least in part—but to let Maria go entirely free? Now, Catalina fretted as she sped through the garden, she would live in fear of Maria following her or lying in wait around every corner. Would she ever feel safe again?

Think of how Maria must feel, her conscience argued.

Slowing her steps, she continued to walk, following the path down to the river. Feeling much calmer by the time she reached the bank, she sat upon a large rock overlooking the streaming water. A wet nose nudged her hand and she smiled at Toro.

"You have not betrayed me completely then, have you?" She rubbed his haunches and kissed him between his eyes.

"That depends," a deep voice said from behind her. "He led me to you at my command, so please show him mercy."

"I am afraid mercy is not something I am good at," she replied, now feeling enormous guilt for the way she had spoken to her father.

"Your father acted as he thought best for everyone. He was not trying to hurt you."

"I know. My wretched tongue! I will apologize later." She turned her head to look up at Felix, who had Midnight tucked into his waistcoat. Only his little head peeped out, nestled among the folds of Felix's neckcloth.

She patted the place on the rock next to her. He joined her and they sat arm to arm, leg to leg; she leaned her head on his shoulder and he wrapped his arm around her. Exhaling slowly, she closed her eyes and listened to the water run.

"This is my special place. I always come here to reflect, to have a picnic, to paint or to nap. I spent a great deal of time here after my mother died."

"It is an enchanting place."

"I am glad you were able to see it."

Midnight made a little squeak and Felix pulled him out of his cocoon inside of his waistcoat.

"Yes, little one?" he asked, holding him up to his face. "I can see you are going to be a demanding master." He rubbed the pup's little nose with a finger and handed him to Catalina, who cuddled him close. There was just something about puppies which lifted one's spirits.

"Are you worried that Maria might come after you?" Felix asked delicately.

She thought for a moment before answering carefully. "I do not know. I suppose I am afraid the nightmares will not end unless there is a proper conclusion to this sordid business. In my mind, I know it would be exceedingly difficult for her to hurt me here, and I do not think her hatred to me extends far enough to kill me. Yet, the way she attacked me, I..."

"Our feelings are not always rational," he finished for her. "I will do my best to protect you."

"I know you will," she whispered.

He stood up and held out his hand to help her to her feet. They began to walk back towards the stables. Catalina felt safe and at peace for the first time in weeks. They left Midnight enjoying a meal and Toro protectively watching over his family.

"Are we to take the entire family with us to Madrid?" Felix asked good-naturedly.

"I do not think so," Catalina answered. "Midnight will have to go with us, of course. Toro would not enjoy being confined in the city."

He chuckled and taking her hand, pulled her along a path behind the stables. Once out of sight, he grinned devilishly at her.

"I am quite certain stealing clandestine kisses is not proper courting, sir," she said primly into his handsome face.

"Whoever wrote the rules on courting can hang," he answered. "It seems to me we should be certain we are compatible."

"If you insist," she said demurely. Standing on tiptoe, she twined her arms about his neck, pulling his head down to hers. The touch of his lips sent fire through her body. She felt alive again and knew this man was her destiny.

They walked hand in hand back to the house after a particularly toe-curling interlude. "What else did you have in mind for this time of courting?"

"I thought we could use it for talking and taking walks, and getting to know each other better, but I keep wanting to kiss you at every opportunity." He smiled roguishly.

"Then I suppose we had better keep our talks and walks near the house and gardens."

"That would be wise, but I imagine I will still find myself stealing kisses."

She looked up with mock exasperation, gave him a naughty smile and then pulled him closer for a quick buss on the lips.

"We would be wise to use our time wisely, then. Is there anything you wish to know about me that has perplexed you?"

He narrowed his gaze in thought. "Perhaps if there was some gentleman you were considering before me. It was no secret you were the most sought-after beauty on the Continent."

She snorted ungracefully. "I think you mean heiress. It would seem to make one more beautiful."

"Do you think so?"

"I am sure of it. I can think of any number of beautiful women who cannot boast such a following—not that I mean to imply such adoration gives me pleasure. The only difference between those ladies and myself is their lack of wealth and title."

"If you will have it so." Felix sounded unconvinced.

"But to answer your question: no, there was no one who had engaged my interest."

"And is there anything you wish to know about me? I have already told you I had not thought to marry."

"Then my question would be, are you certain you are not offering for me out of honor?"

"Did you listen to my words earlier? I confessed my soul to you."

She sighed. "Forgive me. I suppose it is hard for me to believe."

"Then I shall spend the rest of *my* life convincing you."

"I do like the sound of that."

CHAPTER TWENTY

F ELIX WAS ENJOYING this week of rest immensely while he adjusted to the fact that he was soon to be married. Leg-shackled—a tenant for life—riveted—caught in parson's mousetrap. The consolation was having Catalina forever. He wrote to his family to apprise them of his forthcoming nuptials and plans to bring Catalina to England for Christmas.

He laughed as he considered each of his siblings' reactions. Rowley's would be the most priceless, but he did not wish to arrive with a bride, unannounced, in order to see it. Besides, Heath had already stolen that apple and Felix was quite content to do things his own way.

He strongly suspected that Catalina and Eugenia would get on famously. He found he was actually looking forward to this Christmastide more than most. First, however, there was the ball and the announcement of their betrothal. The guests were expected to arrive that day and the ball would take place on the next.

He sealed the packet of letters to send to England with the next set of dispatches, and then he tucked Midnight back into his waistcoat and went downstairs. He would be sad when the little fellow grew too big to wear inside his coat. He was not certain Midnight could walk, either, but if that was the case then he would find a way to carry him about. Hopefully, he would not be as large as his father.

"How do you fancy a trip to England, Midnight?" he asked the black-faced pup, who looked up at him adoringly.

"You do not care, as long as you are with us, do you?" he chuckled and scratched him behind the ears.

Catalina was in the ballroom, directing the placement of the flower stands, chairs, tables and what must have been thousands of candles. She smiled when she saw him enter.

"You have done a beautiful job," he said gratuitously.

She put her hands on her hips and eyed him with severity. "You need not offer false flattery," she scolded.

He could feel his lips twitching. "What would you have me say? It looks silly and frivolous?"

"I would prefer you say nothing at all to that, certainly," she snapped.

"Have we interrupted a lover's quarrel?" the insouciant Captain Owens asked from the terrace doors.

"I do not care," Captain Everleigh promptly remarked as he walked in and bowed before Catalina. "Forgive our dirt, but it is lovely to see you again, my lady."

"You two have only come for the food," Catalina remarked, accepting a kiss on the hand from each of the dashing captains.

"May I at least say how well you look?" Owens asked. "Before we decamp to the kitchens to grovel at Cook's feet, that is."

"Sincere compliments are always welcome." She cast a knowing glance at Felix. He feigned disinterest with a shrug. There was no winning that argument so he would not demean himself by trying.

"Are the others following behind you?" Felix asked.

"I believe there will be a deluge soon. We rode ahead, claiming prior acquaintance, but passed several carriages on the way."

"Then make yourselves useful and charm Cook. She can be temperamental when cooking for a large gathering." Catalina made a shooing motion and the three of them took themselves off to the kitchens. As Felix led his friends away through the chaos in the house caused by guests arriving, along with their baggage and servants, Toro came bounding at him with Midnight in his jowls.

"Excuse me a moment, gentlemen. Good boy, Toro," he said, accepting his new charge. "It seems it is my turn to take watch."

"The fellow delivers his offspring to the nurse?" Everleigh remarked. "Remarkable."

"Is it not? There are four more, but they do not require as much care."

"And he knows this?" Everleigh could not seem to fathom such a remarkable creature.

"He seems to. He brings Midnight to Catalina or myself after he has fed. The mother does not seem to want him, but at least she feeds him. Toro has taken it upon himself to look after him."

"Fascinating," Everleigh said. "Perhaps I should take one or two of them."

"I am sure you will be welcome to them when they are weaned."

The smell from the kitchens was wondrous as they drew near, Toro following close on their heels.

"I have died and gone to Heaven," Owens said dramatically as they crossed the threshold into Cook's domain. Instantly charmed, she motioned the "three diablos guapo" inside. After sitting at her worktable, where she showered them with mountains of food to sample, Everleigh switched to English.

"Are the rumors true, then?"

"Enlighten me on what they might be," Felix answered as he placed a goxua cream pastry in his mouth that melted to perfection on his tongue.

"Marriage. Diplomacy. Need I say more?" Everleigh raised an arrogant brow.

"Yes, yes, and emphatically no."

"Hoist with your own petard, Everleigh! You owe me fifty quid," Owens taunted.

"You bet against me? Felix asked in disbelief, sneaking a piece of cheese to the mastiff begging at his feet.

"I would say I bet *for* you," Everleigh replied smugly.

Owens shook his head. "The fool would rather lose money than admit a woman could defeat the brotherhood. I saw the way you looked at each other and I would never bet against a sure thing."

Everleigh sent Owens a scathing look. "How is my lady doing after all that transpired? It was her first kill, I assume?"

Felix nodded. "Hopefully, it is also her last."

"It is a shame you are removing both her and yourself from the field. She was an excellent spy. You are an excellent spy."

"Her ladyship was in particular, mostly because it was so unexpected, if you ask my opinion," Everleigh added.

"We did not," Owens jibed.

"I think she is recovering, but she was not pleased with how her father dealt with her maid," Felix said in an even tone.

Owens and Everleigh both looked at him inquiringly. "Indeed? What did happen? I do not believe I have heard about this," Owens said, scrunching up his face.

"Do not make that face." Everleigh scowled at Owens.

"You two sound like old fishwives," Felix complained.

"Precisely. Let that be a warning to you, Knight," Everleigh said, his voice dripping with sarcasm and amusement in the way that he had.

Felix cleared his throat to bring the two to order. "To answer your question," he said, a note of reprimand in his voice such as he would use with subalterns, "the general let the maid go."

"Scot-free?" Owens asked, wide-eyed.

Felix inclined his head. "He felt as though she had been punished enough and did not have the wits to concoct such a scheme on her own."

Everleigh frowned.

"Catalina was vexed, to put it mildly."

Owens whistled, drawing the eyes of every servant in the kitchens. He smiled brilliantly, causing several of the young girls to blush. Cook shook her head and sent them back to work with a tirade in Spanish that almost made Felix himself blush.

"What do we know of the maid?" Everleigh asked, still apparently cogitating on the matter of the general having freed Maria.

Felix shrugged. "Very little, I am afraid. Servants are excellent at being nondescript. Catalina seems to think her intellect lacking, although apparently she has an excellent left hook. My lady assures me the maid looked worse after the altercation, but the fact that she was attacked by her own servant in the first place is disturbing."

"Why do I always miss the excitement?" Owens bemoaned.

"Only you would dream of watching two females fight," Everleigh drawled.

Owens looked disparaging as he shook his head. "I do not think so, my friend. You need to leave the spying world on occasion." He patted him on the back.

With a saucy smile, the middle-aged Cook placed a platter of something black and slimy before them. Was it perhaps squid? Owens put one piece in his mouth, chewed for a moment. Standing up, he then placed his hand over his heart and knelt before her in dramatic fashion. Cook was basking in the praise.

"This is probably some type of medieval aphrodisiac," Owens muttered in English for Felix and Everleigh's ears only.

Felix would have to remember to tell Catalina to thank him later. If these samples were anything to go by, she need not worry.

Everleigh stood up and Felix joined him. "Do you intend to remain here for the rest of your stay?" he asked Owens, who looked as though he was giving the matter serious consideration.

"I suppose I should leave the magician to her work," he said, casting a look at the cook.

That did it. Felix was sure the cook had fallen in love. He pretended to pull the captain from the kitchens while Owens sang her praises on the way out. When they were above stairs again, Owens flashed a grin.

"Too overdone?"

"As usual," Everleigh agreed. They went into the study and Felix noticed that, despite the caustic response, Everleigh was deep in thought.

"What is it, Philip?"

He walked over to the window and looked out at the view over the valley and vineyards, his hands shoved into his pockets.

"I think we have given Maria the perfect opportunity for revenge. A hundred English soldiers gathered in a ballroom."

Felix and Owens stood there watching, a little stunned. But, by God, he was correct. "We can hardly cancel at this point. More than half the guests are here."

"True, and nothing may happen. It is only a feeling," Everleigh said.

They all eyed each other. Spies did not ignore presentiments.

"What do you propose we do?" Owens asked.

Felix answered. "Alert all of the men and servants. Designate guards… but whatever you do, do not tell Catalina."

⇥⟫⟨⇤

THE AUTUMN NIGHT was divine; not too cold, not too warm. The ballroom was charmingly decorated like a starry night and smelled like a Spanish garden. Jasmine wafted through the room, which would soon be pleasantly full yet should not be overly crowded. Stringed instruments would soon strum romantically in the background.

Cook had outdone herself even beyond Catalina's expectations.

Even Catalina's hair had cooperated with alarming ease. She was wearing her favorite violet silk gown, fashioned in the English style, which she thought Felix might appreciate. She knew she looked well.

It would be perfect if she did not have that nagging, eerie feeling again.

As hostess, she arrived downstairs early in order to survey the preparations were complete, as she had always done. Often, she and her father would make a late entrance, as was fashionable when they were at other events, but she preferred to know everything was running smoothly beforehand.

"Dare I compliment you?" her favorite deep voice whispered into her ear, sending shivers down her spine.

She turned about to face him and almost gasped aloud. God had certainly been in fine form the day he created this man. He was in formal regimental regalia, like the very first time she had seen him. Catalina did not believe in coincidences, and thanked God that he had seen fit to choose her for this man.

"I will say you are the most beautiful woman I have ever seen, and the ballroom is enchanting. In a word, perfect."

"That will do, my lord." She smiled up into his eyes.

"Will you walk with me for a moment?" he asked, extending his arm.

"Only for a moment. The guests will be arriving soon," she said, taking his arm and wishing the guests would not be arriving soon.

He walked her through the doors from the ballroom out onto the terrace, where it seemed their most wonderful moments had occurred. Before she knew what he was about, he dropped to one knee before her and held out a single rose.

"I told you here a sennight ago that I wanted this time to court you and allow you chance to change your mind. This week has only convinced me more thoroughly that you are the woman for me. Catalina, will you do me the great honor of becoming my wife?"

"Oh! Si, si, si!" She wrapped her arms around his neck and fastened her lips to his. Felix stood up and, lifting her off her feet, twirled her around before setting her down.

"Why now?" she asked, placing her hands on her hips. Still a little dizzy from the kiss, she looked up at him.

"Is it not the perfect time to announce a betrothal?"

"Yet what would you have done if I had said no?" she teased.

"Then I would have been desolate."

Playfully, she hit him on the arm. "I think we should tell Papa first," she said as they walked back into the ballroom, then through the house to his study.

Catalina felt as though she were floating on air. Her father seemed delighted and unsurprised, as did Wellington, who was with him.

"Does this mean I shall be losing you to Henry?" he asked Felix.

Felix looked down at her and she gave a swift nod.

"Oh, well, I suppose I only have myself to blame." He extended his hand to Felix. "You are a lucky devil." He bowed over Catalina's hand. "I imagine you are to be considered fortunate as well. He is one of my best men."

"I know," she answered coyly. They all laughed comfortably before repairing, after a few moments, to the entrance to form a line to greet the other guests.

Catalina opened the dancing with her father, who was a bit sullen and almost tearful.

"At least we will be living mostly in Spain, Papa," she told him, guessing at the cause of his melancholy.

"I know, *mi querida*, but it is more than that. I will be giving you to him. You will no longer be mine."

"Oh, Papa, I will always be yours." Her throat thickened with unshed tears.

"I do believe he is the right man for you. It is not easy for me to say that, but seeing you together this week has made me realize the truth of it."

"Thank you, Papa."

The dance ended and while the servants handed out glasses of champagne, her father quieted the assembled.

"Good evening, I thank you all for joining us to celebrate the removal of France and *Pepe Botella* from our borders!" Loud cheers followed this proclamation. "I would also like to announce, with great pleasure, the joining of my daughter, Catalina, to Major Lord Felix Knight. It is a wonderful night for celebration, and I hope you will enjoy our Spanish hospitality. It has been an honor to serve along with all of you." Another wild cheer greeted this toast and they drank to Spain and England and the upcoming marriage.

"May I have this dance?" Felix bowed before her.

She held out her hand. "I should be delighted, sir," she said formally, but with an impish smile.

He twirled her into a waltz, and for a time, nothing else existed but the two of them. She closed her eyes and savored the moment of being in her beloved's arms. Then the strange feeling intruded and the hairs on the back of Catalina's neck stood on end. She opened her eyes and began to look around her.

"What is it?" Felix asked in concern.

"I do not know. I expect I am worrying about nothing, since Father told me Maria was released to return to her family."

"But?" he probed gently.

"I have that sensation that she is here, watching." She continued to look over Felix's shoulder as they danced. "Is it my imagination or are there men guarding the doors?"

A flicker of guilt crossed his face.

"Do you know something?" she demanded.

"No," he answered emphatically. "We are just being careful. Knowing Maria was set free, and there being such a large gathering of English soldiers in one room... we thought it wise to be prudent."

"Yet you did not think to tell me?" Her accent always grew stronger when she was upset. She was barely containing her fury.

"I did not want you to worry. You had enough on your mind."

They made an entire circle of the ballroom floor before she spoke again, having succeeded in calming herself.

"I cannot imagine what Maria could do to us here. She always seemed rather slow. Perhaps it was an act."

"She did not become angry with you until you began to consort with me?"

"That is correct." She tried to think back. "Perhaps I mistook her sadness for sluggishness. She always had eyes for Dion, and if she spoke, it was often of him."

The music drew to a close, and Catalina felt sad and wary at the same time, having been reminded of Maria. She did not want to think of her or Dion on a night that was meant for celebration and happiness, yet they had intruded.

"Promise me you will not go anywhere alone," Felix ordered. She looked into his eyes, so filled with concern, and gave a slight nod of agreement. As he led her from the dance floor, she did not want to take another partner.

"Walk with me on the terrace for a moment, please?" she asked.

He looked at her in an assessing fashion, but agreed.

She stopped to take a deep breath, willing the sensation of unease to go away, but it only heightened.

"Something is going to happen, I can feel it," she said softly.

"Every door is being watched."

"Yes, but remember Maria lived here with me. If she wishes to enter, she will find a way. I am certain some of the servants are sympathetic."

"What do you think she could do?" he asked earnestly, not in a patronizing way.

"I do not think she knows how to shoot or throw knives. I was trained before she became my maid, but I do not know. We never discussed it."

"If she means to harm only you or Colonel Hill, then I suspect she will attempt to catch you alone."

Catalina began to look around, the hairs on her neck standing at attention as though something ominous was happening. "Perhaps... but if we are well guarded..." She sniffed the air. "Felix, do you smell smoke?"

They looked at each other with alarm and began to run.

CHAPTER TWENTY-ONE

O F COURSE, IT *would be fire,* Felix thought to himself as he and Catalina ran to try to find the source of the smoke.

He should have thought the maid would try something like that. Maria could well be desperate if she felt as though she had lost everything.

Truly, he could not blame Mendoza for being lenient. The girl had suffered enormously and now had not only lost her sister, she had also lost her love. When someone was desperate, they had nothing to lose, and if they were bent on revenge, then they were deadly. Maria would not care if she died.

Felix tried to assess the situation quickly. Thankfully, the house was made of stone, but it did not mean everything inside could not go up in flames.

"Quickly, alert everyone in the ballroom to leave the house," he said to Catalina, "and inform the servants. I will look for the fire." It did not appear that the smoke was coming from the house, so he continued on around the perimeter. Everleigh and Owens came running after him, with a few other men.

"Smoke," Everleigh said at once.

"I cannot tell where it is coming from. Split up and we will go in both directions. Catalina went to get everyone out of the house," Felix explained.

"I will check the kitchens," Owens said, hurrying away in that direction.

"Where is it coming from?" Felix shouted, becoming frustrated.

Everleigh stopped him with his arm. "Look," he said, pointing down the hill.

Felix cursed as he realized what was happening. There were a hundred or more ropes which, already alight and blazing brightly against the night sky, were climbing up the hill towards the house.

"Fuses," Everleigh said.

There were so many that it would be nigh impossible to put them out. As one, they sped towards the buildings, yelling for help. The men had been on alert and at once came running. Everleigh bellowed short orders of explanation to superiors and inferiors alike and they all ran towards the fuses. Grooms and stable boys flocked from the buildings, all alerted by the commotion. Some of them immediately went for water, but even that from the stables would arrive too late.

"Clear the ballroom!" Everleigh and Owens shouted, even though people were leaving. With the thousands of candles inside, the room would go off like one of Prinny's firework displays.

As the officers and gentlemen worked to stop the fuses before they reached the house, Felix and Everleigh began searching for what must be gunpowder or explosives.

"I do not want to imagine how she has come by any of this," Felix muttered as they looked everywhere, from the cellars, undercrofts, to the wood and food stores.

"She followed the drum with her mistress for years. She must have learned the quartermaster's habits or seduced him," Everleigh conjectured.

"She certainly duped Catalina into thinking she was slow-witted."

"This," Everleigh said, spreading his hand out towards the rows of fire approaching the house, "is anything but slow. To set multiple fuses is a masterly stroke. One of them is bound to take." Then they hurried up the steps to the terrace, flattening themselves against the hand-rails as a flood of guests scurried to safety, many of them in a panic. Wails and sobs of frightened women mingled with the shouts and commands of the military men.

Felix and Everleigh sped into the ballroom and frantically began to search behind pillars, chairs and screens. Felix had not seen Catalina, and he prayed desperately that she was out of harm's way. Maria must be somewhere nearby, watching. Several minutes later, satisfied that the ballroom did not hold the explosives, they went back outside.

"Help me with this door!" Everleigh shouted. The heavy wooden barrier was situated under the steps to the terrace. Did it lead beneath the ballroom?

"Of course, it is locked," Everleigh grumbled as he thrust his shoulder against the door. The thick oak did not move an inch. "Stand back!" he ordered, and taking out his pistol, he shot the lock off with unerring skill.

They pried the door back, but it was obvious that no one had opened the door in years, by the creaking and amount of debris dislodged.

Everleigh took a taper and climbed down the steps and muttered a curse. "Nothing here," he called out.

The smell of smoke grew stronger and Felix's sense of urgency grew. He ran back up to the terrace to see if the men were making any progress. It appeared as though some of the fuses had been put out, but almost before his eyes, they seemed to be multiplying.

There were no large wagons or storage rooms to hold a large amount of explosives. With the assistance of several gentlemen, every door was opened and every potted plant was looked inside. There was nothing.

"Time is running out. What do we do?" Felix asked his friend. He could see some of the fuses climbing over the ridge of the hill towards the house.

"Perhaps it is simply a diversion?" Everleigh asked out loud.

"Catalina!" Felix exclaimed. Spinning around, he ran back into the house to search for her, Everleigh right behind him.

"Stop and think, man! If you were a maid bent on revenge, where would you take her?" Everleigh demanded.

Felix shook his head. "I cannot think. Her bedroom? Catalina's bedroom?"

They ran through the house and up the staircase, but Catalina's bedchamber and the adjoining dressing room, with the maid's cot, were both empty.

"What do we do now? She could be anywhere!"

"Perhaps I was wrong and she is outside. It is hard to think like a mad woman," Everleigh said calmly.

"Wait! There is a balcony to my sitting room. It overlooks the terrace." Felix directed Everleigh to follow him. As he entered his room, he heard voices. He held up his hand to stop Everleigh, who nodded his head. He could hear the voices as well.

When Felix reached the doors, the scene before him was his worst nightmare. Not only did Maria have Catalina bound and gagged, but also Colonel Hill. He had no idea how she had managed such a feat on her own, nor how she had lured them away whilst both were in full knowledge of Maria's possible presence.

It was almost *déjà vu* with Dion's attack, except Catalina had not been at the center of Dion's ire that day.

"These people are without honor!" Maria shouted hysterically to the crowd from the balcony to the terrified guests, saying much the same as Dion had that day at Vitoria.

"This man raped and murdered my sister! And she," Maria waved a torch toward Catalina, "murdered my love."

Felix could hear some gasps from the crowd.

"I seek justice for Leonora! And for all of those who died for the bloodlust of the Ingles!"

Felix exchanged glances with Everleigh, who gave a brisk nod of understanding. Maria was an easy target as long as she faced the crowd. However, she was waving a flaming torch in her hand... if there were explosives near at hand, one wrong move and they could all go up in flames. He had to release Catalina and Hill before they captured Maria.

The maid was waving her arm wildly and Felix kept a worried glance on the torch as he crawled silently through the shadows to Catalina and began to saw through her bindings with his knife. The maid had done a devilishly good job of tying the knots and it sounded as loud as a swarm of bees to his ears, along with the nervous thrumming of his blood. Once she was freed, he released a slow breath and motioned for her to sit still. He began on Hill's ropes, whereupon Maria turned their direction. He froze and prayed he was hidden well enough in the darkness behind the other two.

The bindings gave way with a bit of a lurch and Maria must have sensed the movement. Her head snapped their way. Maria's gaze was blank as if there was no soul left inside. In that moment, Felix knew she intended to kill them all.

"What is this?" she spat. "Has your lover come to see you die?" She stared at them without emotion and, with deliberation, moved her torch towards a fuse in her other hand and lit it. The fuse sparked into life.

"Now!" Felix shouted. Everleigh threw his knife at Maria from where he stood, waiting, in the shadows by the door.

Felix did not wait to see what happened. He picked Catalina up and ran with her through the door, hoping Hill could manage on his own.

A loud cacophony of explosions began to go off, one after the other, behind them, but Felix did not stop running. He did not stop to think that they would be faster running separately. He held her as tightly as he could and kept going until they reached the front door, went through it and outside onto the steps.

Hill and Everleigh stumbled out after them and then they all began to run towards the back of the house, where a stunned crowd of guests and servants stood watching the ballroom burning.

Catalina found her father and he threw his arms around her. "Forgive me, *querida*. Forgive me.

This is all my fault."

"You could not have known, Papa. I would not have guessed she could be capable of this."

Mendoza held one arm open to Felix and hugged them both as though his life depended on it.

"When I think I could have lost you both."

"We are here. It is over now."

Indeed, the soldiers, gentlemen and servants were throwing buckets of water on the fire, led by Wellington himself. Thankfully, the ballroom protruded at the back of the house, rather like an orangery, with only the balcony above.

Felix made to go and help, but Catalina's hand on his arm stayed him. "I need you more," she said desperately and clung to him.

He kissed the top of her head. "I will never let you go."

"THE LAST WEEK has passed like a daydream," Catalina said to Midnight, as she rubbed behind his ears. Thankfully, Maria had been the only one to die. Catalina prayed the girl had finally found peace. She could still not believe her maid had orchestrated such an act of destruction, including strapping explosives to herself along with setting the diversionary ropes of fire.

She had stolen the explosives from under their noses. It was almost incomprehensible to Catalina, and she would never underestimate anyone again.

Thankfully, the whole dreadful experience was over and, with her father and Felix to comfort her, she was faring better than on the previous occasion. Most of the damage from the fire had been cleared away, and before long, the stonemasons and some paint would have all the evidence erased.

"It is hard to believe what happened here, is it not?" Felix remarked, coming up beside her on the terrace.

"Yes," she whispered. "I am grateful the terrace was unharmed. It has always been my favorite place and now it holds even more meaning for me." She looked up at the balcony above the ballroom, which still had the large hole created by the explosion.

"Are you certain you wish to go ahead with the wedding?" he asked.

"Yes. Father needs to rejoin his men and I am ready for a new chapter in my life. I cannot wait to see England and meet your family."

"They will love you," he said, reaching down to kiss the top of her head.

"You should not be here; it is bad luck to see me before the service," she reprimanded half-heartedly.

"Do you actually believe in those superstitions?" Felix sounded unconvinced.

"Not really, though as a nation, the Spanish tend to be superstitious."

Midnight had begun to squirm at the sound of Felix's voice. His little face poked out from his wrap.

"Are you to join us at the ceremony?" her betrothed asked the pup as he stroked behind his ears.

"I do not see why not," Catalina replied. "There are only to be a few people present and none of them will mind."

"The priest might," Felix pointed out.

"He is paid well to overlook such things."

Felix smiled down at her. He was to be hers in a matter of hours.

Hers.

"We had better go and dress. I will await you at the chapel, my dear."

There was to be a small ceremony in the estate chapel, no one quite feeling comfortable with a grand occasion after the sober events of the past week.

Catalina could have worn her mother's wedding gown, but it was far too elaborate. Felix had always said he preferred her simple guise to her society façade. Besides, her parents had wed in the summer. She selected a light blue gown decorated with intricate embroidery and added a darker blue velvet gilet for warmth. Her new maid, Betsy, a recent army widow, had tamed her curls and topped the coiffure with a matching silk mantilla, securing it with a peineta. It seemed a little formal, given the understatement of the occasion, but she wished to pay some homage to her Spanish heritage. Her father tried to hide his tears as he escorted her from the house to the chapel, Toro bounding alongside. Midnight was tucked safely inside her gilet, just where he should be. He had grown a small amount and was starting to move around. Perhaps soon, her little miracle would be able to walk after all.

Owens and Everleigh had stayed to witness the event and enjoy Cook's divine creations. They had already set out, escorting Aunt Esmeralda to the chapel, and she seemed delighted with her two handsome escorts. They were to wait inside with the priest and some of the household servants. The white stone chapel was small and charming, with only two pews and an altar, plus a stained-glass window of the Virgin Mary kneeling at the foot of the cross.

Her father led her down the small aisle and placed her hand in Felix's. He wore a single pink rose in his lapel, which made her smile. He remembered.

The ceremony was Catholic and long, despite Catalina's wishes for brevity. However, at last she had her wish and they had both agreed to love, honor and cherish each other in sickness and health.

"I feel as though we have tested many of our vows already," Felix muttered, with a twinkle in his eye.

"As long as we both shall live," she reminded him in a severe undertone.

Somehow, Felix had managed to find a beautiful amethyst and diamond ring to place on her finger.

"It is beautiful," she whispered as the priest continued to read the ceremony. "How did you know this is my favorite?"

"It was the only one that would do... because it matches your eyes."

The priest cleared his throat, causing Felix and Catalina to smile at each other.

"I now pronounce you man and wife."

"Gracias a los cielos!" Mendoza said as he crossed himself, causing those present to laugh... except perhaps the priest.

Felix was indeed thanking the heavens!

After the communion, they signed the register and received congratulations from everyone in the chapel. Despite the smallness of the wedding party, Owens and Everleigh helped to keep it jolly. Along with the servants, they showered the couple with rose petals as they left the chapel.

Cook had prepared a feast for their wedding breakfast, but there would be no grand celebration or ball this time. Felix had assured Catalina his family was certain to do something of the sort when they reached England.

As soon as the breakfast ended, Catalina went to the stables to bid farewell to Toro and his family, the four pups now walking and romping about playfully. Toro's eyes grew sad as she said adios. Animals always understood that word.

"I will take excellent care of Midnight and we will visit on the return journey to Spain." He nuzzled both her hand and Midnight sadly, and then turned away as though he did not wish to prolong the inevitable.

Few words were said as they took their leave of her father. He hugged her long and hard, then shook Felix's hand. Catalina was grateful, because she found her throat too constricted to speak.

They departed from the villa to catch a ship from Bilbao to England in the hopes of reaching Devonshire and The Grange in time for Christmas.

"It will be strange not to be spying anymore," Catalina remarked as the ship sailed through the crystal blue waters, her eyes on her homeland while the familiar Pyrenees and craggy cliffs faded from view.

"You do not have to completely retire your skills, my dear. There will be plenty of opportunities for listening and observing in diplomatic circles, I assure you."

"I suppose that gives me something to look forward to," she said.

"Ah, my love?"

"Yes?" She very much liked the sound of that.

"There is one more question," he continued, as though he had just recalled it.

"Is it not a little late for that?"

He did not answer. "What training in espionage did you receive, exactly? Your knife skills surprised me, rather."

Catalina laughed. "I think I will keep that a secret."

"Is that any way to start a marriage?"

"Of a certainty. I must have some mystery left to me," she teased. "Although, I could perhaps give a small demonstration."

"Well, we do have some time to ourselves before we reach England…" He raised his eyebrows suggestively. He led her down to the Captain's cabin, which he had procured for their journey. It was entirely masculine—paneled wood with dark curtains and one small window—and while the linens were fresh, the odor of tobacco lingered.

"I do not think I would care for living on a ship. It is small and dark," she said, looking around at the cabin.

He came up behind her and wrapped his arms about her. "Oh, my dear, we will not be needing much space or light."

"No?" She looked up at him encouragingly.

"No," he reassured her. "The best things happen in the dark of night."

EPILOGUE

"**I**T IS VERY cold and cloudy in England, but the cliffs are beautiful," Catalina said, surveying his island country with a critical eye as they finally neared land.

"England is not known for its sunshine, but it has other redeeming qualities," he responded, completely captivated by seeing his country through her eyes.

"Such as?" she asked, unconvinced.

"The Knight family?" He smiled. "The weather, certainly not, but I promise you will like England."

"Will your family be very surprised?"

"Oh, yes," he said gleefully. "Because my letters were not posted."

"You are enjoying this greatly, are you not?"

"Which part? Being married or surprising my family?" he asked.

"Both, I hope."

"If you have any doubt as to my enjoyment of our marriage, I am obviously not doing my job properly."

"I have no complaints," she said primly, while a telling blush covered her cheeks.

"That is my family's land right there," he said, pointing to a wide area starting at the edge of the ocean and continuing up to the cliffs topped with grassland. "The estate goes from there all the way to the river, and includes the village. Down in the valley, the house is more protected by the trees. The wind can be quite fierce on this side of England."

The smaller ship docked at the quay near the fishing village. Once they had disembarked, they let Midnight down for a few minutes, then walked up the hill to the village to seek transportation.

The villagers greeted Felix with pride, asking after him and Napoleon. He used to feel strange when people would praise him or ask after his duty, but he now realized it helped them feel better about it all. He introduced Catalina to them and many seemed more awed by her than they did Rowley. She had that presence about her, and her beauty truly was something to behold. If they saw her in her finery, they would probably bow to her like a queen, which amused him greatly.

They took a hired cart from the small tavern to the estate. If his family had known they were coming, they would have sent a carriage for them, but Catalina did not seem to mind, and he knew the ordinary folk would love her more for not being too high in the instep.

As they took the steep, narrow, winding road to the estate, Felix found that he was proud to show Catalina his heritage. The small and colorful fishing huts looked as though they were built upon each other and might fall into the ocean. Yet they had been there for hundreds of years, weathering the severe storms and winds of the coast. It was a harsh, extreme beauty... and it was home.

Smoke wafted from the chimneys on this cold December day, the smell of burning oak one of his favorite memories of winter in England.

He cast a glance at Catalina.

"This is utterly charming," she said, looking around at the place which had helped form him as a man. This place and these people were why he fought for England. It was a good reminder that the sacrifices were worth it for their freedoms.

They pulled into the gates of the estate and took the long tree-lined drive up to the house. Felix did not expect Catalina to be awed by The Grange's magnificence, since she had been brought up in such a manner herself, but her large violet eyes were wide with wonder as she looked around her.

The somewhat shabby cart stopped before the front door to the grey stone manor house and Felix smiled when he saw his brother walk down the steps behind Banks, the longtime butler. Rowley's study looked over the front drive, and he never missed a thing. He would already know that Felix had brought home a wife.

"This is the duke," Catalina remarked, taking Rowley's measure before she had even been handed down from the cart.

Rowley walked over to do the honor himself. He held out his hand. "Welcome to The Grange, my lady," Rowley said, bending over her hand. He then cast a curious glance at Felix as Catalina climbed down. "You are also welcome, Felix," he added, giving him one of his rare smiles.

"May I introduce you to Lady Catalina Knight y Mendoza, the future Duchess of Riojas? Catalina, this is my eldest brother, Rowley, the Duke of Knighton."

Rowley's lips twitched; this small display of his humor would be missed if one did not have the good fortune to see it.

"Indeed, please come inside. You are most welcome. It has been an age since we were all together here at The Grange."

"All five of us are here?"

"All five, plus some additions. I am surprised no one else has noted your arrival," he answered dryly.

"And grandmother. Is she...?" he was afraid to ask. She had always been the matriarch, the invincible one. But when last he'd visited she'd been frail in body, even though still mentally sharp.

"She is alive and well," the duke reassured.

It was more than Felix had hoped for, to have everyone together again.

"I hope our arrival does not inconvenience you or your duchess," Catalina remarked politely.

"Not at all," Rowley answered as they handed their coats and hats to Banks. "The rooms for my siblings are always ready. Not that there are many surprise visits, out here in Devon, but today my preparedness pays off."

Catalina smiled at him and Felix could not contain his pride. This was right.

"Would you prefer to meet the family or go to your room to rest?" Rowley asked.

"It seems as if we have been on a boat forever. I would very much like to meet everyone I have heard so much about!" Catalina answered eagerly.

"As long as you are prepared..." Rowley's voice trailed off as he led them into the drawing room.

Afterwards, Felix could only describe the next few moments as insanity.

"Felix?" one sibling asked.

"Felix!" another shouted.

Eugenia simply threw herself at him and wrapped her arms about him. He could not help but laugh. When he had peeled her arms away and set her back, it seemed that everyone had finally noticed Catalina. The entire family stood around them, but apparently Rowley was going to allow him to do the honors.

"May I present Lady Catalina, my wife?"

For a moment, there was stunned silence, but only for a moment.

Emma, the duchess, was the first to speak. She stepped forward and curtsied. "Welcome to the family, my lady. I am Emma."

He could see Catalina visibly relax, though he doubted she was truly daunted by much of anything. They went down the line of Heath and Cecilia, then Edmund and Isabella.

"And you must be Eugenia," Catalina said with a twinkle in her eyes.

"What has he said about me?" Eugenia immediately demanded, casting an annoyed glance at Felix.

Catalina glided over and took Eugenia's arm. "Only that you and I are very much alike and that I would adore you."

"Oh, well done," Edmund remarked softly, as the rest of the family watched Eugenia lead Catalina to his grandmother, the dowager.

"Who is this?" the dowager barked.

Felix was glad he had warned Catalina about his grandmother's sharp tongue. He followed his wife and sister, and bowed before kissing each frail, withered cheek of his beloved grandparent.

"Grandmother, this is my wife, Catalina."

She curtseyed low enough for a queen and smiled at the dowager with enough charm to slay legions. "I am very pleased to make your acquaintance."

She raised a glass to her eye and surveyed his bride from head to toe, which put him much in the mind of Beau Brummell. "You sound foreign."

"I am Spanish, Your Grace."

The dowager looked askance at him. "What did you go and do that for, Felix?"

"Why not?" He knew better than to make excuses she would not appreciate.

"Why indeed." She gave a shrug. "I suppose if she can make you settle, then I have no objection."

He kissed his grandmother on the cheek. "She makes me happy." He led Catalina to the sofa next to Eugenia and walked back to his brothers. Emma, Cecilia and Isabella followed and sat on another settee across from them. The duchess rang for tea.

Felix turned to look at his brothers without troubling to hide the huge grin on his face. "It seems the ladies have matters in hand. Shall we repair to the study?"

Banks brought in a tray for the gentlemen as well, and Edmund went straight for the biscuits. He had always been Cook's favorite and she pampered him.

"This is quite a surprise, I must say," Edmund remarked, before he took a bite of a warm orange and cinnamon biscuit. "You did not mention a wife when last we saw you in Spain."

"The marriage is a more recent event, though I was working with Catalina even then."

Rowley raised his brows with evident interest, but did not comment.

"Welcome home, Felix. Will you be staying long?" Heath finally spoke. He was looking much healthier. Marriage seemed to suit him well.

"Not terribly long, I am afraid. I have accepted a new post under Sir Henry Wellesley."

"An excellent position. I assume Wellington arranged this?" Rowley asked.

"He did. It was his suggestion. He is rather fond of Catalina."

"I never thought to see you leg-shackled," Heath remarked, "but then again, I never thought to see myself in parson's mousetrap either."

Felix shook his head. "I can only say it was divine intervention. When I look back, there was never any other possible outcome for me."

The brothers all raised their glasses. "Hear, hear."

"Now to see Eugenia settled," Rowley muttered.

"You might have to raise her dowry."

"And attract more lechers? No, thank you. It is not that Eugenia lacks for suitors. Only suitable ones," Rowley quipped.

The brothers carried on ribbing each other good-naturedly. Even Rowley let down his guard enough to laugh with them. Felix treasured the moment, because he knew the times they would all be together again would be few.

Little George came through the open door and toddled straight to his father's lap, in no doubt of his welcome. The ducal heir had grown considerably since Felix had seen him at Heath's wedding, where all he had done was sleep.

Felix was a little in awe of seeing Rowley thus, but it was nevertheless good to see his too-often stoic brother seem young once again.

"You have arrived just in time for the festivities," Edmund said cheerfully.

"What do you have planned?" Felix asked.

"The usual gathering of holly and mistletoe; lots of good cooking; church, of course... not in order of importance, mind you. Perhaps skating, if the weather cooperates."

"I wonder if Catalina has ever skated?" Felix thought out loud.

"We need another hard freeze tonight," Rowley proffered, as little George decided to chew one end his father's neckcloth.

Felix could not stop the laugh that bubbled up from deep within at the sight. A little bark came from within his waistcoat, and he pulled Midnight out.

"By the way, this is Midnight."

"Ni, ni," George tried to repeat the name. Apparently he also thought he was very clever and gurgled as he made his way towards the dog.

"Just wait, Felix."

The thought did not frighten him as much as he thought it would. One day, perhaps. Children had never really been an option before— nor had he considered the likelihood. George wriggled down from his father's lap to investigate the puppy.

"What have we here?" Rowley asked, moving closer to observe.

"The runt of a litter that Catalina nursed when the mother would have abandoned him. He cannot quite walk yet."

Eugenia entered without knocking, not intimidated at all by the masculine domain her brothers had found in the study.

"Are you going to stay in here all day?" she asked. "Tinsley is here and we have greenery to gather!" Tinsley was their neighbor and nearest friend. He had been kind enough to escort Eugenia to events in London while the brothers were gone.

The brothers exchanged glances of fondness and exasperation, then with good-humored reluctance, stood up to prepare themselves for the outdoors and greet Tinsley.

"I had not realized how close to Christmas it was. One loses track of days on the ship," Felix said while gathering his coat and hat.

"And when newly wed," Heath retorted.

Once properly clad for the cold, the family gathered in the entrance hall. Felix took Catalina's arm as they marched outdoors towards the best holly and mistletoe in the home wood.

"Are you regretting your choice of husband yet?" he asked as a rush of brisk wind hit their faces, bringing the scent of fresh pine and cedar to his nose.

"Not yet," she quipped. "I must confess I am fascinated."

"How so? Eugenia's lack of color sense is daunting, I grant you. But not, I would have thought, fascinating."

She laughed. "Having grown up without siblings, the different relationships are intriguing."

"I daresay I can see that. Not having known anything else, it is hard to imagine any other way. What did you think of Eugenia? You handled her wonderfully, I must say."

"She is a breath of fresh air—quite an original. I can see why you thought we would suit."

"I am happy to hear that."

"Why are we going outside in the cold?" she asked.

"Do you have traditions in Spain for Christmas?"

"Oh, yes. We have special foods we make. We go to mass, of course, and exchange gifts."

"Gathering greenery and decorating the house is one of our traditions. I think you will enjoy our Christmas."

"It will certainly be lively," she said, watching the brothers begin to climb trees.

"Excuse me, my dear," Felix said, letting go of her arm. "Tradition!" he explained as he went to join his brothers. Not for years had he climbed trees with them to fetch mistletoe.

"Race you to the top!" he shouted as he tried to catch up with them. He had always been the fastest climber and knew that was why they had hurried off before him. He was soon panting and sweating—and his gloves and boots were doubtless scuffed beyond repair—by the time he reached the top, but the look of annoyance on his three brothers' faces was worth it when he looked down at them with satisfaction.

"I still beat you old codgers, even though you stole a head start!" he gloated.

"Just wait, marriage will make you soft as well," Heath shouted back good-naturedly. It was only natural for there to be some competitiveness amongst four boys, and even Eugenia, Felix mused. In the past, she would have donned trousers and joined them in the climb. He wondered why she had not done it this time.

Could the London Season have changed her so much? He did not think he liked the thought of that.

It must look to Catalina as though there were four large monkeys in the trees. He chuckled as they tossed down balls of greenery to the ladies. A cart had been brought in readiness, and they soon had it filled for a servant to return to the house later.

Felix quickly slithered back down the tree and rejoined Catalina. He flashed a huge grin at her.

"This is a strange tradition," she said doubtfully, examining the mistletoe. "You decorate the house with this?"

"I always thought it silly until now," he said, taking a bunch of the plant and holding it above their heads. "Let me demonstrate its usefulness."

He brought his lips to hers before she could expound upon the oddness of such a thing. He heard a few cheers, but when he looked up, his brothers and their wives had joined them in kissing under their own bunches of mistletoe. Catalina's cheeks flushed delightfully as she looked around. Felix noticed Tinsley staring at Eugenia strangely before giving her a quick kiss. Felix shook his head. He must be imagining things. *Tomfool*, he chastised himself, turning back to his delectable wife.

"If you find yourself under the mistletoe with someone, you must give them a kiss. Then you pluck one of the white berries."

"I would have thought this too scandalous for the reserved British!" she exclaimed.

"Occasionally, we lose our reserve," he teased.

"Now for the holly!" Eugenia declared. She began to lead them deeper into the wood.

"I am afraid to know what tradition you have with the holly," she said as she put her arm in Felix's.

"Oh, that is only for decoration. No one wants to touch it again for it pricks your fingers."

She shook her head. "Very well. Let us pick this holly. Must you climb trees for it?"

"No. It is a tree, but grows close to the ground."

"That is a relief."

With ten of them gathering, it did not take long to fill a second cart with holly and other greens. By the time they tramped back to the house, their cheeks were all bright red. The warmth inside the house was blissful, and the smell of spicy baking and wassail made every minute of being outside worth it.

Reluctantly, they shed their hats, coats, and gloves, and then Felix rushed Catalina towards the fire. They stood holding their hands out

to the flames and before long, Felix felt the familiar prickling aware-
ness of returning sensation to his limbs as they thawed.

"What do you think now?" Felix asked Catalina.

"I think you will ask me this several times every day," she mused.
"Do not worry. I like your family and I like your England. I am not so
fond of the cold and damp, but I will grow accustomed."

Banks entered with a tray of warm gingerbread and Edmund instantly rubbed his hands together with glee.

He handed one to Catalina. "Have you ever tried gingerbread?"
Edmund asked. "It is delicious."

"Then I must have some, of course. I approve of this wassail," she
remarked, completely slaughtering the pronunciation of the word.

Felix watched her take a bite and the expressions that crossed her
face were delightful.

"This is very strange, but I think I like it."

Edmund laughed. "Do not worry. We have plenty more goodies if
you do not like that one. Do you have any special foods you would
like us to have which are your traditions?"

"That is a wonderful idea, Edmund," Emma said. "I am sure Cook
would be happy to oblige."

"We do have a special cake that is not too difficult," Catalina said,
looking pleased. "It is in the shape of a crown with a cream filling and
candied fruit on top. It is to represent the wise men. We celebrate that
with the Epiphany in Spain."

"I love hearing about how other cultures celebrate Christ's birth,"
Edmund said.

"That reminds me. I have something. Please excuse me, I will be
back in a moment," Catalina said, gathering her skirts to leave.

"Shall I assist you?" Felix asked, rising to his feet.

"No, I believe I can find my way, thank you." She hurried off and
Felix turned to watch his entire family staring at him. It was the first
time he had been alone with them.

"Yes?" he asked warily.

"I think she is an absolute delight," Cecilia said. Felix knew her the least, but if she had brought Heath back to them, he was inclined to adore her.

"I am hardly one to speak on the matter of surprise marriage," Heath added dryly.

Isabella entered the room just then, holding George. Felix had not even noticed her leave. She had been George's nurse when she was hiding from her father, and was still clearly attached to the boy.

Immediately, he began to point to Felix and repeat syllables. "Ni, ni."

"I think he wishes to see Midnight," she said, as she brought his nephew to him and placed him on the sofa where Catalina had been sitting.

"You wish to see the puppy?" Felix asked as he pulled him from his waistcoat. He held him out and George tried to pat him with all of the awkwardness of a toddler. However, the happiness that came to his face when Midnight kissed his cheek was infectious.

"Be careful or you will have a hard time leaving with him," Rowley said over Felix's shoulder, looking fondly upon his son playing with the dog.

Midnight had learned to rock back and forth on all fours and even take a step or two.

"I will let him argue with Catalina about that," Felix chuckled.

He decided to put the boy and the dog down on the carpet where they could play more freely. Emma produced a ball and George and Midnight somehow managed to roll it about together. The little puppy seemed encouraged to move more towards the object.

Catalina entered the room holding one of the large boxes she had insisted on bringing to England.

A footman held open the door and looked up at them apologetically, as though he had tried to assist her. Felix walked over and took the box from her, not bothering to comment upon her stubbornness.

Catalina noticed Midnight and George playing together on the floor and she held her hands to her chest.

"I fear you might have competition for Midnight, my love," he teased. "Where would you like this box?"

Catalina looked around. "A table out of reach of puppies and Georges would be best."

Quickly the table was cleared where the remnants of their biscuits had been.

"This is for you," she said to the duke and duchess. "I apologize the presentation is not better," she added with a shy smile.

Rowley held out his hand for Emma to do the honors. She opened the box carefully and began to pull out intricately carved, beautiful pieces of a nativity, painted and decorated with amazing detail. It even had the stable and houses surrounding it.

"How thoughtful! I have never seen anything like this," Emma said.

"When I realized we would be here for Christmas, this is what I thought to bring you. Beautiful nativity scenes are something the Spanish do very well. We call it a *portal de Belén*."

"We will find a perfect place for it. Thank you very much."

"You are most welcome. Now you can think of us for the Christmases when we cannot be here. Perhaps some time in the future you may all visit our home."

"That would be wonderful," Emma said as she finished placing all the pieces on the table.

Tomorrow was Christmas Eve, but they had only just arrived this day and it had been full and exhausting.

"I think we shall retire, if you will forgive us. It has been rather a full day," Felix said, over the din of all eight of them speaking, it seemed. "It is time for Midnight to be let out and fed, at any rate."

Isabella had been cuddling the pup, and she placed him down on all fours. He rocked and took two awkward steps forward. She clapped her hands.

"I do think he will be walking soon!"

He gathered Midnight and held out his arm for Catalina as they said goodnight. Slipping her shawl about her shoulders, she joined him and they went for a turn about the garden while their dog took care of business. Catalina leaned against him as they stood admiring the clear, crisp, starry night.

Suddenly feeling amorous, he put both arms around her and drew her to him for a kiss.

"Why, Felix, I thought you were tired." She gave him a saucy look, which never failed to wake him up.

He would make her pay for that impertinence. His lips descended, crushing hers with need, and she wound her arms around his neck and kissed him back with the sweet, fierce passion of her fiery Spanish nature. Felix did not care that they were within sight of the house; in actual fact, he could not think at all until a bark interrupted them and Catalina pulled her lips from his.

Somehow, Midnight had reached their feet, and gave a bark at them, his little tail wagging merrily. Felix bent down to scoop the dog up.

"We are going to have to discuss your timing, Midnight."

Catalina laughed. "But how clever he is! He must have walked to us."

Felix sighed dramatically. "I suppose he is."

"It is too bad that we did not see it for ourselves in the darkness, though."

"I do not think that is the reason we missed it," he remarked with a wry, heated look at her. It was wasted on her. She was looking up at the sky.

"You know, I used to be afraid of the dark. Now I think it is my favorite time of day."

"We have several more hours of darkness," he said with a knowing grin, and with no more ado, he pulled her back to the house.

About the Author

Like many writers, Elizabeth Johns was first an avid reader, though she was a reluctant convert. It was Jane Austen's clever wit and unique turn of phrase that hooked Johns when she was "forced" to read Pride and Prejudice for a school assignment. She began writing when she ran out of her favorite author's books and decided to try her hand at crafting a Regency romance novel. Her journey into publishing began with the release of Surrender the Past, book one of the Loring-Abbott Series. Johns makes no pretensions to Austen's wit but hopes readers will perhaps laugh and find some enjoyment in her writing.

Johns attributes much of her inspiration to her mother, a former English teacher. During their last summer together, Johns would sit on the porch swing and read her stories to her mother, who encouraged her to continue writing. Busy with multiple careers, including a professional job in the medical field, author and mother of two children, Johns squeezes in time for reading whenever possible.

Made in the USA
Coppell, TX
23 November 2022

86924416R00134